DARK HORSES

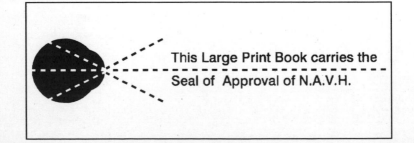

This Large Print Book carries the
Seal of Approval of N.A.V.H.

DARK HORSES

RALPH COTTON

THORNDIKE PRESS

A part of Gale, Cengage Learning

Farmington Hills, Mich • San Francisco • New York • Waterville, Maine
Meriden, Conn • Mason, Ohio • Chicago

LIBRARY OF CONGRESS CATALOGING-IN-PUBLICATION DATA

Cotton, Ralph W.
 Dark Horses / by Ralph Cotton. — Large print edition.
  pages ; cm. — (Thorndike Press large print western)
  ISBN 978-1-4104-7236-6 (hardcover) — ISBN 1-4104-7236-1 (hardcover)
  1. Horse dealers—Fiction. 2. Mexico—Fiction. 3. Large type books. I. Title.
 PS3553.O766D37 2014
 813'.54—dc23   2014019849

Published in 2014 by arrangement with NAL Signet, a member of Penguin Group (USA) LLC, a Penguin Random House Company

Printed in Mexico
1 2 3 4 5 6 7 18 17 16 15 14

For Mary Lynn, of course . . .

Part 1

CHAPTER 1

Dark Horses, the Mexican hill country, Old Mexico

The horse trader Will Summers stood with his rain slicker buttoned all the way up to his chin, his wet black Stetson pulled low on his forehead. His boots were muddy and soaked through his socks. His wet gloved hand was wrapped around the stock of his equally wet Winchester rifle. Behind him stood his dapple gray and a string of four bay fillies. The animals held their heads bowed against the rain.

Summers read a bullet-riddled sign he'd picked up out of the mud. He slung it free of water and mud and read it again as if he might have missed something.

Bienvenido a Caballos Oscuros . . . , he said silently to himself.

"Welcome to Dark Horses," he translated beneath the muffling sound of pouring rain.

But how far? he asked himself, looking all

around. The rain raced slantwise on a hard wind. Thunder grumbled behind streaks of distant lightning. Night was falling fast under the boiling gray sky. The horse trader frowned to himself and looked up and down the slick hillside trail.

To his right he looked along a boulder-clad hillside to where the long, rocky upper edge of an ancient caldera swept down and encircled the wide valley below. The lay of the land revealed where, thousands of years ago, the lower valley had been the open top of a boiling volcano. Over time, as the belly of the earth cooled, the thin, standing pipe walls of the volcano had weathered and aged and toppled inward and filled that once-smoldering chasm. All of this before man's footprints had ventured onto this rugged terrain.

Behind the fallen, honeycombed lava walls, over those same millennia past, dirt and seed of all varieties had steadily blown in and sculpted a yawning black abyss into a rocky green valley — a valley currently shrouded beneath the wind-driven rain.

On the valley floor, snaking into sight from the north, Summers recognized the Blue River — *El Río Azul.* The river's muddy water had swollen out of its banks and bar-reled swiftly in and around bluffs and lower cliffs and hill lines like an unspooling ribbon of silk. As he studied the hillside and the valley below him, a large chunk of rock, gravelly mud and an unearthed boulder broke loose before his eyes and bounced and slid and rumbled down to the valley floor.

Whoa. Summers turned his eyes back along the wet hillside above him, knowing the same thing could have happened up there at any second. It didn't matter how much farther it was to Dark Horses; he had to get himself and the horses somewhere out of this storm — somewhere safer than here, he told himself. Blowing rain hammered his hat brim, his boots, his slicker and the glassy, pool-streaked ground around him. Lightning twisted and curled. Behind it, a clap of thunder exploded like cannon fire.

"Welcome to Dark Horses," he repeated, saying it this time to the dapple gray who had pressed its muzzle against Summers' arm.

The gray chuffed, as if rejecting both Summers' invitation and his wry attempt at humor. Behind the gray, the four black-point bay fillies milled at the sound of thunder. Then they settled and huddled together behind the gray. The fillies were

11

bound for the breeding barn of an American rancher by the name of Ansil Swann.

Once dry, the fillies' coats shone a lustrous winter wheat red, highlighted against black forelegs, mane and tails. But the animals hadn't been dry all day. Summers intended to rub them down and let them finish drying overnight in a warm livery barn. Get them grained and rested before the new owner arrived in Dark Horses to take the delivery. But so much for his plan, he thought, realizing the storm would no doubt pin him down out here for the night.

"Let's find you and these girls some shelter," he murmured to the gray. The gray slung water from its soaked mane.

But where?

Summers looked around more as he gathered his reins and the lead rope to the fillies. Swinging himself up across his wet saddle, he reminded himself that he'd seen no sign of a cliff shelter anywhere along the ten or so miles of high trail behind him.

"We'll find something," he murmured, nudging the gray forward. The fillies trudged along single file behind him, their images flickering on and off in streaks of lightning.

He rode on.

For over an hour and a half he led his wet, miserable procession through the storm along the darkened hillside trail. Twice he heard the rumble of rockslides through the pounding rain ahead of him, and twice he'd had to lead the horses off the blocked trail around piles of stone wreckage. But what else could he do? he reasoned. Stopping on this loose, deluged hillside was out of the question.

Find shelter or keep moving, he told himself. There was no third choice in the matter.

Beneath his wet saddle the gray grumbled and nickered under its breath at each heavy clap of thunder. Yet the animal made no effort to balk or pull up shy, even with its reins lying loose in Summers' hand. Following the gray's lead, the four fillies stayed calm. For that Summers was grateful.

Good work. He patted a wet hand on the gray's withers as they pushed on.

Moments later, at a narrow fork in the trail, he spotted a thin glow of firelight perched on the hillside above him.

"Thank God," he said in relief. He reined the gray and pulled the string of fillies sidelong onto the upward fork.

During brief intervals between twists of lightning, his only guide through the pitch-darkness came from the sound of rain splattering on the rocky trail in front of him.

Three feet to his left the trickle and splatter of rain against rock fell away silent. So did the trail itself. The caldera valley lay swaddled in a black void over three hundred feet below.

Summers had no idea what might lay in store around the firelight above him, but whatever situation awaited him there could be no more perilous than this trail he was on. Or so he told himself, pushing on blindly in absolute darkness, water spilling from the brim of his hat.

Another hour had passed before Summers had worked his way up the rocky trail through the storm and the darkness. High up where the slim trail ended, he stopped and stepped down from his saddle at the entrance to an abandoned mining project. Following the glow of firelight that had drawn him like a moth, he led the horses out of the rain and under a stone overhang trussed up by thick pine timbers. Wet rifle in hand, he tied the five animals to an iron ring bolted to one of the timbers and stood in silence for a moment listening toward the flicker of fire along a descending stone wall.

Hearing no sound from within the hillside, he ventured forward into the mouth of the shaft.

"Hello the fire," he called out. He waited, and when no reply come back to him through the flickering light along the stone walls, he called out again. Still no reply. "Coming in," he announced.

He looked back at the shadowy horses standing in the dim, sparse light. Then he walked forward, his rifle lowered but held ready in his hand.

Twenty feet into the cavern he heard a horse nickering quietly toward him, the animal catching the scent of an encroaching stranger.

"Hello the campfire," Summers called out again. But he did not stop and wait for a reply. He walked on as the flicker of firelight grew stronger. He stopped again when he came to a place where the shaft opened wide and smoke from a campfire swirled upward into a high broken ceiling. A smell of cooking meat wafted in the darkness. A small tin cooking pot sat off the flames on the edge of the fire. A spoon handle stuck up from it. Having not eaten all day caused Summers' belly to whine at the scent of food.

Looking all around, he heard the chuff of the horse and saw the animal standing shadowly among rocks on the far side of the campfire. Then he swung his rifle quickly at the sound of a man coughing in the darkness to his right. The cough turned into a dark, raspy chuckle as Summers saw two red-streaked eyes glint in the flickering fire.

"Bienvenue . . . mon ami," a weak, gravelly voice said in French from the dark corner outside the firelight. Then the voice turned into English. "Do you bring . . . a rope for me?"

Summers heard pain in the voice. He stepped closer.

"I'm not carrying a rope," he said, already getting an idea what was going on here. "I saw your fire. I came in out of the rain."

"Ah . . ." The voice trailed.

Summers waited for more. When nothing came, he stepped in close enough to look down at the drawn bearded face. "Are you hurt?"

"I am dying, thank you . . . ," the voice said wryly, ending in a deep, harsh cough.

Summers looked around at the fireside and saw a blackened torch lying on a rock. He stepped away from the man, picked up the torch and stuck the end of it in the flames, lighting it. Then he stepped back and held the light out over the man lying on a bloody blanket on the stone floor. The man clutched a hand to a blood-soaked bandage on his chest.

16

"Are you shot?" Summers asked.

"*Oui* . . . I am shot to death," the man said with finality. He stared up at Summers. "Are you not with *them*?" He gave a weak gesture toward the world outside the stone cavern walls.

"Them?" said Summers. "I'm here on my own."

"The man with the bay horses?" the man asked.

Summers gave him a curious look.

"We saw you," the man said.

We? Summers looked around again into the darkness beyond the circling firelight. Nothing.

"Yes, that was me," he said. "Is somebody hunting you, mister?"

The wounded man shook his head slowly.

"Never mind," the man said. He seemed stronger; he tried to prop himself up onto his elbows, but his strength failed him.

"Why don't you lie still?" said Summers, stooping down beside him.

"Water . . . food," the man said weakly. "There is liver stew. . . ." He collapsed onto the blanket; he cut his eyes toward the fire, where a canteen stood on the stone floor.

"I'll get it for you," Summers said.

He laid the torch on the floor, went to the fire, rifle in hand, and brought back the

17

small tin pot and the canteen. The smell of the hot food tempted him. But he set the pot on the floor by the blanket and uncapped the canteen. He helped the man up onto his elbows and steadied the canteen while he drank. When he lowered the canteen, he capped it, laid it aside and picked up the small tin pot.

"This will get your strength up," he said, stirring the spoon in a thickened meaty broth. He held out a spoonful, but at the last second the man turned his face away and eased himself back down on the blanket.

"You eat it, *mon ami.* I will need . . . no strength in hell," the man sighed, and clutched his chest tighter.

Summers wasn't going to argue.

"Obliged," he said, even as he spooned the warm, rich stew into his mouth. "Who shot you?"

"It does . . . not matter," the man said. He paused, looked Summers up and down, then said, "What are you doing . . . in this Mexican hellhole, *mon ami*?"

"Delivering the four bay fillies you saw me leading," Summers said. He spooned up more liver stew; he chewed and swallowed hungrily. "Taking them to a man named Ansil Swann." He spooned up more stew,

18

held it, then stopped. "Are you sure you don't want some of this?" he asked, just to be polite.

The man shook his head. He looked away toward the darkness and gave a dark chuckle.

"What a small and peculiar world . . . I have lived in," he said, as if reflecting on a life that would soon leave him. He chuckled again and stifled a cough. "I know this man, Swann."

"You do?" said Summers.

"Oh yes, I know him . . . very well," said the dying man. "It is his *viande de cheval . . .* you are eating."

"His what?" Summers asked. He looked down the pot in his hand.

"Viande de cheval," the man said.

"Speak English, mister," Summers said, getting a bad feeling about the conversation.

"Horse meat," the man said in a laughing, rasping cough.

"Horse meat?" Summers said, staring at the rich meaty broth in the pot.

"Yes, my friend," said the chuckling, dying man. "You are eating Ansil Swann's . . . prize racing stallion."

CHAPTER 2

Summers stuck the spoon back into the pot and set the pot aside. He wiped a hand across his lips and looked down at the pot. Prize stallion or no, it was some tasty stew, he had to admit. He looked away from the pot and all around the shadowy cavern as if making sure he hadn't been seen.

"You killed the man's prize racing stallion?" he asked drily.

The wounded man's weak laughter fell away into a cough. Summers watched the man as he collected himself and clutched tighter at his chest.

"I — I did not . . . kill him," he said brokenly. "He suffered a leg break. We . . . butchered and boned him." He cut his dark eyes toward the pot and said, "Is damn good racehorse stew, eh? I cooked it myself."

"I have to say, it is," Summers replied, resisting the smell of hot liver stew rising and wafting around his face.

"Then, *bon appétit,*" the man said, his strength seeming to come and go. "He is . . . horse steak and spick roast now." Again his dark chuckle.

"Obliged, but no," Summers said. "I don't make a practice of eating horse."

"What?" the man said. "It is a matter . . . of your religion?"

"No," Summers said, "it's a matter of principle. I'm a horse trader."

"So?" the man said.

"Never mind." Summers shook his head, seeing no point in trying to explain. He went back to the matter of the racing stallion. "So you stole this man Swann's stallion?"

"*Oui, mes partenaires* and I . . . stole him," he said.

"Speak English —"

"My partners and I . . . stole the animal," the man translated. "When my wound worsened . . . they left me here." He gave a sudden violent cough. Blood trickled from his lips. He collected himself and gestured a nod toward the outer circle of darkness farther back in the cavern. "See . . . for yourself, *mon ami.* It is no . . . trail mule's liver you were eating." He gave a weak shrug. "I regret I had no onion . . . no garlic, or even sage —"

21

"It tasted fine," Summers said, cutting him off. He didn't want to talk about it. He picked up the torch and pushed himself to his feet. Rifle in hand, holding the torch out in front of him, he walked back into the cavern until he saw the grizzly remains of the butchered stallion lying on the stone floor.

"Jesus," he whispered in the flickering glow of the torch, recalling his conversation with Ansil Swann at the auction barns in Denver City. Swann had purchased his bays as breeding stock for a black stallion, intending to develop racing stock equal to any animal on either side of the Atlantic. Summers' wet gloved hand tightened around his rifle stock at the sight of a big stallion's blood-streaked carcass lying boned to its skeletal core. Its severed head lay three feet away, a bullet hole gaping in its forehead, its tongue a-loll; its innards lay in a loose pile beside it. The animal's skin had been peeled back as necessary and lay spread on the floor around it.

Summers stepped closer, just enough to see if what the dying man was telling him was true. Beneath his boots the stone floor was slick with blood. He held the torch down and saw the stallion's broken right foreleg. Seeing it, he eased his hand on his rifle. At least the man wasn't lying about the leg break. The break was as bad as any he'd ever seen — maybe worse. He let out a breath and pushed up his wet hat brim.

All right. . . .

There could be no excuse for the man and his *partenaires* stealing Swann's stallion, yet, from the looks of the foreleg, Summers realized that the animal had had to be put down. *No question about that.*

He turned with the torch and stepped over to the fire. The stallion's shiny black mane and tail lay in a heap on a flat rock. Summers reached down atop the pile and picked up a twelve-inch riding quirt the same color as the dead animal's tail and mane hair. Inspecting the quirt, he noted the quality of the person who had braided it.

"It is . . . good work my *partenaires* do, eh?" the man said brokenly from his blanket.

"Yes, they do," Summers replied, taken by the craftsmanship of the work. He slipped the loop of the quirt onto his wrist and ran the length of it between his thumb and fingers. It was flawless, as smooth as silk. The person braiding it had not used a simple three-strand plait, he noted. This was four strands, perhaps even five — the fifth strand woven into the body of the quirt in a way undetectable to the human eye.

23

"Is this what your partners and you do when you're not stealing horses?" he asked.

Instead of replying the man coughed deep and wetly and fell silent. Summers left the quirt on his wrist and reached down and picked up a half-finished horsehair bridle from the pile of shiny hair. He shook his head slowly and had started to lay the bridle down when a voice called out from the dark entranceway.

"Freeze right there, mister," the voice said. "Let that rifle fall from your hand!"

Summers froze, but he hesitated for a second before turning loose of his rifle.

"Suit yourself," the voice said. "I'll save us both a hanging."

"Wait," Summers said, sensing the man behind the voice was ready to pull a trigger. He let the Winchester fall to the floor cushioned by the pile of horsehair. "There, it's down, see?" he said, still half-bowed at the waist. Now he would explain who he was, that he had nothing to do with any of this.

"Sidestep away from it, easy-like," the voice demanded. "Get your hands up high."

"Done . . . and done," Summers said quietly, stepping away slowly, straightening and raising his hands above his shoulders, the shiny black quirt still hanging from his wrist. "I want to tell you straight up that I have nothing to do —"

"Shut your mouth, mister!" the voice snapped, cutting him off.

In a flash of lightning, Summers saw the man's silhouette in the cavern entrance. A wide blackened hat sat above a long blackened duster. An aimed rifle. All of it vanished as the flash of light blinked back into darkness.

"I got one for you, Sheriff Bert!" the man called back over his shoulder. He cut a glance at the pile of horsehair lying beside the fire, then kept his eyes and his gun fixed on Summers. Behind him Summers saw torchlight appear in the cavern entrance and move forward.

"Hold him right there, Endo. We're coming," a voice called out in reply.

"Mister, you have stepped in a deep pile of it," the posse man Endo Clifford said. "See this?" He patted a wet deputy badge pinned to his chest.

"I see it," Summers said. "I can explain being here." He nodded toward the cavern entrance. "The fillies and the dapple gray you saw back there belong to me. I saw a campfire and I came back in here to get out of the storm."

"I just bet you did," the man said. He

25

jerked around quickly as a cough and a deep groan emitted from the darkness where the wounded man lay on his blanket.

"Ask him," Summers said, nodding toward the sound.

"I bet I will," the man said. As he spoke he stepped around the cavern and looked down where the man lay as still as stone, his dead eyes staring blankly at the dark ceiling. "Ha! He just coughed out his last breath," he said. "If ol' horse-thieving Hendrik here is your alibi, you best reach down into the jar again."

Horse-thieving Hendrik. . . .

"What?" Summers said.

"Hendrik's dead." The rifleman chuckled. "Looks like you're having one of them days, mister."

"I've got paperwork here," said Summers. He gave a nod toward the inside lapel pocket of his wet riding duster.

"I just bet you do," the man said. "Reach for them and see how quick I start cutting you in half." Thunder rumbled along the hillside above them.

Summers stood still and kept silent until five other men stepped into sight, the first one holding a torch above his head. Three of the five men were Mexican. Their sombreros drooped, soaked with water. Two were Americans, dressed in slickers, tall hats and range clothes.

"Well, well, look what we've got here," said the torchbearer, stepping in and stopping a few feet away from Summers. He held the torch in his left hand and a long-barreled nickel-plated Remington Army revolver in his right. As he spoke, four more men stepped into the cavern, rifles up and cocked. One of the men moved all around, searching the cavern.

The leader looked away from Summers for a second and scanned the cavern, taking note of the horsehair, the half-braided bridle, then the quirt hanging from Summers' wrist. "I hope that's not what I think it is," he said, staring at the quirt.

Summers didn't answer; he realized how bad this looked for him. He never should have looped this shiny new quirt over his wrist, he told himself. Now the thing had trouble written all over it.

Before Summers could reply, the man searching the cavern stopped at the place where the stallion had been killed and butchered. He struck a long match and held it out.

"My God, Sheriff Bert, come look at this," he said. "These sons a' bitches have stripped Swann's stallion to the bone."

The man, Sheriff Bert Miller, glared at Summers as he sidestepped over toward the darkness with his torch.

"Keep your sights pinned on him, men," he said to the others. "He makes a move, kill him."

Summers stood watching as three men kept him covered and three men searched all around in the cavern. After a moment, the leader walked back over calmly from the site of the slaughtered stallion and stood in front of him.

"That's a hell of a mess," he said. He took off his hat, slung water from it and put it back on. "I saw the leg break. But it never would have happened had you boys not stolen him."

"I didn't steal him, mister," Summers said. "I saw the —"

"It's not *mister,*" said the rifleman Endo Clifford, cutting him off. He stepped in close to Summers. "He's Sheriff Bert. Call him *mister* again, I'll feed you this rifle butt!" He jiggled the rifle in a threatening manner. Summers just stared at him.

"Easy, Endo," Sheriff Bert said.

Summers continued, speaking to the sheriff while he stared hard at Endo Clifford.

"Like I said, I came in out of the storm, Sheriff," he said. "I found everything you see here . . . except the dead man over there was still alive. I gave him some water —"

"Sheriff, look at this," one of the men called out from beside the dead man's blanket. He held up the tin pot of horse liver stew and stirred the spoon around in it. "Him and Hendrik were eating Swann's stallion when we got here. The pot's still warm."

"You son of a bitch!" said Clifford, his rage overcoming his self-control. He drew back his rifle, ready to stab the butt into Summers' face.

But the sheriff threw out a hand, stopping him.

"Whoa, Endo," he said. "Don't knock the man out while I'm talking to him. What the hell's wrong with you?"

Clifford cooled down.

"Sorry, Sheriff Bert," he offered. "I just hate a damn horse thief, is all."

"I'm not a horse thief. I've got paperwork, Sheriff," Summers said. "Inside my duster, here." He nodded at the lapel of his wet duster.

"This is Mexico. Your paperwork doesn't mean much here," the sheriff said. "Hector," he called out to one of the three

Mexican riflemen, "tell this gringo how much his paperwork is worth around here."

"Ha," said the stocky Mexican, "your paperwork don't mean *chit* here, gringo."

The sheriff chuckled under his breath at the Mexican's pronunciation. *"Chit . . . ,"* he said, quietly mocking the man's accent, grinning just between Summers and himself. He reached out and opened Summers' duster. His hand went inside and rummaged for the paperwork on the four fillies.

"This is a bill of sales from the Denver City stock auction for the bays," Summers said. "I've got one for the dapple gray in my saddlebags somewhere."

"In your saddlebags somewhere," the sheriff said casually, unfolding and rustling through the paperwork. He read it silently to himself.

"So what? You've got paperwork from El Paso City," said Endo Clifford. "They're the damnedest thieves and liars in the world at the El Paso Horse Auction."

"He didn't say El Paso City, Endo," the sheriff said without looking up from reading. "He said Denver City. Pay attention, Endo."

"Oh," said Clifford. He looked stumped, but only for a second until he retaliated.

"Well, they're *even worse* thieves in Denver City!"

The sheriff finished reading the paper-work.

"Looks like everything's in order," he said. "Question is, is any of it true?"

"It's all true, Sheriff," Summers said. He wanted to lower a hand and reach for the paperwork, but something told him not to. "You can ask Mr. Swann. He'll vouch for me." He kept his hands raised.

Sheriff Miller folded the paperwork and shoved it inside his wet rain slicker. The glint of a five-point tin badge showed on his chest, then went out of sight.

"I've got another idea," he said. He turned to Clifford and said, "Bring in the Belltraes. Let's hear what they've got to say about this one."

"The Belltraes . . . ?" Summers said, looking back and forth between Clifford and the sheriff.

Clifford gave him a tight, menacing grin. He stood with his rifle tense in his hands, as if eager to swing the butt around into Summers' face.

"That's right, horse thief," he said. "We got your pals Ezra and Collard right outside the cavern — fixing to hang them soon as the storm lets up."

"I don't know any Ezra and Collard Bell-trae," Summers said.

"Yeah, we'll see about that," said Clifford.

"Bring the brothers in," Sheriff Miller called out to the two Mexican riflemen standing nearby. "Let's see what they can tell us about Mr. Summers here."

CHAPTER 3

As the storm continued to rage outside the cavern, one of the Mexican riflemen ran out into the stone causeway, holding up a torch to light his way. In a moment he returned with two more riflemen, who prodded two bound and wounded prisoners ahead of them with their rifle barrels. Thunder jarred the cavern like a cannon blast, then rolled away along the Mexican hill line. Summers stood watching in silence, his hands still chest high, the shiny black quirt hanging from his wrist.

Beside Will Summers, Endo Clifford gave a dark chuckle and spoke sidelong to him.

"Now you're going to be sorry for every lie you ever told in your life, horse thief," he said.

Summers just looked at him. He was getting an urge to hammer a fist into the deputy's face.

The two prisoners staggered into the open

cavern on the end of ropes drawn tight around their waists. Their arms were pinned to their sides, their hands tied behind their backs.

Ready to hang, Summers thought, from the looks of them.

The two were dressed in black, bareheaded and soaked from the storm. Their wet black hair hung in long strands partly covering their battered and swollen faces. The riflemen shoved them to the ground near the fire. Sheriff Miller stepped over and grabbed one by his loose shirt collar and dragged him upward to his feet.

"Don't you pass out on me, Ezra!" he said, shaking the half-conscious man. To the rifleman nearest him he said, "Julio, help me hold him up." He shook the battered prisoner again and swiped wet hair back from his marked and purple face. "Pay attention, Ezra!" he said in the man's face. "You'll get plenty of sleep once that rope jerks around your neck." He drew back a hand as if to slap the man again. But he held back as the man struggled to hold his head up.

"I'm . . . awake," the prisoner said over swollen lips.

Summers winced at the sight of split lips, cuts, welts.

"Good," said Miller. He chuckled and shook the man again for good measure. "Now look at this man and tell me his name." He roughly jerked the man's face around toward Summers. "We know he was with you. Just tell us who he is. Save us from beating it out of you."

"Wait a minute, Sheriff —" Summers started to protest, but his words were cut short as the butt of Endo Clifford's rifle clipped a sharp blow to his ribs. He buckled slightly at the waist.

"Keep your mouth shut till you're spoken to," Clifford warned him. "Now straighten up." He yanked Summers upright. Summers managed to keep his hand clutched to his ribs.

Miller gave them a glance, then looked back at the prisoner.

"Come on, Ezra, what's his name?" said Miller. "Spit it out, and you can go on back to sleep."

The prisoner looked at Summers through blackened swollen eyes, as if trying hard to recognize him.

"I — I don't know his name," he said weakly. "I never . . . saw him before."

"Lying son of a bitch!" shouted Endo Clifford. He stepped away from Summers and closer to the prisoner. "Let me swat him a lick or two, Sheriff." He drew back his rifle butt.

"Simmer yourself down, Endo," Miller warned him. "We've got time to get the truth before we string them up."

"This man is telling you the truth, Sheriff," Summers cut in. "I don't know these two men. Him either." He nodded over toward the body lying on the blanket.

Miller ignored Summers and directed his words back to Ezra Belltrae.

"Here's the thing, Ezra," he said in a more reasonable tone of voice. "You know you and your brother, Collard, are going to hang, first thing when the storm lets up." He looped an arm up onto the battered prisoner's shoulders as he spoke. "There's no two ways about it." He shook his head. "You were seen stealing horses from Swann's corral." He gestured a hand toward the spot where the stallion had been butchered. "You've butchered and boned out his stallion. That's the meat we caught you carrying, right?"

"We did . . . all that," the prisoner admitted freely. "We take meat to the people at the old hill ruins." He tried to stretch a thin smile onto his split and swollen lips.

"See, that's the way," said Miller, sounding encouraged. "Own up to what you did and be done with it. Get yourself hanged out here and save yourself the trip to Dark Horses. None of us wants to drag this thing out." He gestured toward Summers. "Identify this man if he was with you and let's hang everybody at once. Makes sense, don't you think? Do it out here, save yourselves a lot of beatings, lots of abuse and getting spat on when you climb them handmade gallows steps in Dark Horses."

"Yes . . . it makes sense," said Ezra Belltrae. He leveled his swollen eyes onto Summers and stood up straighter.

"All right, now we're getting somewhere," said Miller with a breath of relief.

"I don't know . . . this man," he insisted, staring into Summers' eyes.

"Damn it to hell!" said Miller. Turning to the gathered riflemen, he said, "Find a beam strong enough to swing a rope over. We're hanging the Belltraes right now." He stared coldly into Ezra Belltrae's eyes. "I'm done with these Mex-Chinook half-bred Indian-French Micmac slope-head — whatever they are — sons of bitches!"

"You heard him, boys," said Endo Clifford, sounding excited. "Let's get to stretching their necks —"

From the ground near the campfire, the other Belltrae brother spoke up in a weak

37

voice, cutting Clifford off.

"I . . . will identify him," he said. "He was . . . with us."

"Say what . . . ?" said Clifford, looking surprised.

Miller walked over to the fire and looked down at the other Belltrae brother's battered face.

"Who is he, Collard?" he asked in a no-nonsense tone. He took out Summers' paperwork and shook it in his hand. "He gave me a name. But I want to hear it from you."

Collard stared up at the sheriff through his purple eyes for a second.

"Smith," he said in a strained voice.

"Smith, huh?" said Miller, not liking Collard's reply. He clenched his big fists at his sides. "I just knew I'd end up kicking you some more," he said, drawing back his wet left boot. "I swear I believe you two like taking a beating better than I do giving it."

"No, wait. . . . It is the name he . . . told us," said Collard. He raised a blue trembling hand to protect himself. "Ol' Hendrik bring him . . . to us."

"Yeah?" said Miller, turning in place, looking from face to face, seeing the men reflect possibility in their eyes. He stared at Ezra with a start of a smile. "Now what do you

38

say? Your brother's decided to do the right thing and —"

"He's lying," Ezra said, stone-faced, cutting him off. "We don't know . . . this man." His voice sounded stronger than it had moments earlier.

"Are you lying to me, Collard?" Miller asked the brother on the ground.

"No," Collard said weakly. "Ezra . . . is lying." He pointed a finger at his brother.

"I am . . . telling the truth," came Ezra's rebuttal. "My brother is lying."

Miller looked back and forth between the Belltrae brothers and cursed under his breath. He shoved the paperwork back into his pocket behind his rain slicker.

"Never mind with those ropes, fellows," he said to the Mexican rifleman. "These two are hardheaded."

"Wait a minute, Sheriff Bert," said Clifford. "You mean we're not even going to hang them?"

"No, we're not, Endo," said Miller. "Not right now, not right here." He looked at the Belltrae brothers. "These two we could hang today. But I want somebody besides me to decide whether or not this one was in on it. As it stands right now, I don't know what to make of it."

"They're doing this on purpose, to keep

39

them from hanging a day or two sooner," said Clifford, staring at the Belltraes in turn. "These sons a' bitches."

"Could be," said Miller. "But he does have these papers on the fillies, and I know for a fact Swann was looking for some breeding stock." He looked at Summers with mixed contempt. "I'm not hanging a man unless I'm certain he's guilty."

"That's not much better than wasting a lot of time having a trial and that whole mess," said Clifford.

"That's how we're doing it this time, Endo," Miller said with a firm stare. "So button your lip about it. Soon as the storm lets up, we're headed to Swann's ranchero on our way to Dark Horses — see what Ansil Swann says about this one." He looked Summers up and down and said to him, "So far the Belltraes are all that's keeping you alive, mister."

Summers just stared at him.

"Yeah, they are," Clifford put in, "but only for a day or two. You'll all three hang when we get you to Swann's ranch." He spat on the ground between them. Then he bumped against Summers as he and Miller stepped away toward the fire and two Mexican riflemen moved in to take their place.

■ ■ ■ ■

As the storm pounded and whaled on the Mexican hillsides, Will Summers and the Belltrae brothers sat leaning against a stone wall in flickering torchlight. The three watched in silence as a Mexican walked out along the stone causeway shaft to where Summers had tied his dapple gray and the string of fillies. The gray sawed its head in protest and jerked against the reins as the man led the five animals inside the cavern.

"That's a fine-looking . . . gray you ride, mister," said Ezra in a hushed and pained voice. He sat the closest to Summers and appeared to be less badly beaten than his brother. He spoke sidelong as his head lolled back against the stone.

"Are we going to talk horses now?" Summers said in a clipped tone without turning to face the man.

Ezra fell silent for a moment. Finally he let out a pained breath.

"We jackpotted you to keep Miller from hanging us," he said.

"I know," Summers said, staring straight ahead, watching the Mexican check his horses over good. "But you heard the deputy. It's only for a day or two. You'll hang soon enough."

"For a living man, a day or two means nothing," he said. "For a man who is to be hanged . . . a day is an eternity."

Summers heard a mixed accent of wilderness French and schooled English in the man's voice.

"You got me there," he replied. "I didn't like the prospect of hanging any more than you did."

"I know," said Ezra with resolve. "And now it is us, not you, who will hang — not if Swann identifies you as a man bringing him horses."

"He will," said Summers. "That is, if we can get to his place without the sheriff's crazy deputy shooting us first." He continued staring straight ahead as he spoke. Across the low-burning fire, he watched the Mexican run an appraising hand down the horse's foreleg.

"Endo Clifford . . . is no deputy," said Ezra Belltrae, sounding a little stronger, "any more than Bert Miller is a sheriff."

Summers cut a sidelong glance at him.

"Then they sure fooled me," he said skeptically. "They're both wearing badges."

"Don't be deceived by . . . badges," said Collard Belltrae, raising himself a little against the stone wall. "They are hired killers. Nothing more."

Ezra helped his brother adjust himself upright. Then he turned back to Summers.

"What my brother, Collard, means is that they are not elected lawmen. They work for Swann," he said. "That's the only reason they're taking all three of us to Swann. They don't want to do something out here . . . that they will have to answer for to Swann. He's the man who pays them. Swann wields much influence with the Mexican government. Without Swann, men like Miller and Endo Clifford know they would be treated like the murderers and thieves they are."

"This is Mexico," said Summers. "But I suppose enough money buys a man like Swann powerful influence wherever his business takes him."

Ezra Belltrae nodded his bruised head.

"Yes, money is the way of the world," he said, rubbing his thumb and fingertip together in the universal sign for greed. "Swann's mining companies are held in high favor by the Mexican government. His mines have brought in the money and resources it takes to turn a poor Mexican hill town like Dark Horses into a prosperous *business* settlement."

"I can't fault a man for making his fortune," Summers said. He turned his head enough to look the two up and down.

"Nor can I," said Ezra Belltrae. "You asked me how he has such influence, so I tell you." As Ezra paused, Collard took up the conversation.

"Dark Horses is Swann's dream of what Old Mexico must someday become — he calls it Little America," he said.

"Does he, now?" said Summers. "And how is it that you know all this?"

The two brothers looked at each other for a moment, then back at Summers.

"We know it because . . . we once worked for him," Collard said, his voice still strained.

"Until we decided to leave his employ and start working for ourselves," said Ezra.

"Stealing horses?" Summers asked.

"No," said Ezra, ignoring the accusation. He nodded at the quirt still hanging from Summers' wrist. "We make bridles, quirts, anything that can be braided from horse-hair."

Summers examined the quirt.

"You do good work," he said. "But you're not making a living at it around here."

"No, we are not," said Ezra. "We sell our goods across the border, in Texas, in Arizona."

"We also break and sell wild mustangs,"

said Collard.

"Like yourself, we are horse traders," Ezra put in. "Only we are Indian and not welcome in the same places as you."

Indian. . . . Summers looked at them closer.

"What tribe are you from?" he asked.

"Micmac —" Collard started to say.

"Chinook," Ezra said over him.

"Right." Summers nodded skeptically, dismissing them both. He turned away.

"Wait," said Ezra. "What my brother, Collard, meant is, we're French-Indian. We have the blood of the Micmac, the Flathead and the Chinook in us." He paused. "We *are* mission-school Indian — look at us. Do you doubt it?"

"No," said Summers, "I don't doubt you." He listened toward the storm outside the cavern, noting it had begun to sound farther away along the hillsides. Good, he thought. The quicker he stood before Ansil Swann, the quicker he could get this situation straightened out. No sooner had he noticed the storm starting to wane than he heard Sheriff Miller call out to his riflemen.

"All right," Miller said, "everybody get saddled and ready. Julio tells me the storm is moving out. When it's gone, so are we." He added, looking all around the cavern,

45

"We're two days from Dark Horses, but only a day and a half to Swann's ranch, maybe less. He sees we've caught these thieves, there's a good chance you men will all get a reward of some kind — his token of appreciation."

Ezra Belltrae leaned over closer to Summers and spoke to him in a guarded tone of voice.

"We could stay right here another week. It wouldn't bother me at all," he said. "I don't want to go to Swann's ranch."

"Me neither," Collard said in his pained voice. The two sat staring at Summers through their swollen eyes.

Ezra's voice fell even quieter; he leaned even closer to Summers as he spoke.

"We might even want to leave before we get there," he said. "Are you interested?"

Summers didn't reply; he only gazed ahead toward his horses as if he hadn't heard Ezra. The shape these two were in, he couldn't see them going anywhere. This was wishful thinking on the part of two desperate men facing a noose.

Ezra read Summers' silence and said nothing more on the matter.

Summers continued to stare straight ahead. He was pretty certain these brothers were going to hang. He was also certain he

46

wasn't. Once Swann saw him and cleared him, he would collect his money and be on his way. For now, the best thing he could do was separate himself from these two, keep his mouth shut and let this situation play itself out.

CHAPTER 4

As the last of the storm still lingered overhead, Miller led the posse and the prisoners
out of the shelter of the mine shaft and into
the gray light of afternoon. A Mexican rifleman had strung a rope from Summers'
wrists to the Belltraes' in turn, keeping the
three with only a short distance between
their horses. Any attempt to make a sudden
run for it would have ended in a tangle of
horse, men and rope. Summers and the
Belltraes knew it.

The three rode along at a walk. Behind
them another rifleman led Summers' string
of fillies. Behind him, bringing up the rear,
a Mexican led the Belltraes' packhorse, the
animal's back covered with canvas-wrapped
bundles of bloody horse meat. Miller had
gotten one of the Mexicans to wrap the
butchered stallion's head in canvas and
brought it along as proof of the animal's
death.

They rode on, winding down the muddy sodden hill trails until at dark they had reached a terraced plain twenty yards back from the roaring river. At the edge of the plain, Blue River splashed high and muddy as it raced past them.

"This is as far as we're going tonight, compadres," Miller called out above the roar of heavy crashing water. "Tomorrow it'll be down some. We'll start early looking for a place to cross."

Summers saw the Belltraes give each other a look, but he thought nothing of it. Given the location, surrounded on two sides by a turn in the raging river, on another side by a long stretch of flatlands that offered no cover from rifle fire, he was convinced the brothers would have to wait until tomorrow to attempt any kind of escape. Their only other direction was to go back the way they came, but that would leave them racing uphill on a mud-slick trail in the black of night.

Huh-uh, I don't think so, Summers assured himself, looking down at the length of rope holding the three together. They knew he wasn't going with them. They wouldn't try to force him along, take a chance on him foiling their getaway. He stepped down from atop his horse as the

Belltraes and the Mexican leading them did the same.

The Mexican led the three to a large rock and seated them on the ground against it and strung their rope around it. They sat watching the posse make camp. Summers saw the Belltraes alternate their attention between the posse and the high raging river to the right. For two men who'd each taken a bad beating, Summers noted how quickly the two had come around. Their eyes were still almost swollen shut, yet they seemed to be fully conscious, undulled by the purple cuts and welts on their faces, their heads.

When a campfire had been made and coffee had been boiled, and food had been cooked over open flames, two Mexicans brought tin plates of red beans and flatbread and stood over the three with rifles while they ate. Over beside the fire Endo Clifford gave the three a harsh stare as they ate.

"Don't see why we're wasting good food on the Belltraes," he called out. "It'll be lying piled on the ground beneath their pants legs when the rope stiffens up around their necks." He ended his grim offering with a dark laugh. The other posse men nodded; some chuckled along with him.

After Clifford's joke the camp fell silent, the saddle-worn men's only interest being to get themselves fed and bedded down for the night. Yet the silence only lasted for a second before Collard Belltrae finished swallowing a mouthful of beans and stared over at Clifford.

"I see you there lapping at that pile like a starving dog, Endo Clifford," he said flatly.

The faces of the posse men turned to Clifford, who seemed to need a second to interpret Collard's words. Then his face suddenly turned blue-red.

"You son of a bitch!" he shrieked. Flinging his tin plate of food aside, he sprang to his feet, charging toward the three prisoners.

"Get back here, Endo!" Miller commanded, trying to stop the enraged deputy. But Clifford was beyond his control. The crazed deputy hurled himself onto Collard Belltrae, barehanded, his fists swinging in a roundhouse fashion. The rope connecting the three prisoners drew tight, yanking Summers and both Belltrae brothers into the fray. Collard caught Endo Clifford in a bear hug; the two rolled back and forth in tangled rope, Clifford's fists pounding wildly.

"Stop him!" Miller shouted at the other posse men.

In a second the posse men become engaged in the melee, three of them tangled in

51

the prisoners' rope as they pulled Clifford back, still kicking and screaming at Collard Belltrae. Summers managed to duck away from a swinging fist. Clifford continued to kick and fight until Miller stepped in, grabbed him by his throat and slung him sidelong to the ground. Two Mexican posse men pinned him to the dirt.

Clifford stopped struggling when he looked up and saw Miller's rifle butt loom menacingly above his face.

"That's all of it, Endo!" Miller shouted. "If you want to keep that badge you'll get control of yourself."

"You heard what he said, Sheriff —" Endo started.

"I don't give a damn what he said," bellowed Miller. He held the rifle butt ready to jam into the deputy's face. "What's it going to be?"

Clifford settled, let out a breath and submitted under the grip of the two posse men atop him.

"All right, I'm done with it," he said. "I lost my head to these horse-eating sons a' bitches, Sheriff, but now I'm good." He spread his hand as if in surrender. "Let me up, damn it," he said coolly to the posse men.

The posse men looked up at Miller for

direction.

"All right, let him up," Miller said.

As the posse men stood up from atop Clifford, Miller reached a hand down and helped the deputy pull himself to his feet. Summers and the Belltraes lay watching in their tangled rope, still tied to the large rock behind them.

"Do something like that again, Endo," Miller threatened, "I'll tear that badge from your chest and chase you out of here."

"I won't, Sheriff," said Clifford, slapping damp dirt from his chest, his trousers. "You've got my word."

Miller looked around at the prisoners' discarded tin plates and cups, the beans strewn on the ground, the coffee spilled.

"That was all the supper you're getting tonight," he said. He looked at one of the Mexican posse men. "Julio, you and Hector march them out a ways, let them relieve themselves. Then bed them down for the night." He turned to Collard Belltrae, who sat wiping a fresh trickle of blood from his lower lip. "Shoot your mouth off again, I won't lift a finger to stop Endo from killing you."

Collard only glared at him as he, his brother and Summers stood for the guards, their hands tied in front of them, the lead rope strung between their wrists.

"My brother has said all he has to say, Sheriff," said Ezra Belltrae.

Summers only stared at the Belltraes until the posse men gestured the three of them toward a stand of brush a few yards away. They walked there and back in silence, and when they returned, even though nothing more was said, Summers noted to himself a new air of resolve about the two brothers. Something had changed for the Belltraes, he noted, yet, as tired and hungry as he was, he put the two out of his mind. He lay back on the damp ground as the guards retied their lead rope around the rock for the night.

In moments, sleep had overcome Summers and the rest of the camp as well. Yet, in the middle of the night, the camp was quickly awakened by shouting from two Mexican riflemen who had come to relieve the guards sitting watch over the prisoners. Summers' eyes flew open at the feel of hands shaking him roughly. He sat up, blinking and staring into the angry face of the stocky guard, Hector, while around the campfire men rose from their blankets and hurried over toward him, guns in hand.

"Tell me where they are, gringo," Hector

demanded, "or I will beat the chit out of you!"

Summers just stared at the Mexican, bleary-eyed, his mind not yet fully awake.

"*Mis* compadres are dead!" he said. Behind him on the ground, the two Mexicans on watch lay dead in pools of blood. One's throat was slashed; the other's head was bashed in by a bloody rock lying three feet away.

The Mexican drew back a pistol and started to swipe the barrel across Summers' face. But before he could make a swing, Miller's hand reached down and grabbed him by his wrist.

"For God sakes, don't knock him out, Hector," he barked. "He won't be able to tell us anything!"

Hector backed away. Miller himself stood crouched over Summers, the end of the sliced rope in one hand. He gripped Summers by his shirt, held the sliced rope in his face.

"How'd they get the knife, mister?" he demanded. "Which way are they headed?"

"Let me at him, Sheriff," said Clifford, moving in close beside Miller. "I'll loosen his tongue — kill two of our men, will they?"

Miller shoved the deputy away and wagged the sliced rope in Summers' face. But before he could say anything more, a man called out from the place they had tied their horses.

"They've stolen our horses, Sheriff!" he shouted.

"Jesus!" said Miller. "All of them?" He looked over at the shadowy darkness the other side of the flickering campfire.

"No, but damn near all," the man called back to him. "The ones tied farthest out of the light — even the packhorse."

"Those thieving sons a' bitches know every trick," Miller said with contempt. He swung his face back to Summers. As he spoke, Endo Clifford ran across the camp and looked at what few horses were left.

"Where are they headed?" Miller demanded of Summers.

"Sheriff, I wasn't a part of this," Summers said quickly, holding up his tied wrists. "If I was, would I still be sitting here?"

That stopped Miller. He stared for a second, then cursed under his breath. He stood up over Summers and looked all around as the men gathered closer.

"How many horses are we left with, Endo?" he called out across the campsite.

"His string and three others," Clifford called out in reply.

"Well, well, what a coincidence, mister.

Your horses and three others," said Miller, glaring down at Summers. Firelight flickered on the dark anger in his eyes.

"I had nothing to do with it, Sheriff," Summers insisted, looking up.

Miller grabbed him by his tied hands and yanked him to his feet. Summers staggered in place.

"Start checking their tracks," Miller called out to the men.

"Buster already did, Sheriff," said one of the Americans, a Texas gunman named Red Warren.

"That's right. I did, Sheriff," a tall, stout Missourian named Buster Saggert called out in reply. "They scattered our horses instead of taking 'em with them."

Miller considered it for a second. He looked at Summers, then back at the two posse men.

"That means they're crossing the river," he said. "Didn't want to be pulling too many horses along in that swift water." He looked back at Summers, checking his expression. "Right, mister?"

Summers kept his mouth shut, knowing there was nothing he could say that would do him any good. But he agreed with Miller. They had scattered the horses to keep the posse men busy as long as they could.

Then they had headed straight for the river — that's what he would have done, he told himself. The Río Azul was high, fast and dangerous, but still a better choice than swinging from a rope.

Miller looked away from Summers, at one of the Mexicans stooped over the bodies of the guards. The body of the guard with his throat cut lay closest. Miller shook his head slowly, seeing that guard's rifle was missing and his side holster was empty, yet his knife still stood in its sheath on his side.

"Where do you suppose they got a knife, Julio?" he asked the stooped Mexican.

The Mexican only shrugged as he stood up. Other posse men had begun to gather in closer.

"I expect we'll never know the answer to that, Sheriff Bert," said Endo Clifford, turning to walk away as he spoke. "These bastards have a way of getting their hands on stuff —"

His words stopped short as Miller's hand grasped the back of his leather vest at his beltline and kept him from walking away.

"Hold it, Endo," said Miller. He jerked Clifford's vest up and stared at the empty knife sheath stuck down behind his belt. "Where's your knife?"

"My knife . . . ?" Clifford's hand went

58

back and clutched at the empty sheath, feeling all around. "Hell, it's right here —" His words stopped short again. "Damn! It was right there, where it always is!" His voice took on an uneasiness.

"Endo, you damn fool!" said Miller. In his rage his hand went instinctively to the butt of his gun. "You let Collard Belltrae wrestle your knife from you!"

"No, no!" Clifford insisted, shaking his head wildly. "He didn't get my knife from me. I don't know what happened to it. But he didn't get it."

"The hell he didn't!" Miller grabbed the shaken Clifford and pressed him down over the body of the dead Mexican guard. "There, did you do that? Did you cut this man's throat?"

"No, damn it, turn me loose!" Clifford shouted, struggling against the sheriff's ironlike grip on his shoulders. "You know damn well I didn't!"

"Then the Belltraes did it with your knife!" said Miller. He looked all around at the other men's faces. "Anybody else missing their knife?"

The men only looked back and forth at each other, touching their hands to their sheathed knives.

"Huh? No?" said Miller. "I didn't think

so." He shoved Clifford away from him. Clifford sprawled on the damp ground. "Just you, you bungling idiot," Miller said to him.

Summers looked down at Clifford as he scrambled up onto his feet.

"Here's the one you ought to be accusing!" he shouted. He lunged at Summers as he shouted, "He's the one —"

His words turned into a deep, painful gasp as Summers anticipated his move, side-stepped and swung a hard kick that planted his boot toe solidly into Clifford's groin. The kick lifted Clifford onto his toes. He hung there for a second as if suspended.

"Holy Jesus," said Red Warren, cupping himself, watching Clifford bow slowly at the waist and finally topple stiffly to the ground.

"*Dios mio,*" said a Mexican named Gorge in a hushed tone, "*ha le patearon la bolas sueltas!*"

"*Sí,*" said Julio, turning his words into English, "he has kicked his balls loose."

Buster Saggert started to step toward Summers, but Miller stopped him with a raised hand.

"Leave him alone, Buster," Miller said firmly. "Clifford had it coming. I wish I'd done it myself." He gestured at Clifford, and said to Saggert, "You and Red get him on his feet." He looked at Summers. "Do something like that again, it won't matter if Swann vouches for you or not. I'll stick a bullet in your head."

Summers only stared at him in silence.

"All right," Miller called out to the posse men, "everybody get out of here, round up our horses. Let's get after these horse-thieving curs!"

"What if they've crossed the Blue River?" Red Warren asked, motioning toward the sound of the rushing water. "It's running high."

"If they crossed it we'll cross it too!" shouted Miller. "We're not going to be turned back. Swann will want those two's hides when he hears what they've done to his stallion."

The Mexican posse men gave each other guarded looks, then moved away at a trot, spreading out, rifles in hand, following the tracks of their scattered horses.

CHAPTER 5

It was full daylight by the time the posse men had gathered the horses the Belltraes had scattered all along the banks of the swollen river. Will Summers stood up when Miller rode in leading Summers' gray behind him. A Mexican, now mounted on his own recovered horse, led the string of fillies behind him, some of the posse men having ridden the young mares out on the search. Summers' gray and the fillies were all mud-streaked and worn out from the hard morning ride.

Miller stepped down from his saddle, watching Summers look his muddy dapple gray over.

"You've got a fine horse, mister," Miller said, handing Summers the gray's reins, "if he's really yours, that is."

"It's my horse, Sheriff," Summers said, returning Miller's harsh stare.

Miller ignored his reply and called out to

the Mexicans leading the four fillies.

"Bring those gals over here, Hector," he said. "Let this man see they're in the same shape they were before you rode them. If those are Mr. Swann's animals, I want him knowing we've taken good care of them for him."

Summers looked the fillies over as the Mexican rode forward and handed him the lead rope. He looked them over closer as Miller and the posse men watched from their saddles. Endo Clifford sat bowed and stiff in his saddle, watching Summers with a dark scowl. The Mexican they had left guarding Summers stood by, his rifle ready in his hands.

"Lajo, cut him loose," Miller said, gesturing at the rope around Summers' wrists. "You and your compadres stick close to him."

Summers looked up at Miller, surprised, as the Mexican reached out with a long boot knife and sliced through the rope.

"I don't want you slowing us down," said Miller. "If you try anything, these men will chop you into dog meat. Do you understand me, mister?"

"The name is *Will Summers*," Summers reminded him, rubbing his freed wrists, keeping his eyes up at Miller.

"Yeah, we'll see about that," Miller replied. "Until we find out more about you, keep in mind there'll be gun sights on you, every move you make." Over a low muddy rise, Red Warren came riding toward them as Miller spoke.

"I understand," Summers said.

Miller jerked a nod toward the mud-streaked gray and the string of fillies. "Then hit your saddle, lead your string," he said. "We're about to cross the river."

Red Warren galloped up closer and stopped his muddy horse a few feet from Miller.

"I followed their prints to the water's edge where they crossed, Sheriff," he said. "But I've got to say, this is awful risky. A few hours and the river will be settling back into its banks."

"I'm not giving them a few more hours," said Sheriff Miller with resolve. "If the Belltraes crossed it, we'll cross it." He nudged his horse forward toward Warren. "Let's get going."

As the horsemen turned their horses in behind Miller and Warren, Summers saw a look of hatred in Endo Clifford's eyes, directed at him. He returned Clifford's stare and gave his gray a chuck of the reins, sending the muddy animal forward, the four fillies strung alongside him.

They descended from damp ground into a sloppy wet plain leading out to the rushing river. Following Miller and Red Warren, the riders splashed along at a gallop until they had skirted over two hundred yards downstream. There they came to a halt and bunched up on a narrow bar of rocky earth with water whipping up and lashing up at them.

"Good God, Red, they crossed here?" Miller shouted above the roar of the water. Summers let the other men move up in front of him and his string, keeping a little more room for himself.

"There they went," Red said, pointing a wet gloved finger down at the tip of the bar where hoofprints led down and fell away in the swirling silt-filled water. He continued shouting, "If you ask me, we'd have to be plumb loco —"

"I'm not asking you, Red," Miller shouted above the muddy raging torrent. He looked all around, then at the grim faces of the Mexicans gathered around him. They stared in dark consternation at the rushing water.

"Es una locura, Lajo?" Miller asked the Mexican nearest him as he gestured at the raging water.

Lajo pulled a ragged blanket tighter

around him against the spray of water.

"*Sí, es de locos, muy, muy locos,*" Lajo said, looking Miller in the eye.

"I never seen a river a Mex can't swim a horse across, Sheriff Miller," Buster Saggert put in. "If these fellows say it's *crazy,* it must be tongue-slapping, bug-eyed nuts."

"Shut up, Buster," said Miller. He looked back at Lajo. Lajo shrugged in his drawn blanket.

"I don't think they cross here," he said.

"Oh?" said Miller. He gestured at the hoofprints leading into the swirling water. "Then what do you make of this?" Water splashed high along the rock bar as he spoke.

"It is, how you say . . . a hunting duck," Lajo said, struggling for a way to explain himself. He looked back and forth among the Americans.

"A *what*?" said Miller.

"A *not real* hunting duck?" Lajo ventured.

"What the blazing hell is he saying, Red?" said Miller, getting impatient.

"Beats me," said Red Warren, also impatient. He looked at Endo, who sat bowed against the lingering ache in his badly kicked testicles.

Endo grumbled and shook his head in disgust.

"I don't know why we brought these Mexes with us," he said. "The whole damn country don't even speak English — most of 'em won't even try."

"A *decoy*," Summers blurted out, getting tired of listening to them.

The posse men all looked around at him.

"He's saying the tracks are meant to fool you," he said, nodding at the hoofprints. "The Belltraes didn't cross here."

Lajo nodded vigorously.

"*Sí*," Lajo said, "*señuelo*, a decoy — a trick, is what I mean."

"Why didn't you say so, Lajo?" Miller growled. But he looked out at the raging water and swallowed a dryness in his throat.

"I try to," Lajo said. He looked back at Summers as if grateful for his help.

"Anyway, it's nonsense. This is no *decoy*," Miller said, ignoring Lajo's reply. "I know a trick when I see one. They crossed here. There's no two ways about it."

Summers just sat listening. So did the Mexicans.

Miller stared out at the raging water in contemplation, until his thoughts were interrupted by Buster Saggert.

"Riders coming, Sheriff," Saggert said, staring back across the wet plain behind them. He raised his rifle from his lap and held it ready. Summers had also looked back and spotted the riders at the same time as Saggert. He pulled on his gray's reins, starting to turn.

Seeing rainwater splashing up in the wake of four approaching riders, Miller quickly jerked his rifle up as he started backing his horse up to get off the thin slice of rocky ground.

"Everybody get off this rock and spread out," he ordered, even as the men had already started turning and backing their horses back onto wider ground. "Get your string the hell out of their way!" he shouted at Summers.

Summers was already turning his gray and his string of fillies. He pulled the animals aside.

The approaching riders were coming fast, not letting the wet, soggy ground slow them down.

As the posse men spread along the edge of the water and began forming a fighting line, Miller stood in his stirrups and gave the riders a closer look through the splashing water.

"Everybody hold your fire," he said to the men on either side of him. His voice took a bitter turn. "It's Swann's child bride." He cursed under his breath and added, "Damn it, this is all I need. Why's she still out here snooping around?"

The posse men sat still, watching as the four riders splashed up across the soggy plain and reined their horses to a halt twenty feet in front of them.

"Morning, Miss Bailey," Miller said politely to the leader of the four. He took off his wet hat. On either side of Miller the posse men touched their hat brims respectfully. "I figured you and your boys would be headed back by now."

Boys. . . .

The three young horsemen glared at Miller.

"Morning, Sheriff," said Bailey Swann. She wore wet range clothes, a tall brown hat, boots and a slicker. "Put your hat on," she said to Miller in a no-nonsense tone of voice. "This is not a social call. We got caught by the storm yesterday," she added. "I thought we'd see how your search is going before we head back this morning and inform Mr. Swann."

"Of course, Miss Bailey." Miller's face reddened. He pushed his wet hat back down on his head. "As you can see we're hot on the Belltraes' trail." he said, his tone turning stiff, a little impatient. He gestured a hand down toward the tracks leading out into the rushing water. "We should have them treed and hanged before noon today."

"We saw you from the high ridges day before yesterday," Bailey Swann said bluntly. "You had them. What happened?"

"Fact is, they got away from us last night," said Miller. As he spoke to her, the young woman dismissingly stepped her muddy horse over in front of Will Summers. She looked him up and down, appraising him curiously. In turn Summers noted to himself the age difference between her and Ansil Swann. The young woman before him was not much older than himself, midtwenties, late twenties. Swann was old enough to be this woman's grandfather.

"We found ol' Hendrik dead back in the mine shafts last afternoon. Caught this one before he had time to get away —" Miller continued, until the young woman cut him off.

"We saw Hendrik's body last night," she said bluntly. "We saw what happened in the cave. Was that my husband's stallion?" she asked.

"I'm afraid so, Mrs. Swann," said Miller. "We've brought the animal's head back for your husband to identify —"

"We rode through your camp a while ago," Bailey said. "We chased away a pack of wolves that had torn into the bundles of horse meat you left there. I expect they returned as soon as we were out of sight. There wasn't much to identify. There'll be less when you get back there."

Miller stiffened, clenched his fists and his teeth to keep from hurling out a curse word. Before he could respond, Bailey Swann nodded at Will Summers and asked, "Who is this one, just another saddle tramp?"

Summers' eyes fixed on hers and stayed. He had nothing to hide. He wasn't going to cower down.

"Will Summers, ma'am," Summers replied before Miller got the chance to. "I wasn't with the Belltraes. I was delivering these fillies to your husband — Mr. Swann, that is," he corrected himself.

"He claims Will Summers is his name, ma'am," Miller cut in. "Even has some papers here on the horses." He patted the lapel of his mud-splattered rain slicker. "Says Mr. Swann will vouch for him as soon as we get him there."

"Oh?" said Bailey. She held a hand out to Miller for the papers as she stared at Summers. "I don't recall Mr. Swann mentioning the purchase of any bay fillies."

"That's what I figured, Miss Bailey," said Miller, taking out the papers and handing

71

them over to her. "Then we should have hanged all three yesterday when we had the chance — saved ourselves a lot of extra riding." He glared at Summers with renewed hatred. "Hector, go scout us a tree."

"Wait!" Summers blurted out to Miller and the Mexican. To Bailey he said quickly, "Take me to your husband, ma'am. He'll vouch for me. He bought these fillies from me — said they were breeding stock for his stallion." He looked back and forth among the three other riders staring at him. "Surely he would have told somebody they were coming."

The three riders continued to stare at him, unmoved.

Bailey Swann had unfolded the paperwork and started reading. She didn't look up at Summers. "You're right. He would have," she said. Then she lifted her eyes to him. "That's my point exactly. Mr. Swann never mentioned it."

"How's that tree coming along, Hector?" Miller said to the Mexican who had stalled for a moment to hear the woman's reply. Hector turned his horse quickly and rode away along the river's edge. Summers sat silent, looking into the woman's cold blue eyes. He saw her fold the paperwork and start to hand it back to Miller.

"We can't hang you quick enough to suit me," Endo Clifford said to Summers in a pained voice.

Bailey Swann looked at Clifford, then back at Summers. Detecting the bad blood between the two, she looked back at Miller for an explanation.

"It's nothing, ma'am," Miller said, reaching out for the paperwork. "Endo kept boning and dogging him. He gave Endo the boot, in the worst possible place, if you know what I mean — pardon me for saying it." His face reddened again.

"Yes, I believe I know," the young woman said. She appeared to consider something. "You know what?" she said, pulling the paperwork back before Miller could take it from her. "Now that I think of it, I do remember my husband mentioning he'd acquired breeding stock for his stallion."

Miller just stared at her; so did Summers.

"Ma'am . . . ?" said Miller. He gave her a dubious look.

"Yes, it's true," she said. "I don't know how it could have slipped my mind."

Summers felt a sense of relief come over him. He almost slumped in his saddle. But he stopped himself and watched and waited, not sure he should believe his own ears.

CHAPTER 6

While the flooded river raged past the wet mud-splattered riders, Summers drew a long, calm breath. He continued to watch the young woman, certain that she was lying, but not about to say so. Anything she said that put some distance between him and a hanging rope, he was all for it. The doubt she saw in Miller's eyes made her turn to the young men riding with her for support.

"Dallas," she said to the nearest one, "don't you remember Mr. Swann telling you last week that there's a man bringing some bay fillies? I'm certain he did."

Dallas Tate, a handsome, tough-looking young man around Will Summers' age, quickly took up the woman's ruse.

"Yeah, come to think of it, I do remember," he said. He stepped his horse forward and inspected the fillies with what Summers saw to be sudden and mock interest. Summers pulled the string forward as if to afford the man a better look. He remained quiet, not wanting to stop anything that was starting to go in his favor.

"He said there were four bays coming — high bred, as I recall," said Tate. He turned in his saddle and looked at another rider. "Lon, is that what you heard?"

"Yep, it is," said Lonnie Kerns, a young Californian cattle drover with a barbwire scar across his left cheek, his upper lips. "I don't recall the number, but I remember they're all bays —"

Clifford listened, boiling with rage, until he couldn't take any more of it.

"Did he, now?" he blurted out with sarcasm, not believing a word of it. "Then did he also mention this man would be riding a waterlogged dapple gray, wearing muddy boots?"

Bailey and the three riders stared at Clifford.

"So you don't believe us?" she said coolly.

Clifford sneered. "Not in a pig's eye —"

"That's enough out of you, Endo," Miller said, still seething over Endo's knife being taken away from him by the Belltraes. He said to the young woman, "Please overlook Endo, Miss Bailey. He's not himself today."

"You should teach him to keep his mouth

shut," said Dallas Tate. "I'll tolerate no rudeness toward Mrs. Swann."

"Why, you . . . ," said Clifford. He stepped his horse forward, but Miller grabbed the horse's bridle, stopping him.

"We'll be escorting Mr. Summers and his horses to my husband," the woman cut in. "Where are his guns?" As she spoke she stuck the folded paperwork into her slicker. Summers stepped his horses forward and stopped up close beside the sheriff.

"I hope you know what you're doing, Mrs. Swann," Miller said, reaching around and taking Summers' rolled-up gun belt, Colt and everything else from his saddlebags and handing them over.

"I always know what I'm doing, Sheriff," the young woman said firmly.

Summers didn't put on his gun belt. Instead he draped the belt over his shoulder, pulled out the Colt, checked it, found it loaded, spun the cylinder and slid it back into holster.

"Obliged you kept it dry for me, Sheriff," he said.

"Anytime I can help," Miller said in a wry tone.

"What about my rifle?" Summers asked.

"Julio, bring this man his Winchester," Miller said over his shoulder. To Summers he said, "Mister, you're a lucky man today."

Summers straightened in his saddle as he saw his Winchester being passed up to Miller.

"It's *Summers . . . Will* Summers," he allowed himself to say. He took the Winchester Miller held out to him.

"I'll remember that," said Miller. He watched Summers back his gray and pull the string along with him. "Mrs. Bailey," he added, "please tell Mr. Swann that I hope he's feeling better. Tell him we've crossed the Blue River, and we'll be hanging the Belltraes before the day ends. I'll be riding out to the ranch to report as soon as we're done out here." He gave her a piercing stare. "I need to discuss drawing my pay."

Drawing his pay . . . ? Summers watched and listened.

Ignoring his words, Bailey looked away from Miller and out on the rushing river.

"You're not fool enough to cross this, are you?" she said.

Miller looked taken aback by her words.

"The Belltraes crossed it. So can we," he replied in a stubborn clipped tone.

The woman looked at her three riders for an opinion. All three shook their heads slowly.

"Ain't a way in the world," Dallas Tate said.

Bailey Swann took a deep breath and smiled cordially.

"Yes, then, I will tell *my husband,* Sheriff Miller," she said. "Good luck." She turned her horse; the three horsemen followed her. So did Summers, him and his horse string flanked by Lonnie Kerns on his right and the third man, Little Ted Ford, on his left.

"If I ever see you again, *horse thief,* you're a dead man," Endo Clifford shouted out at Summers. But Summers rode on at a walk without looking back. Beside him, Little Ted Ford held up an insulting hand gesture back toward Clifford and gave a short laugh.

"Don't tease that fool, Little Ted," said Kerns. "Not with your back to him. No matter how little you think of him, he is a back-shooting murderer. Keep that in mind."

"Ha, he doesn't scare me," said Little Ted. As he spoke he lifted his canteen from his saddle horn, uncapped it and handed it to Summers.

"Here, Will Summers," he said, holding out the canteen. "Looks like you've got the *dries.*"

"Obliged, I do," Summers said, taking the canteen. He raised the canteen to his lips and drew a long gulp of cool water from it. Then he passed it back to Little Ted, who looked at, shook it and grinned as he capped it.

"I expect there's nothing like the threat of hanging to give a man the dries," he said.

"You're right there," Summers said, wiping his sleeve across his lips. He raised his voice enough for the woman and Dallas Tate riding in front of him to hear. "I'm grateful the four of you showed up when you did. I've never come that close to a hanging rope."

Without turning in their saddles Dallas Tate and Bailey Swann gave each other a sidelong look.

"How close have you come?" Dallas asked flatly.

The question caught Summers by surprise. He considered it.

"I've never had to think about it," he said. "I've never been a horse thief."

Beside him, Lonnie Kerns gave a thin smile and held his gloved finger and thumb up close together.

"Not even a little bit?" he asked.

Summers looked around at the four before answering.

"No," he said after a second, "not even a little bit."

"Pay them no mind, Will Summers," said the young woman, still without turning in her saddle. "Nobody's concerned what you do for a living. We're not your judge and jury — not the way Miller and Clifford think they are."

Summers let her words sink in.

"But it's true, ma'am," he said. "I'm no thief. You saw the paperwork. You saw your husband's signature."

Bailey shrugged in her rain slicker.

"Anybody can fake a signature on a handful of paperwork if they've a mind to," she said. Beside her Tate's hat brim nodded in agreement.

Summers thought about it some more, puzzled by her actions on his behalf only moments earlier.

"If you didn't believe me, why'd you vouch for me back there?" he asked.

"Because Miller and Clifford are idiots," she said. "And because nobody riding with the Belltraes would go to all that trouble to steal horses in Mexico." She added with a half chuckle, "Anyway, my husband is always looking for good breeding stock. I figure it's a good bet he bought them from you." She finally turned her head slightly and glanced back at him. "But that doesn't say much about where you got them, does it?"

Summers fell silent for a moment.

"No, ma'am, I expect it doesn't," he said finally. He drew the fillies closer alongside him and rode on, deciding once again that it was time to keep his mouth shut. He was grateful to the woman and her ranch hands for saving him from the sheriff's posse. He could wait until they reached Ansil Swann's ranch and let Swann clear everything up.

After a moment of silence, Little Ted said to everyone, "All right. I've got a dollar says Miller tries to swim the posse across the river. Any takers?"

"I've got two dollars says they'll drown if he does," Lonnie Kerns chuckled, "leastwise, everybody but the Mexicans. Those vaqueros can swim a horse to China if they took a notion."

"Maybe Miller and Clifford will get out there and drown themselves," Bailey Swann said, staring straight ahead. "That would be the best thing for everybody."

A strange thing to say. . . . Summers looked curiously at her and Dallas Tate as they rode on.

In the afternoon the last of the lingering clouds had moved away and the hot Mexican sun had reclaimed its reign in a clear blue sky. As Summers and the other four riders crossed stretches of flatlands, the long-thirsting ground seemed to suck up the remnants of last night's storm waters. Flooded streams fell back inside cut banks. The horses' hooves, which had sounded muffled on the damp ground earlier in the day, now clacked on the hardening terrain. Dust had already begun to rise along the trail behind them. A moderate breeze flurried in across the desert hills.

"Enjoy the cool air while it lasts," Dallas Tate said as the five settled on a campsite and stepped down from their saddles. They led their horses just off the trail into the shade and shelter of rocks. In the west the sun painted the sky purple-red.

After a meal of heated beans from tins, thick-sliced salt pork and flatbread from a trail sack, the five sat around a low fire sipping hot coffee. Summers had eaten like a man starved. The four took note, knowing he'd been a prisoner. When he'd finally set aside his tin plate and relaxed back against his saddle, Bailey looked at the others, then at him.

"So, Will Summers," she said, "were you there when the Belltraes killed and butchered my husband's stallion?"

"No, ma'am," Summers said. "When I got to the mine shafts the Belltraes had done their worst and were gone. I found the man they call Hendrik there dying." As he spoke he reached inside his trouser pocket and pulled out the horsehair quirt that the posse men had overlooked. "Far as I know, this is all that remains." He held it out. Little Ted, sitting nearest him, took it and passed it on to Lonnie Kerns. From Kerns to Tate, who examined it for a second and passed it sidelong to Bailey.

The young woman turned the shiny black quirt in her hands and sighed quietly. As she examined it, Tate stood up from beside her and stepped away from the fire to retrieve his saddle lying on the ground a few yards away.

"Such a waste," she commented almost to herself. "Mr. Swann will take this hard. He loved the stallion." She nodded toward the four fillies standing at a rope line with the other horses. "He was convinced that with the right mares he could produce some fine racing stock."

"I know," said Summers. "He told me as much when he bought the bays from me." He sipped his coffee.

"I'm afraid seeing these bays is only going to make him feel worse," the woman said.

"I'm sorry for how this turned out for him," Summers said, watching her pass the shiny quirt back to Lonnie Kerns in Tate's absence. Kerns passed it on in turn to Little Ted. "But being a serious horse breeder, I'm sure he'll find himself a stallion to replace the one he lost." He took the quirt when Little Ted held it out to him.

"I don't think so," said Bailey Swann. "He was so fond of the black stallion, I believe this news will crush him."

Crush him? Summers gave her a curious look. The man he'd met at the Denver City horse auction hadn't impressed him as a man easily crushed, even under these circumstances.

"Ma'am," he said, "your husband —"

"Please, call me Bailey, at least while we're on the trail," she said, interrupting him. "May I call you Will?"

"Yes, certainly," said Summers. "As I was saying, *Bailey* —"

"She's *Mrs. Swann* to you," Tate said, stepping in with his saddle and dropping it beside the young woman.

Summers just looked at him, seeing jealousy fueled by white-hot anger flare in his eyes. Tate's right hand almost made a move to the Colt on his hip. Summers caught the gesture and prepared to make a grab for his own Colt that he'd strapped around his waist earlier in the afternoon.

"Dallas," Bailey said firmly, "don't correct Will. I asked him to call me Bailey while we're on the trail. You weren't listening." She sounded as if she was reprimanding him.

" 'Will,' is it?" said Tate, softening his stare a little as he turned from Summers to the young woman.

"Yes, it *is,*" Bailey said firmly, with a glare that left room for no more discussion of the matter. She looked back at Summers as Tate stomped away from the fire to the horses. "You were saying, Will?"

Summers set his coffee cup down by his left hand and kept his right hand near his holstered Colt. The other two ranch hands looked at each other knowingly, in silence.

"I was saying," he continued, "your husband struck me as a hard-fisted business-man —"

"In most cases, yes, he is," Bailey said, cutting him off. "But breeding racehorses has always been his overriding passion. I regret having to bring him this terrible news."

"I understand," Summers said. As he spoke he kept Dallas Tate in his peripheral line of sight, not liking the way things had just gone between them.

"I wish I could tell him about the stallion and have you just take the bays back with you. He wouldn't even have to know."

"I've come a long way to deliver them," Summers said. "I need to get paid."

"Of course you do, and I will pay you," Bailey added quickly. "You can give me your address and I'll submit a draft to you by mail."

"I'm sorry, ma'am," Summers said, back to *ma'am* now that the talk had turned businesslike. "It doesn't work that way."

"But it could," the woman insisted. "I assure you the draft will be on its way." She leaned forward. "Oh, please, Will. It would be so very helpful."

"I'm sorry, ma'am," Summers said. "I wouldn't be holding up my end of the deal if I did that. I promised your husband I'd deliver these fillies to him. That's what I'll have to do."

"I was afraid you'd feel this way," she said, sounding crestfallen over the matter. She sat back and sipped her coffee, gazing into the low flames as night closed around them.

CHAPTER 7

Summers forced himself to sleep lightly in spite of his weariness from the trail and from being held prisoner. In the night, his saddle pulled back from the light of the low-burning fire, his hat brim low over his face, he awakened and raised his brim enough to see Dallas Tate standing by the fire, his rifle in hand, getting ready to relieve Little Ted from standing guard up in the rocks a few yards away.

Tate stared over in his direction for a moment. As he did so, Summers tightened his hand around his Colt, which he'd tucked inside his blanket, until Tate finally turned and walked away. Then Summers eased his hand off his Colt and closed his eyes. Yet he opened his eyes again and watched as Little Ted walked into the firelight a moment later. Little Ted dragged his saddle away from the fire and lay down out of the fire-light.

As Summers settled back in his blanket and started to close his eyes again, he caught sight of the woman walking slowly through the firelight and stopping and sitting down on the ground beside him.

"Are you asleep, Will?" she asked in a whisper, as if knowing he would be watching Tate and Little Ted change guard.

Summers waited a few seconds before answering. Then he raised himself on an elbow facing her.

"Dozing," he said quietly in reply. "I try not to sleep too soundly on the trail."

"A good idea," she said, leaning in a little closer. "I saw your hat brim up. I thought we might talk."

All right, Summers thought, knowing she would not have seen his raised hat brim had she not come looking. He let it go.

"About your husband's bays?" he asked. "Because I really would rather discuss them with him —"

"No, I understand that," she said, getting away from the subject of her husband's purchase. "I agree that's better left to you and Mr. Swann when we get to the ranch."

Summers nodded and relaxed a little, glad she'd come to see the horse transaction his way.

"What can I do for you?" he asked quietly.

"I — I want to apologize for Dallas Tate, the way he acted earlier," she said. "He works for my husband. I feel a responsibility."

"No need, Miss Bailey," Summers said.

"He's a jealous young man," she said. "Although there is no basis for it, I must assure you. I am a faithful wife to my husband."

"I understand," said Summers. "I would not have thought otherwise. Some men get ideas in their heads for no reason."

"Yes, that's true," she said. "There has been nothing untoward between the two of us, in spite of how it may look. I am a progressive woman. But I have nothing to hide."

"I understand," Summers said again.

She fell silent for a moment; she looked off into the night. Then she finally sighed and turned back to him.

"May I be perfectly honest with you, Will?" she asked. She didn't wait for a reply. "There was something between Dallas Tate and me. It was a terrible mistake — I saw it, and I ended it."

Summers didn't reply. It was none of his business, and he didn't want to invite himself into it.

"It has been over for some time now —

for me, that is," she said.

All right, here goes. . . . "Not for him, though," Summers said, getting the picture.

"No, not for him. He knows our indiscretion is over, yet he still insists on being my protector," she said, "especially now while my husband is under the weather."

"Mr. Swann is ill?" Summers asked.

"Yes, he's been ill ever since returning from his trip to Denver City," she said. "That's why I'm out here instead of him. I'm trying to hold things together until he's back on his feet."

"Of course." Summers nodded in the shadowy moonlight.

"I know I should more firmly discourage Dallas Tate. I shouldn't have him riding beside me. I know how that must look." She paused for a moment, then added, "But I dare not push him to a point that he would do something hotheaded and foolish — maybe go to my husband." She sighed again. "I'm afraid I am at the mercy of a foolish, angry man."

Summers just looked at her.

"I should have known better," she continued. "Dallas has been more jealous and possessive of me than Mr. Swann ever has. Perhaps that was part of what drew me to him. But by the time I saw his dark nature,

90

it was too late. Now I am stuck in a mess of my own making."

"That's too bad, ma'am," Summers said.

"Yes, it is." She paused and glanced over her shoulder in the direction of the guard post up the rocks a few yards above them. Then she looked back at Summers and gave a short lilting laugh. "Look at me, Will," she said. "Even now, I'm worried, hoping he didn't see me come over here to you. If he saw me I know he would think the wrong thing."

Summers glanced at the low firelight he'd watched her walk through, then looked back at her, seeing her eyes in the shadowy moonlight.

"He *is* standing watch over the camp, Miss Bailey," Summers said in a knowing voice. "He must have seen you in the firelight."

"Yes . . . yes, you're right," she said. "I should have waited until morning to talk to you. I just wanted to warn you about him. It was silly of me. With poor Ansil ill, I must not be thinking clearly. I have never felt so alone. . . ." She let her words trail. "Please don't think I'm some foolish woman."

"Not at all, ma'am," Summers said. "I'm obliged you warned me about Dallas. I saw the jealousy. Now I know why." He fell quiet and waited, knowing the awkwardness of silence would prompt her next move, her next words. After a moment it did.

"Well, then," she said finally, "enough of my troubles. I'll let you get to sleep." She stood and dusted the seat of her trousers. She gave a short nervous giggle and added, "I'll just see myself out."

"Night, Mrs. Swann," Summers said. He smiled, touched his hat brim. He watched her walk away into the shadowy darkness, not taking the same path back though the light of the campfire.

Curious . . . Then he lowered his hat brim over his closed eyes.

At dawn, as the first glow of sunlight mantled the eastern hill line, Summers was awakened from his light sleep by the tip of a rifle barrel jammed into his side. He tried instinctively to roll away from it, but the iron barrel came down onto the center of his chest as if to pin him in place. Behind Tate at the fire, the other two men stood up staring, coffee cups in hand. Bailey Swann was on her way toward him. Summers saw a rifle in her hands.

"Wake up, you son of a bitch!" Tate growled, standing over him. Summers' eyes sprang open, his blanket still wrapped around him. He looked up at Tate.

"What did you do to her?" Tate demanded. In his rage, he flipped Summers' blanket open with his rifle barrel as if doing so would prove his accusation. But when the blanket flipped open, Summers' Colt came up cocked and pointed into his face.

"Back off," Summers warned.

But Tate was having none of it. He stood as if frozen in place, his finger on the trigger of his cocked rifle.

"Stop it, Dallas!" Bailey screamed as she quickened her steps, her rifle in both hands, ready to use. "He didn't do anything to me!"

"I saw you come over here in the night," he said to Bailey, not taking his eyes off Summers. "Don't lie! You lay down with him. I heard you giggling, the two of you having a gay ol' time!"

Summers thought Tate's anger was at the point of no return. So be it, he told himself, his hand tightening around the butt of the Colt, his finger already squeezing back on the trigger. He wasn't going to wait for Tate to make the next move. Once that happened it would be too late.

"I didn't sleep with him, Dallas," Bailey said. She jerked to a halt. "I only talked with him."

"Oh yeah?" said Tate. "I suppose you lost

this in the conversation, then," he said. He pulled his left hand away from the front stock of his rifle and held up a thin, ornate hair comb, which he'd held clasped in his palm. "I found this here beside his blanket. That's why I'm here. He's going to answer for what he's done."

Summers had eased back on his trigger finger, seeing Tate look away from him, at Bailey. But at the slightest move, he had resolved himself to still pull the Colt's trigger and kill Dallas Tate where he stood.

The woman looked stunned. She raised one hand from her rifle and felt her hair.

"It — it must have come loose while we were talking," she said, looking astonished at the silver hair ornament.

"Yeah, I bet," said Tate. "It came loose while the two of you rolled around in the blanket —"

"Stop it, Dallas!" Bailey shouted. "Nothing happened. We talked. Now put down that rifle before Will decides to shoot you dead. None of us would blame him if he does." Her eyes flashed to Summers, then back to Tate. Summers held the Colt level, ready, yet he waited.

"Will. . . ." Tate sneered. He said Summers' name as if it created some bitter terrible taste in his mouth. He glanced down at

Summers, then back to her. "You'd like that wouldn't you, Bailey?" he said in a low, level tone. "Seeing me dead would solve a lot of problems for you, wouldn't it?"

Summers waited, watched, kept ready to fire at the slightest sign of Tate's finger twitch inside the rifle's trigger guard.

"But I'm not going to do that, not this time," Tate said, suddenly pulling his rifle away from Summers and holding it one-handed, pointed down at the ground. "Last night was free, Summers," he said with a dark twisted grin. "Call it on the house."

"Watch your mouth, Tate," Summers warned, coming to his feet now that the rifle was aimed away from him. "She told you nothing happened. . . . Nothing did." He still held the Colt aimed at Tate, only more loosely now.

"I'm not a fool, Summers," Tate growled. Pitching his rifle away in one direction, the ornate hair comb in another, he brought a hand back and knocked Summers' Colt away from his belly. Summers saw he had changed his mind. He'd wanted a killing; now he would settle for a straight-up fist-fight.

Suits me, Summers told himself. He pitched the Colt aside onto the blanket just in time. He caught Dallas Tate as Tate lunged, fists flying, hammering at him. Summers took a glancing blow to the side of his head, another to his shoulder.

Charging forward recklessly, the enraged Tate gave no regard to his balance. All he wanted was to get his blows in on Summers, spill blood, break bones. But Summers, still coolheaded, kept his balance and took a stance. As Tate charged, Summers pivoted, allowing the man's weight and anger to propel him forward and down. Summers stuck out a boot, worsening Tate's fall by tripping him. Tate hit the ground on his face and chest in a puff of dust and a loud grunt.

But he wasn't through; neither was Summers. Tate hurled himself upward onto his feet. Summers aimed and delivered a solid straight punch to his face. Tate's face came up, giving Summers a perfect target for a long right cross. Summers swung and connected, sending Tate sideways and back onto the ground. Tate landed in a position that offered Summers a perfect kick to his exposed ribs. Summers didn't take the kick. Instead he stepped back and stood ready for whatever move Tate made when he got to his feet.

"I'll kill you!" shouted Tate, blood streaming from his lips, his nose. He staggered in place for a moment, his head unclear.

Summers didn't respond. He circled slowly, five feet away, his fists tight, his hands spread in low guard, waiting for Tate's next move.

Instead of charging again, Tate rocked on his feet unsteadily. Realizing he'd taken on more than he could handle, he slapped his hand against the gun in his holster. He started to raise it. Yet, before he could, Summers moved in suddenly, as if he had already anticipated Tate reverting to gunplay. His hand wrapped around Tate's gun hand, Colt and all, as it came up from the holster.

"Jesus!" said Little Ted. He and Lonnie Kerns were a few feet away. They watched Summers swing Tate's arm out and up high. Then he stepped forward under Tate's upraised arm and twisted his gun hand hard. Tate screamed as he turned a forward flip and landed hard, flat on his back. Summers stood holding Tate's twisted wrist in one hand and his discarded Colt in his other. Tate floundered and wallowed and gasped for breath in the dirt at Summers' feet.

"Jesus!" Little Ted repeated.

He and Lonnie stood staring in awe. Summers stooped a little over Tate's chest, took a fistful of his shirt and raised him up and down on the ground, helping him catch his lost breath.

"Breathe," he told Tate calmly. "Come on, take it easy. In and out. . . . That's it." He turned Tate's wrist loose and let his arm flop to the ground.

"My — my arm is broken?" Tate managed to ask in a raspy voice, starting to catch his breath.

"No," Summers said, "but it will be, and so will your neck, if you try a stunt like that again." He stepped back, opened Tate's Colt and let the bullets fall to the ground.

"He won't," Bailey said firmly, "not around here anyway." She stepped forward, her rifle in her hands. "On your feet, Dallas. Gather your gear and ride out. Don't let me see your face around here again."

Tate struggled to his feet, his right arm still numb and weak, hanging useless at his side. He looked back and forth between Summers and the woman, his eyes still filled with hate, but it was hatred now kept in check. He stooped and picked up his hat with his left hand and slapped it against this leg. Summers reached out and stuck his empty Colt into its holster. Tate walked away toward his horse, his back covered with dirt, his right arm held against his side.

Lonnie and Little Ted stood in silence,

watching until Tate stepped up into his saddle and rode his horse away at a walk, a blanket trailing from his bedroll, down the horse's side.

"Jesus," Little Ted said again as Tate rode out of sight over a rise in the trail.

"Will you stop saying *that*?" said Lonnie Kerns. "We ain't in church here."

"I know, but, Jesus!" said Little Ted, still stunned by what he'd seen. He looked at Summers. "What was that you did to him?"

"Nothing," said Summers, "just something I learned from my pa a long time ago."

"Was your pa a magician or something?" asked Little Ted.

"No," said Summers, still staring ahead the trail. "He was a lawman — one of the good ones. He taught me a lot of things."

Little Ted considered it for moment, then asked quietly, "Think you could teach a fellow my size how to do that?"

"Size wouldn't stop you from learning," Summers said, a little surprised. He considered it for a moment himself.

"What's wrong?" asked Little Ted.

"Nothing," said Summers. "Nobody's ever asked me to teach them how it's done." He looked Little Ted up and down. "You're not wanting to learn it just so you can shove people around, are you?"

99

"Look at me," said Little Ted. "Do I look like I'm ever going to be able to shove anybody around?" He spread his thin arms and turned a full circle. "I'd like to know how to put some bullyboy in his place if I have to — if I can learn how, that is."

"You can learn," said Summers. "The question is, will you remember it when you need it?"

"Then — then you'll do it, you'll teach me?" Little Ted said, sounding excited at the prospect.

Summers nodded and looked off in the direction of the Ansil Swann Ranch.

"Sure, I'll teach it to you," he said, "soon as we get where we're going and Ansil Swann tells everybody I'm all right." He looked at Bailey Swann as if for approval.

"Don't worry, Will," she said. "I'm certain my husband will confirm everything you've said."

"Good," said Summers. "I want to get there as soon as I can and get things settled once and for all."

PART 2

CHAPTER 8

In the late afternoon, Summers led his string of fillies into the front yard of the Swann hacienda. The woman rode beside him. The two ranch hands, Little Ted and Lonnie Kerns, rode a few feet behind. Summers and the others stopped their horses at a row of iron hitch rings attached along a waist-high stone wall. The two ranch hands remained in their saddles; Summers and the woman stepped off.

Summers looked all around, impressed. The stone wall enclosed an elaborate two-story Spanish-style main house overlooking a flat stretch of terraced land on a wide hillside.

"You have a beautiful home, ma'am," he commented, tying off the string's lead rope. From the house a thin, elderly Mexican came trotting with a limp.

"Thank you, Will," Bailey Swann said coolly, an authoritative tone coming into her voice. Standing beside her horse, she took off her hat and touched her fingers here and there, fluffing and arranging her hair as best she could. "Perhaps you'd like Lonnie and Ted to show you to the bunkhouse. You can wash up and relax awhile while I have Bedos and Rena prepare dinner for us." She turned away from Summers to the thin Mexican as he stopped and took her horse's reins from her.

"*Gracias,* Bedos," she said idly as the elderly Mexican stood ready to lead her horse away.

"If it's all the same, ma'am," Summers said, "I'd like to meet with Mr. Swann before anything else. I need to get this matter cleared up —"

"Yes, of course you do," said Bailey, cutting him short. She looked at Little Ted and Lonnie. "You two go on," she said. "Bedos will show Will to the bunkhouse after he's had a chance to speak to Mr. Swann."

"Yes, ma'am," said Lonnie, and he and Little Ted touched their fingertips to their hat brims. They both looked at Summers, then turned their horses and rode away toward a stone and plank bunkhouse eighty yards away.

"Bedos, please lead the string to the hacienda barn with my horse," she said.

"Mr. Swann will be right along to look them over."

Summers saw the elderly Mexican give the woman what he considered to be a questioning look. Yet, as quickly as Summers saw the look come to the Mexican's eyes, it disappeared.

"Sí, señora, en seguida," the thin Mexican said. He stepped over and untied the string and led them alongside Bailey's horse, walking a few steps behind Summers and the woman until he veered away with the horses toward a small stone and plank barn to the right side of the sprawling hacienda.

"I'll give Mr. Swann your paperwork, Will," she said, patting the shirt pocket where she'd put it when he gave it to her on the trail. "Anything you need while you're here, you have only to ask Bedos or his daughter, Rena," the woman said sidelong to Summers as they neared a wide front porch. "We recently sold off our market herd, so we'll be short of vaqueros for the season. But we always keep Bedos and his daughter to attend to the hacienda, and any guests of course."

Understandable. . . . Summers nodded. Having already looked around, he noted to himself that there appeared to be little work going on, no line of drovers' horses at the hitch rail out in front of the bunkhouse. Stepping onto the porch, he looked up and saw that the thick Spanish window shutters along the second floor were all closed save for one overlooking the trail they'd ridden in on. The shutters each had a gun port cross in its middle, for the sake of defense.

On the porch, the woman stopped and turned to Summers.

"If you will be so kind, Will . . ." She gestured toward a row of comfortable-looking chairs. "Please have a seat, and I will tell my husband you're here. Meanwhile, I'll have Rena bring you a pitcher of water — some wine, some mescal perhaps?"

"Obliged, ma'am," said Summers, taking off his hat. "Water sounds fine."

As Summers seated himself and laid his hat on his crossed knee, Bailey Swann walked into the house and closed the front door behind herself. He relaxed now, glad his problem with the bay fillies would soon be over. Summers sat looking all around the large ranch, a corral of cattle ponies at the side of a weathered barn only a few yards from the bunkhouse, a better-kept breeding barn with rows of private stalls for the Swanns' and their hacienda guests' personal horses.

A business baron's cattle ranch in Old

Mexico, he told himself, sizing the place up. The mark of big money, he observed, of power, success. And yet he knew that to a businessman as wealthy as Swann, while this was a working ranch, it was also a play ranch, a *rancho de lujo* — a luxury ranch. Something to remind himself and the world of how far he'd come in a life where so many had barely scratched themselves out a meager living.

My compliments, Ansil Swann, Summers said to himself. As he sat waiting, he saw a single horseman ride in from the west and stop his horse atop a low rise two hundred yards away. The rider sat staring toward the hacienda, a black flat-crowned hat atop his head. He wore a black linen suit coat behind a tan trail duster.

Summers returned the horseman's stare for a time. His attention then went back to the front door as it opened and a young Mexican woman his age stepped out carrying a tray with a pitcher of water and a drinking gourd on it. She only glanced at the watching horseman in passing, showing no concern.

"Water for you, Señor Summers," she said, stepping over to the table beside Summers' chair. Even though she was the Swanns' kitchen help serving him water, her dark striking beauty brought Summers to his feet instinctively. He dismissed the single horseman for the moment.

"Begging your pardon, ma'am," he said, as if he hadn't risen quick enough.

"Please, sit down, *por favor,* Señor Summers," she said in clearly refined English. There was the hint of a playful lilt to her voice. Summers suspected it was not the first time her looks had brought a man to his feet. "I am Rena — Señora Swann told me your name." She straightened from setting the tray on the table, then raised the water and filled the drinking gourd for him. She set the pitcher down and gave him a level gaze. "Please summon me if I can do anything for you."

"Yes, ma'am," Summers said. There was not the faintest hint of suggestion in her words or manners, yet he saw how wishful thinking might lead a man to take it that way. "This is fine, *gracias,*" he added, taking the drinking gourd as she held it out to him.

"De nada," she said. As she turned and stepped past him, she smiled demurely. But then she stopped abruptly and looked back out at the horseman. Now there were two of them, both in the black hats, both in black suits, tan dusters.

"Expecting company?" Summers asked,

checking her expression, beginning to see signs of concern.

"I must ask the señora," she said dutifully, shaking her head a little. She still wore the smile, but with a little tension at work in it now.

Summers stood watching as she walked inside.

Easy, he reminded himself, you're here on horse business, no other kind.

A few moments went by as he sat sipping the cool water from the gourd. Then Bailey Swann stepped out onto the porch and closed the door quietly. She leaned against the door for a moment and sighed, giving him a weary smile. She looked out at the low rise and appeared to be relieved the two riders were gone.

Summers watched her smile strengthen, then turn weary again.

"Will, I'm very sorry," she said, ignoring the low rise. "My husband is still not feeling very well. He sends you his apologies." She tried to appear brightened. "But on a good note, he did verify everything you've said." Her smiled continued. "That is, you are who you say you are, and he did indeed purchase the bay fillies from you. He sent out the money he still owes you upon delivery, as the contract so states."

Summers watched her unfold some cash in her hand and count out three hundred dollars for him to see. "So I can settle up with you on Ansil's behalf."

"Obliged, ma'am," Summers said, taking the money as she held it out for him.

"Oh, and here is a letter with his signature, instructing Sheriff Miller or any of his men to allow you safe passage."

"Obliged again, ma'am," Summers said. "I'll go to Dark Horses first thing and show it to the sheriff." He folded the paper and put it away inside his shirt. He couldn't help seeing how tense she was in spite of how hard she tried to hide it. Something was wrong here, he told himself. He had suspected it a couple of times before, but never so much as now.

"Well, then, that concludes our horse venture, Will," she said. "I hope we can —"

"One more thing, ma'am," Will said, gazing down at the money on his palm. "Did your husband mention that we had agreed on a hundred-dollar bonus if I got the bays here sooner than the time we estimated?" He looked her levelly in the eye.

She hesitated to answer, but only for a moment.

"Oh yes, he certainly did," she said as if catching herself. Her smile turned nervous.

"It must've slipped my mind. I beg your pardon, Will." She stepped away toward the door as she spoke. "I left it lying on his desk. I'll just go get it."

Huh-uh. . . .

Summers stood watching as the door swung shut. At the last second he stopped it with his hand before it closed entirely. Quietly he opened it and stepped inside. He knew he had no right going inside the Swann hacienda uninvited. But he had nothing but trouble ever since arriving in the Mexican hill country with Swann's bays. He had nearly been hanged. He was making it his right to know what was going on here. He moved forward quietly, following the sound of the woman's riding boots on the clay-tiled floor.

Inside Ansil Swann's lavish office, Bailey Swann hurriedly unlocked the cash drawer on her husband's wide polished desk. With a worried look she rummaged through the remaining cash, counting, recounting, scratching all around to find money she might have missed finding earlier. In a tall-backed chair behind the desk Ansil Swann sat in silence, his eyes staring down at the floor, a dejected look on his aged and craggy face.

"For God sakes, Ansil, there's more cash here somewhere! I know there is. There has to be!" She gave up searching the drawer and hurried across the room to a hand-carved wooden box sitting on the mantel above the fireplace. She had to step onto a footstool in order to reach it.

Behind the desk, Ansil sat motionless. An ivory-handled engraved Army Colt lay atop the desk. As Bailey took the wooden box in hand and stepped down from the footstool, she heard a footstep creak just outside the office doorway where the tile floor turned into broad-plank polished oak.

"Rena, is that you?" she said in a hushed tone as she turned with the wooden box in her hands. "I need you to go to the porch and stall until I —" Her words stopped short as she stared into Summers' watching eyes. "I mean, uh. That is —" She stopped again as she hurried to the open office door, forcing Summers back a step with the wooden box.

"Here we are, Will," she said, talking fast, trying hurriedly to take charge. She reached a hand back to shut the office door, seeing Summers look past her at Ansil Swann. "We mustn't disturb poor Mr. Swann! He's not doing very well at all — but I have your hundred dollars right here, I believe. Mr.

Swann must've put it away when I left —"

"Stop it, ma'am," Summers said, cutting her off. He reached a hand past her and shoved the big door open.

"Please, Will, what are you doing? I have your hundred-dollar bonus —"

He cut her off again as the door creaked wide open, revealing Swann at his desk, his downcast eyes, the big Colt lying there.

"There was no bonus agreed to, ma'am," Summers said as gently as he could, or as gently as he thought she deserved. He eased her around and ushered her back into the office, over to the desk. He took the box from her and set it on the desk.

"Mr. Swann, sir," he said, "it's me, Will Summers — from the horse auction, Denver City?"

Swann only stared blankly at the floor. Summers eyed the ivory-handled Colt. He saw that it was cocked, ready to fire.

"Mr. Swann?" he said in a louder voice. He saw Swann's head move, but only a fraction, a twitch in the side of his neck. He picked up the ornately engraved Colt and looked at Bailey as he tried to uncock it.

"The hammer is frozen," she said. "It hasn't worked for years. It's worthless, merely a keepsake, a desk piece."

"Can he hear me?" Summers asked.

"Yes, he can," she said defensively. "I told you he simply isn't feeling well today!" Her voice rose impatiently.

"I believe *that,*" Summers said cynically. He turned to Swann and slapped his palm down loudly top the desk.

"Mr. Swann!" he shouted loudly. But still the man only sat staring at the floor. At that moment Summers saw the linen bib hanging on his chest, the wet circles on it. Swann's chin glistened wetly above it. Will saw two handles atop the high-backed chair.

A wheelchair. . . .

"You have no right to barge in here like this!" Bailey said. "Now leave! Get out of my house this instant!"

"Your husband has had a stroke, ma'am?" Summers asked her in a quiet tone.

"Yes," Bailey said, "I mean, no, he's just feeling ill —" She stopped herself, seeing that her denial wasn't going to work. Her eyes welled with tears. "I don't know . . . ," she said. "I haven't had a doctor look at him. I haven't dared."

Summers looked at her curiously as he laid the broken Colt atop the desk.

"Why not?" he asked.

She produced a lady's handkerchief and touched it to her eyes.

"He — he wouldn't want me to under our

circumstances," she said, keeping herself from crying.

"He wouldn't want you to get him a doctor?" Summers asked. "Then just what *are* your circumstances, ma'am?"

"I've been afraid to tell anyone, Will," she said. "But I can see it's time to trust someone, before my situation gets worse. I only hope I can trust you to keep silent about what I'm going to tell you."

"Anything you confide in me stays with me," Summers said. "You have my word on that."

She nodded and looked down and shook her head. Then she backed away from him and put away her handkerchief.

"Shortly after returning from Denver City," she said, "my husband revealed to me that the financial empire he's created is crumbling before his eyes." She paused as if to see what affect the news would have on Summers.

Summers looked impassive.

"You mean all of his wealth, the mines, the railroads, everything?" he asked.

"Yes, everything," the woman said. "Most of it embezzled by the very men he paid to protect and manage his interests. And now those same men have banded together to take everything we have — our mine holdings here in Mexico, our hacienda, everything. They have already legally taken possession of Ansil's railroads north of the border. Learning he lost the railroads is what brought on *this*." She gestured a hand toward the dejected man in the wheelchair.

"You mean they've taken everything they could seize from him legally," Summers said. "Now they can come to Mexico and take everything else by force. When you lost your money you lost your influence with the Mexican government."

"Yes, that is our situation, Will," she said. "Ruthless men become even more ruthless in Mexico. I'm trying to keep his condition a secret and salvage whatever I can before these men arrive and begin taking over our mines and our ranch. Even my hired hands don't realize how bad his health is." She paused, then said, "That's why I wanted to postpone paying you the three hundred dollars."

"You weren't going to mail my money to me, were you?" he said.

"That's true, Will. I'm sorry," she said. "It wasn't so much about not paying you your money as it was about people hearing that we could not come up with three hundred dollars."

"But you did come up with it," Summers said.

"Yes," she said. "It is every penny we have. But I paid it to keep the truth from being known — to buy myself time while I figure a way out of this mess I'm in." She paused, then said, "Ansil did come up with a plan that would help. But now that he's ill, I don't know if I can carry it out."

Summers glanced out through an open window and searched along the low rise for the two horsemen. They were not only back; they had two more horsemen with them, the same black suits, string ties, tan dusters. Behind the horsemen an empty wagon rolled up into sight and stopped.

Summers nodded at the window.

"These are debt collectors?" he asked.

Bailey rose and stood close to Summers' side, looking out.

"Yes, they are. I've been expecting them. They work for Finnity and Baines, the company who bought my husband's bank-notes in Chicago. They call themselves debt collectors," she said, "but they are more like hired gunmen, marauders out to take what-ever they can." She gripped his forearm firmly, seeing the four men riding toward the hacienda at a gallop, the wagon close behind. The four drew rifles from their saddle boots as they rode closer. Summers looked toward the bunkhouse and saw Kerns and Little Ted jumping atop their tired horses at the hitch rail. He saw them boot their horses toward the hacienda at a hard run.

"Ma'am," Summers said in a quiet tone, "it looks like these fellows have their bark on. You'd best wheel your husband out of here. Get Rena and her pa and all of you take cover." He stepped over and pulled the thick shutters closed on the office window. "Collecting a debt is one thing, but these men appear to be out for blood."

"You — you're going to face them for me, Will?" she said, sounding surprised.

"The closer they get, the more it looks that way," Summers said, looking out, seeing the four men slow their horses a little and spread out as they neared the front yard, the wagon right behind them. He watched as Kerns and Little Ted rode hard, out of sight around the far end of the hacienda. Taking their horses out of the line of fire, he decided. He stepped over to a wall rack of firearms and took down a shortened double-barrel shotgun. He checked it, found it loaded.

Bailey had hurried over, grabbed the handles on her husband's wheelchair and

118

pushed it across the floor. She stopped in the doorway and looked back at Summers. Ansil Swann sat with his head bowed, a string of slobber hanging from his gaping lips.

"Will," she said solemnly, "they're going to tell you they have every right to collect what my husband owes."

"They can say what suits them," Summers said. "I don't listen well when charged at with rifles." He clicked the shotgun shut and walked out the office door behind her. "Now get out of sight, please," he said, turning toward the front door.

CHAPTER 9

At the front door, Summers waited, listening, until the sound of the four horses' hooves stopped a few yards away from the porch and the big, empty wagon rattled to a creaking halt. Still he waited, shotgun in hand, his free hand on the doorknob, listening to the metallic sound of a rifle levering a round up into its chamber. A second passed, and then he heard a strong voice call out from the front yard.

"You in there," the voice shouted. "We saw you. Come on out. There's nothing you can do to stop us doing our job."

Summers opened the front door slowly and stepped out onto the front porch, the shotgun down at his side. He glanced at the far end of the porch, but he didn't see either Lonnie Kerns or Little Ted.

How long could it take them to tie their horses?

Seeing him look for the two ranch hands,

120

the man who had spoken gave a dark chuckle.

"Looks like your two pals went off to find themselves a shady spot," he said. The other three horsemen and the wagon driver gave the same dark chuckle.

Summers watched the lead horseman step his big chestnut forward. He was the only man not wearing a wide-brimmed hat. This one wore a black derby sitting at a rakish cock above his left eye. Instead of a black string tie, this man wore a wide black necktie with silver stripes across it — the same black suit, the same tan duster, Summers noted.

"Where's Swann? Where's his woman?" the man asked in a more somber tone. "We've come to gather furniture, household goods and the four bays we heard about. We'll be taking them back to Dark Horses with us." He sounded cocksure of himself.

Where had he heard about the bays? Summers asked himself. Dallas Tate, he realized.

He raised the shotgun and stared at them, his feet planted shoulder width apart. The horsemen looked him up and down.

"So, that's how it's going to be, huh, hombre?" the man said, emphasizing the word *hombre.* He looked all around. "You'd be making a bad mistake thinking we won't chop you down right where you stand."

Summers cocked both hammers.

"You'd be making a mistake not holding that horse from taking another step," he replied.

The sound of the shotgun cocking caused the horseman to tighten the chestnut's rein. The horse stopped in its tracks.

"Hombre, this is Mexico," the horseman said. "We don't need a court order to take what's owed to us. These furnishings and those horses belong to Finnity and Baines now. We're taking them."

"I didn't ask you for a court order," Summers said flatly, making his intentions clear. "Turn your wagon and ride away. That's the last I'll say on the matter."

The horseman gave a short chuckle of disbelief.

"Case you haven't noticed, hombre, there're four of us, five counting Tubbs." He gave a short nod toward the man driving the empty wagon. The man stood up with a rifle he raised from beside his wagon seat.

Summers stood staring, having spoken his piece. But from the left corner of the hacienda came Little Ted's voice.

"Case *you* haven't noticed, *hombre,* there're six of us, counting the two at the upstairs gun ports," said Little Ted, in a mocking tone.

Standing on the porch, Summers saw the riders' eyes turn to the second-floor row of shuttered windows above him. Summers had no idea who might have been at the gun ports up there. But what Little Ted said was working.

The leader looked back at Summers. A stiff smile showed beneath a pencil-thin mustache. But Summers could see through the smile. There was fear in the man's eyes.

"Well, well," he said, keeping his voice confident, calm. "We seem to have a Mexican standoff, in Mexico of all places." As he spoke, Summers kept watch on the rifle in his hands. He noted the man pulled his horse sideways to him, the rifle barrel in his direction. "Maybe this is a good time for me to explain to you why you shouldn't start trouble with me and these gentlemen behind me —"

Summers saw the man's thumb go over the rifle hammer as if to cock it. He didn't hesitate. The shotgun roared in his hands.

The leader did not flip backward from his saddle with the impact of the blast as Summers had expected.

Weak load, he told himself quickly. He watched the man wobble in his saddle, his face and chest covered with blood, his shirt and necktie shredded. His buckshot-riddled bowler hat spun away in the air.

"Good God!" one of the horsemen shouted.

The bloody leader managed to climb shakily down his horse's side, the reins slipping from his hand. He fell onto his knees. His frightened horse, suddenly given free rein, nickered loud and spun and bolted away at a full run. The man tittered on his knees and pitched facedown into the dirt. Summers swung the shotgun at another horseman whose horse had also spooked a little at the sound of the shotgun blast. But instead of swinging his rifle up, the man balanced it across his lap and threw his empty hands chest high.

"Hold it!" he shouted at Summers and the two ranch hands. "Don't shoot!" But his request came too late. Both Little Ted and Kerns saw the wagon driver swing his shotgun into play and fired as one from both corners of the hacienda. The driver fell back into the empty wagon bed. The other two riders grabbed the wagon horses and held them in check. "This wasn't supposed to turn into a bloodbath!" the man continued. "We've got a right to come here and take possession! Our company is owed money! We need to talk about this, for God sakes!"

Summers noted that the man kept his hand away from his rifle hammer as he spoke. The three remaining horsemen appeared stunned at how Summers had blasted the lead man from his saddle without hesitation.

Kerns and Little Ted both held their fire. Summers took a step forward on the porch. The three horsemen appeared to be frozen in place, their hands in full view. They didn't want a fight. They were used to getting their way; they hadn't expected this.

Interesting, Summers thought.

"I warned you that I had no more to say on the matter," he said in a cool, level tone. In the dirt, the leader groaned and pushed himself up with his palms.

"You'll . . . pay for this," he growled at Summers, blood running down his face.

Summers only stared. He'd brought the fillies here for breeding stock. He wasn't about to see them led away by a group of debt collectors — men whose only course of law was to apply force and fear in equal measure.

"Can we get him up from there?" a horseman asked, gesturing down at Darren Crayley.

Summers gave his approval with a jerk of the smoking shotgun barrel.

"Boot your rifles first," he said. Then he watched as two riders slipped their rifles into their saddle boots, stepped down and walked to the man who was struggling in the dirt.

The two pulled him to the feet. He staggered in place between them and wiped blood from his eyes. Summers saw buckshot holes bleeding on his forehead, his chin, down the right side of his chest. His right ear, which looked partly severed, hung down the side of his head. One man stooped and picked up his chewed-up bowler hat and held it.

"I'll ki-kill you for this," the wounded man said. "As sure as there's . . . a devil . . . in hell, I'll kill you —"

"Keep it up," warned Summers, "I'll shoot you again." He half raised the shotgun to his shoulder.

"You men, *rush him,*" Crayley commanded the two holding him up. But the two horsemen shook him by his shoulders.

"Shut up, Darren," said one. "You heard the man. He's already shot you once. He ain't bluffing."

"His shotgun loads . . . are low powdered. They have no strength," the man, Darren

Crayley, said. "Look at me. I'd be dead if they did. Now rush him, damn it!"

"Step away from him," Summers said calmly, leveling the shotgun, taking tighter aim at the bloody man. "We'll go again."

"Please, mister, no," one man said, even as he took a step away from Crayley and held him at arm's length. "He don't know what he's saying. Let us take him, get him looked after. We were just doing our jobs here."

"So are we," Little Ted called out, he and Kerns stepping out from the corners and moving slowly along the front of the porch. The two men looked at the rifles pointed at them, then glanced up warily at the second-floor gun ports.

"Tubbs is bleeding bad over here," the third man called out from the wagon. Groans of pain rose from the wagon bed.

"Jesus," said one of the two horsemen. He looked at Summers and said, "Can we take them both out of here, before they both bleed to death? Call this whole thing quits?"

"Get them out of here," Summers said, lowering the double-barreled shotgun an inch. This wasn't what these four had expected. Watch out next time, he thought to himself.

"Obliged, mister," said the same man.

"What about Crayley's horse?"

Summers stared at him, narrow-eyed.

"Get it on your way out," he said.

Crayley started to complain, but both men shook him, warning him to keep his mouth shut. They looped Crayley's arm over their shoulders.

"You can ride in the wagon bed with Tubbs," one of them said, jerking a handkerchief from his suit coat pocket and giving it to Crayley to hold to his bloody face.

"Lie there beside stinking Tubbs . . . all the way to Dark Horses?" asked Crayley. "Huh-uh, I'm taking my horse." He struggled against the two as they turned and motioned for the third rider to lead the wagon forward toward them.

"Don't push it, Darren," one said. "You're lucky we're getting you out of here alive."

Summers and the two ranch hands watched as the wagon rolled out of sight across the low rise, the three horsemen flanking it. One of the horsemen rode over and gathered the loose frightened horse and brought it back to the wagon as the group moved on. Darren Crayley remained in the wagon with Tubbs.

"Man oh man!" Little Ted said to Summers, the three of them standing out front on the hacienda, "You shot the hell out of Crayley. He'll never look the same. We make up a powerful force, us three!"

Summers just looked at Little Ted.

"He made a move for his rifle," Summers replied. "If I didn't stop him then, when would I?"

"I agree," said Little Ted, excited. "I just wasn't expecting it is all. They must be so used to getting their way, I don't think they knew what hit them."

"They'll be back, though," said Kerns, "now that they know about the four bays. Those fillies are too fine for them to pass up." He gazed out at the empty low rise. "Next time they'll know what to expect. They'll bring more guns with them."

Little Ted looked at Summers.

"Are you going to stick around now, stand with us when they show up again?" he said.

Summers didn't answer.

"Because if you don't, they're going to be harder to stop next time," Little Ted added. "We'll have gotten them riled up for nothing."

"Leave him alone, Little Ted," said Kerns. "We're the ones who shot the wagon driver. Summers has to do what suits him. No need in you pressing him on it."

They both looked at Summers for a reply.

Before he could answer, Bailey Swann and Rena both stepped out onto the porch, each with a rifle in her hands.

"Leave Will alone, boys," said Bailey. "He brought Mr. Swann's bays here the way he agreed to do. He didn't ask for all the trouble that's found him. I'm certain he has business obligations across the border that need attending to."

Summers didn't respond. Instead he nodded at the rifles in the women's hands.

"That was you two up there at the gun ports?" he asked, looking back and forth between them.

Bailey gave a thin smile.

"Yes, it was," she said, "but the collectors didn't know that. Besides, our bullets would have done just as much damage as anyone else's."

"Yes, ma'am," Summers said respectfully, "I realize that." He paused in thought, then asked, "Who's the boss behind these collectors?"

Bailey and Rena looked to Kerns.

"That would be Evert Crayley," said Kerns. "He's Darren Crayley's own pa, but all the men call him *Dad.* He's the top security man for Finnity and Baines. He's got himself an office set up in the Dark Horses Hotel while they sort through taking Swann's holdings."

"Dad Crayley used to be a gunman for Mr. Swann's railroad," said Little Ted. "Now he makes his living taking back everything Ansil Swann worked for all his life."

"Hell of a way to make a living," said Lonnie Kerns. He spat in disgust.

Bailey turned to the two ranch hands and said, "Lonnie, you and Ted go fetch us some beef for dinner. We could all use a good meal, after today's activities."

"Yes, ma'am," Kerns said, touching his fingertips to his hat brim. "Come on, Little Ted."

"After dinner, I'm hoping you'll show me that flip you did on Dallas Tate," Little Ted said to Summers.

"We'll see," said Summers. He stood beside Bailey and watched as the two ranch hands walked away.

"The fact is, Evert Crayley used to be among my husband's closest friends," Bailey Swann said to Summers. "Yet he was the first one to jump over to the side of Finnity and Baines when Ansil's business interests began to falter."

"That's a shame, ma'am," said Summers. "I hope everything works out for you and your husband."

"It would mean a lot to me, *personally,* if you stayed here for a while, Will," she said quietly, just between the two of them. She put a hand on his forearm as she spoke. She gave a glance to Rena on the porch. Rena turned and walked back inside the hacienda and closed the door behind herself.

Summers took note of the two women's silent exchange. He also took note of Bailey Swann's hand on his arm, how close she now stood to him.

"With Dallas Tate gone, I have no one to take charge of things here." She paused, then added, "I'm in need of a strong man who isn't afraid of these collectors — who will tell Lonnie and Little Ted what to do when these collectors return."

A gunman, a top gunman. . . . That was what she was asking him to be, he told himself.

"Ma'am, I'm a horse trader," he said. "I know how to use a gun, but I'm no gunman, and I'm afraid a gunman is what you're looking for."

"I need a man who can take charge," she said. "A man who can stand up to these collectors the way you just did."

"Your two ranch hands did just as much as I did —" Will said before she cut him short.

"They had to be led to do it," she said. "Don't be so modest, Will. They respect you. They see you're a leader. They'll follow your orders."

Will shook his head slowly.

"Ma'am, I don't want to cause you to have any false hope," he said. "I believe these men will run you and your husband over sooner or later. Without any influence with the Mexican government, or the money it takes to hire guns, it's just a matter of time."

"I know, Will," Bailey said, letting her hand drop from his forearm. "I don't have to be reminded."

"Ma'am, I'm sorry," Will said. "Earlier, you said your husband had a plan?"

"Yes," Bailey said. She looked all around, then said, "Later tonight, when we can speak more freely, I want to tell you everything."

Summers looked off toward the trail as if anxious to get under way.

"Please," Bailey said. "It'll be getting dark soon. We've got plenty of room in the bunkhouse. Stay the night with us. We'll send you off after a good breakfast in the morning."

Summers nodded. He had to admit he was curious what sort of plan she had in mind to fend off the debt collectors and save her and her husband's holdings.

"A good dinner, a hot breakfast . . . ," he said, offering a thin smile. "I'd be a fool to turn that down."

Chapter 10

After a dinner prepared in the outdoor *cocina* by Rena and her father, served beneath the paling afternoon sky, Summers sat on the porch swing sipping from a hot coffee mug, his hat lying on the swing beside him. A red sun melted slowly on the western sky. Ansil Swann sat in his wheelchair as still and silent as a corpse, with a shawl hiked on his shoulders and covering his lap against the cool evening air.

Summers watched Little Ted gallop his horse toward the house from a watch point out above the main trail, where Lonnie Kerns had relieved him only moments earlier. Ted swung down from his saddle and reined his horse at a hitch ring.

"All right, Will Summers," he said as he took off his hat and hung it over his saddle horn, "you said you'd teach me. Now let's get to it before we run out of light." He grinned and stretched his arms as if loosening up.

Seated in a swing beside her husband's wheelchair, Bailey sighed under her breath. She watched Summers put his coffee cup down, stand and step off the front porch in the fading light. He slipped a leather trail glove from behind his gun belt and pulled it on.

"I can teach you how to do it in less than two minutes, Ted," he said. "But you might have to practice it awhile until it becomes second nature to you. Fair enough?" He stopped and stood three feet from Little Ted, facing him.

"Fair enough," said Little Ted. "I'm a fast learner when it suits me." He stood facing Summers, who towered a head above him.

"Unload your six-shooter," Summers said, nodding at the Colt holstered on Little Ted's hip.

Ted grinned and cocked his head a little to one side.

"Why?" he said. "Dallas' Colt was *loaded* when you took it from him."

"That's right," said Summers, "but yours won't be. Not if you want me to show you."

"All right," said Little Ted, "here I go." He raised the Colt, unloaded the bullets into his hand and dropped them into his pocket. When he slipped the Colt back into the holster, he looked expectantly at Will Summers.

"Now draw on me like you mean it," Summers said.

Without a second of hesitation, Little Ted's hand made a dive for his Colt. The tip of the gun barrel cleared the edge of the holster and started to swing up. But as quick as a whip, Summers' left hand wrapped over the top of the cocked gun and clamped down in front of the hammer, to keep it from falling should the trigger be pulled.

But there he stopped instead of following through and throwing Little Ted for a flip.

"See that . . . ?" he said, gesturing Ted's attention to his gloved hand. "Even if you pull the trigger now, it's not going to do anything." The two stared at the cocked hammer for a second.

"Yeah," said Little Ted, "but won't it hurt if I pulled the trigger right now?"

"Not as bad as getting shot would," said Summers. "That's step one," he added. "Here's step two." He reached his other hand over and clasped it onto Ted's gun as if shaking hands with it. He swung Ted's arm out, back and up slowly in one long circle, stopping when he saw Ted was on the verge of losing balance.

"Whoa, that's good," said Ted, feeling

himself ready to pitch forward with the slightest pressure from Summers' gripping hands.

"Now, if I wanted to flip you," said Summers, "I'd step in under your arm, twist hard and swing your gun hand back the rest of the way. You'd have no choice but to flip forward. It you were a heavier man, I might have to kick your right foot back like this to get you started." He swung the side of his boot against Ted's foot at the ankle, then stopped short of following through. "Have you got it?" he asked.

"I think I might," Ted said.

Watching from the porch, Bailey saw the two change positions, Little Ted putting on the trail glove, Summers holding Little Ted's unloaded gun down at his side, ready to draw it. Beside Bailey, Rena walked up and stood watching. She laid a hand gently on her mistress' shoulder.

"What are they doing?" she asked quietly.

"It's something we saw Will Summers do to Dallas Tate before I sent him away with his arm hanging at his side," Bailey replied just as quietly. Beside her in his wheelchair, Ansil Swann sat with his face half-raised but his eyes blank and staring straight ahead. A nerve twitched twice in his slack jaw, then stopped.

"He is handsome and capable, this Will Summers?" Rena said. She squeezed Bailey's shoulder a little for emphasis.

"Yes," said Bailey, "he is."

"But he is leaving in the morning?" Rena said.

"Not if I have anything to do with it," Bailey said.

"Oh . . . ?" said Rena, sounding concerned.

"Don't worry. I know how to handle men," Bailey said. She raised a hand, laid it over Rena's and patted it softly. "Your only concern is taking care of poor Ansil and me." She laid her head over briefly atop her and Rena's hands. Then she straightened and looked at her husband's hollow eyes staring at her blankly from his wheelchair.

In the night, only moments after the ranch hands and Summers had gone off to the bunkhouse, Bailey Swann lay awake in her bed while Ansil rested in a small bed against the wall where Bedos Reyes had carried him. She had left orders for Little Ted and Lonnie Kerns to ride out after dinner and watch over the main trail until the first light of dawn. The ranch hands had only given each other a look, and followed their orders.

When she'd heard the sound of Kerns'

and Little Ted's horses heading from the barn toward the main trail, she rose on the side of her bed. Standing, she slipped out of her sleeping gown and wrapped a long coat around herself. Naked now save for the long coat, she stepped into a pair of soft moccasin house slippers and walked quietly down the stairs and through the darkened house.

When she had walked out the front door, she closed it quietly behind her and walked across the yard and down the moonlit trail connecting the front yard to the bunkhouse. On her way, she saw the fiery red eyes of a coyote stare at her as it moved along through a stretch of sparse brush. But what she did not see were the two pairs of human eyes watching her from deeper within that same stretch of brush.

She looked back over her shoulder through the light of the half moon as she stepped onto the plank porch. Seeing only the purple night, a half moon the color of molted gold lying suspended in a bed of diamonds, she turned back to the door and inched it open slowly, moonlight spilling slantwise across the pine flooring. She closed the door equally slowly. Yet, in spite of her stealth, as she stepped quietly across the floorboards, she heard the cocking of a gun hammer from a corner bunk.

She stopped and froze.

"Will, it's me, Bailey," she whispered. She paused, then took another slow quiet step. "Will, did you hear me? Where are you? You're not going to shoot, are you?"

A pause; then Summers' voice came quietly out of the darkness.

"No, I'm not going to shoot," he said. "I'm over here."

She watched a match flare in the darkness and go to the wick of an oil lamp on a small table beside the bunk bed. A glow of light rose, then damped low and glowed in a pale gold behind the lamp's black-smudged glass.

"I came to talk," she reminded him, "to tell you my plan." She moved closer, holding the front of her coat closed.

Summers looked her up and down, getting the picture why she was really here.

"I'll dress," he said, holding the blanket against him. He reached the Colt up and slipped it into his holster, his gun belt hanging on the bedpost. Then he reached out toward his trousers lying over a wooden chair, having to stretch some to get there.

"No, wait," she said, stopping at the side of the bed, looking down at him, her hair undone, falling around the collar of her long coat. "I didn't come here *only* to talk." She opened the coat, stepped out of it in the soft lamplight and let it fall to the floor behind her. She shook out her long auburn hair; it fell around her bare shoulders, down her upturned breasts.

Jesus! Sweet Mother of —

Summers withdrew his outstretched hand and lay staring, his back hiked up against a pillow, his holstered Colt hanging beside his shoulder. Here was a rich man's woman standing naked before him. He had noted her striking beauty all along, but he'd tried not to dwell on it. He knew about her and Dallas Tate, and he knew how she had used him to taunt the jealous young ranch hand.

Yes, a rich man's woman, something a man like Ansil Swann strove for as one of his many rewards in life. The kind of woman Summers knew a man like himself could never have, except under these dire circumstances. Yet now, seeing her here, in *his* world, standing naked before him, in a dusty bunkhouse, the two of them alone in the middle of a quiet night, he could not ignore her beauty; now he could no longer put it aside as something he could only admire and hunger for but never have. She had brought herself to him — a gift, a reward? Either way, how could he refuse?

Jesus, he couldn't refuse, he thought to himself. If he did he would regret it the rest of his life. It wasn't as if he owed Ansil Swann a thing. Besides, from all outer appearances, Swann was a dead man. Anyway, this was not something of his doing, Summers told himself as Bailey eased down to lie atop him, the heat of her already closing around him. She'd been unfaithful to Swann long before he arrived here. Who was he to —

"Wait," he said suddenly, stopping her as she lowered her lips to his. She stopped and opened her eyes and gazed at him as if in disbelief, a woman not used to being denied what she wanted, not in matters such as this.

"Wait?" she asked, as if not certain she'd heard him correctly. She started to say more, but she felt Summers clasp his left hand over her mouth. She saw him reach his right hand up and slip the Colt from its holster. Her eyes widened slightly.

"Someone's there," he whispered. He eased her quickly from atop him and reached over and killed the lamplight with a twist of the wick wheel. Just as the corner of the bunkhouse went black, a plank creaked on the front porch.

As the front door swung open wide and moonlight seeped in across the floor, Summers moved in a crouch, his Colt cocked, aimed and ready. Bailey Swann leaped up from the bed and stood back in the other black corner.

"We hear you in there. Don't shoot," said a hushed voice from outside the open door.

"You don't shoot, we won't shoot," said another voice. Summers had heard those voices before, but he couldn't place where right away. But he didn't have to wonder long. Bailey let out a sigh of relief and stepped back over the bed.

"It's the Belltraes," she said. She reached down, pulled up the bedcover and wrapped it around herself.

"The Belltraes?" Summers said, seeing that as no good reason to lower his Colt. He stared at the two shadowy silhouettes stepping into the dark bunkhouse.

"Yes," said Bailey, "they're here to see me." She stepped around to the table, picked up a match, struck it and lit the lamp.

To see her?

Summers held his Colt level, but he felt dumbstruck.

"I hope we're not interrupting anything here," said Collard Belltrae. The lamplight rose and spread back into a circling glow.

"Call it just a wild guess," said Ezra Belltrae, "but I'm betting we *are.*"

144

"You're right, Ezra. You *are* interrupting," Bailey said, sounding exasperated.

"For that you have our apologies," said Ezra.

Both Belltrae brothers stood grinning at Summers and the woman as Bailey slipped on her moccasins and gestured for Summers to lower the Colt and put on his trousers. When both were adequately covered, Bailey wrapping her coat around herself and dropping the bedcover from under it, she looked at the brothers and pulled back her long auburn hair.

"This had better be good, fellows," she said. She held her open hand out toward Collard as she spoke. Collard stepped forward and handed her a bag of tobacco with a card of rolling papers stuck down in it.

Summers stood watching, in bewilderment. "I realize the three of you have already met," she said, taking out a paper and smoothing it in her fingers.

"Yes, we have," said Collard. He said to Summers, "I'm sorry we had to leave you behind that night. Fact is, you didn't seem real keen on cutting out."

Summers looked at their faces, still bruised and swollen, but not as bad.

Summers still hadn't found a basis of

understanding on what these two were doing there. He looked at Bailey as she expertly rolled herself a smoke and ran it in and out of her mouth.

"I know I owe you an explanation, Will," she said. "I'm sorry these two arrived at such an inconvenient time."

"I could use an explanation," Summers said, still watching the Belltraes, but lowering his Colt a little.

She paused as she leaned over, picked up another match, struck it and lit her cigarette. She shook out the match as she blew out a puff of smoke.

"They did a job for me," she said. "They stole my husband's racing stallion . . . to keep it from getting taken by Finnity and Baines' collection men."

"Oh?" Summers lowered the Colt a little more.

"Yeah, that's right," said Collard, to Summers. He turned to Bailey and added, "The stallion is safe and sound at Don Manuel's place, by the way." He looked back at Summers. "That wasn't the stallion you and ol' Hendrik ate. That was a desert mustang, happened to be the same color — they all look about alike dressed out." He shrugged.

"We only broke his leg over a rock after he was shot and dressed out," Ezra put in.

Summers just stared at him, getting the idea.

"I know how terrible this sounds, Will," said the woman, "but my back was against the wall. I had them steal the stallion, and I reported it to Sheriff Miller. I managed to sell the stallion to Don Manuel, who has a spread thirty miles north of here. No one doubted it. With the stallion butchered and eaten, no one would go searching for it."

"Us being known to scalp and fillet other folks' horses for hair and steak," said Collard, with a sharp grin, "that slaughter in the cave and the quirt you found was all we needed to seal the deal."

Summers let out a breath and gave Bailey Swann a look.

"Is this the idea you were going to tell me about — ?" he asked.

"No," Bailey said quickly, cutting him short. She looked at the Belltraes as if to explain. "I had thought we might do the same thing with the bays. But we can't."

"We've seen the bay fillies," said Collard. "Don Manuel would give top dollar, if we could get them to him."

"Too risky," Bailey said, shaking her head. "The stallion was a onetime thing. If the bays go missing, it'll start looking peculiar.

147

Finnity and Baines' men will start searching."

"Suit yourself, ma'am," said Ezra. "We just wanted to report, let you know the stallion made it to Don Manuel's." He reached inside his shirt, took out a leather bag of gold coins, shook it, rattled the coins and handed it to her. "Here's your money — less our fee, like you promised. You be sure and let the don know we brought this to you like you paid us to. We don't want our heads on a stick. Do we, Collard?"

"No, we don't," Collard agreed, shaking his head. The two looked at Summers and Bailey and touched their dirty fingers to their sagging hat brims.

"And a good evening to you both," Ezra said. As the brothers stepped toward the door, Ezra turned and said, "I almost forgot. If I was you I'd be shying away from Dark Horses. Your man Miller is going out. Evert Crayley is putting a Finnity and Baines man in his place." He grinned. "You might say Ansil Swann's days of glory are coming to a close."

"Thank you, Ezra," Bailey said stiffly. She and Summers sat watching as the brothers left and closed the door behind them.

CHAPTER 11

No sooner had the Belltraes gone than Will Summers uncocked the Colt and let it hang loosely in his hand. He walked to the bed and shoved the gun down into its holster. He buckled his loose belt at his waist and passed up the cigarette when Bailey offered it to him. He looked squarely at her as he sat down in the wooden chair. Seeing the look on his face, Bailey sat in silence for a moment; then she shook her head and held it in her hands. Looking at her, Summers thought he saw a tear fall from her cheek.

"Well, now you know about the stallion," she said. "You are the only person here who knows it. I deliberately kept it from the ranch hands, even Dallas Tate." She shook her head as if in shame. "What a terrible person you must think I am, Will," she said in a hurt voice, "all these things I've done, just to keep the body and soul together."

"I haven't judged you, Bailey," he said.

But he knew he was not seeing her with the same eyes now that he'd learned what she and the Belltraes had done. "You and your husband are in trouble. I've seen the kind of men you're up against. If you try to play fair with these men, they'll eat you both alive."

But what he said wasn't completely true. Moments ago she had been the rich man's woman, some creature of grace and beauty standing above the fray of the world. Now she was cheapened somehow, he thought, a scheming woman, doing whatever it took to pull herself forward. He didn't know why he felt this way, but he did, and he was certain that what had almost happened only moments the Belltraes arrived was not going to happen at all.

"I'm glad to hear you say that, Will," she said. "It means a lot to me."

Damn it! Of all the times to start feeling guilty, he chastised himself.

He didn't know why, but somehow he even felt like a lesser person himself, as if while she took advantage of her husband's unfortunate condition, he would be taking advantage of hers. No matter how badly he wanted her, it was not the same now. She stood and walked over to him, letting her long coat fall open on its own. He watched her reach out to turn out the lamp. She gave him a look as she reached.

"They're gone," she said. "It's still early. I sent the hands away until morning. . . ." She let her words trail.

"Leave it on," Summers said quietly. "It's time you tell me about this plan you mentioned."

"Oh," she said. Summers saw the mixed feelings in her pale blue eyes. Surprise, relief, but some disappointed. "Well, all right," she said, tightening the coat at her throat. "I can tell you my plan." She leveled her gaze at him. "Please, Will, promise me you'll keep it a secret."

"I promise," Summers said.

She glanced at the window, then at the closed door. She gestured for Summers to move his chair closer. He did, yet she still spoke in a lowered, guarded voice.

"In the shaft of one of my husband's closed mines is a strongbox he hid there. The box contains a large amount of cash and gold ingots. The cash is what he received for gold when he sold to the Dutch and the French Belgians. They bought the gold with American greenbacks to keep the transactions from being easily traced by the Mexican government. The cash was never taken to the bank in Dark Horses." She paused and took a breath. "The gold is what he still had on hand when the new *federale* regime took over Mexico City and declared individual gold sales illegal."

Summers just looked at her as she continued.

"Don Manuel had agreed to purchase the remaining gold from him, but Ansil had the stroke. I haven't yet been able to risk moving it across the hill country to Don Manuel. The *federales* turn a blind eye to everything, but not when it comes to gold — gold they haven't taken their cut from," she added.

Summers considered it.

"Why doesn't Don Manuel come get the gold?" he said. "Take the risk himself for a lesser price?"

"Oh, he wanted to," said Bailey. "But Ansil wouldn't trust him, not now that Don Manuel has plenty of manpower and we only have Kerns and Little Ted working for us."

"I understand," said Summers. "The most guns win."

"Exactly," she said. She leaned out to him and took his hands in hers as she studied his eyes.

"Go with me, Will," she said. "Take charge for me. Help my ranch hands and me take the gold to Don Manuel and I'll pay you five thousand dollars."

Five thousand dollars? Summers stared at her.

"How much cash and gold are we talking about?" he asked.

"A lot," she said. "I honestly can't say how much. But a fortune, according to Ansil, and Ansil doesn't think small." She studied Summers' eyes intently.

"Do Lonnie and Little Ted know about this?" he asked.

"No, not yet," she said. "They don't need to know until we're well under way. Then I'll tell them *where* we're going. Once we arrive I'll tell them *why.*"

A careful woman, Summers reminded himself.

He took a deep breath and let it out, considering her proposition. For a lot less money he'd been nearly hanged bringing four bay fillies to the Mexican hill country. Looking into her pale blue eyes, he saw the wild desperation there, the willingness to do whatever it took to keep from losing everything she owned. "How far are the strongbox and the gold from here?" he asked. "How far is it to Don Manuel's?"

"The gold is a day's ride," she said. "From there to Don Manuel's, three days, four at the most with a slow-moving wagon."

153

Summers nodded, considering it.

"All right," he said after a moment.

"You'll — you'll do it?" she stammered, surprised.

"I'll do it," he said quietly. "But you'll have to pay Kerns and Little Ted more than ranch-hand wages for this. If you don't you'll be taking the chance of them turning on you. When we go to the mine, you need to clear the air with them. They need to know their reward as well as their risk."

"Yes, yes, I agree," she said, sounding excited. She squeezed his hands in hers. "And, Will, I want you to know," she added, gesturing sidelong at the bed she sat on. "This? What we were going to do before the Belltraes interrupted? I wasn't going to lie with you just to entice you into doing this for me. It was more than that —"

Summers doubted it, but he wasn't going to say so.

"It doesn't matter what we *might have* done here tonight," he said, "but for now, we'd best stick to business."

Again, he thought he saw a look of both relief and disappointment come to her eyes.

"Will," she said, still holding his hands in hers, "please tell me you're not doing this *only* for the money. Please tell me, if only because I need to hear it?"

"It's not *only* for the money, Bailey," Will said. He slipped his hands from hers. "Nothing I do ever is."

At first light in Dark Horses, Evert "Dad" Crayley, walked into the doctor's office flanked by two gunmen. The three men who'd ridden with Darren to the Swann hacienda stood up quickly, like soldiers called to attention.

"Where is that son of a bitch son of mine?" Dad asked. All three pointed a finger down a long hallway. Dad and his two flanking gunmen walked on without stopping. The three waiting gunmen stood and watched in silence, then gave one another wary looks. Dad and his two flanking gunmen walked straight down a hallway to a recovery room where a young Mexican girl sat picking buckshot from Darren Crayley's shoulder with a long pair of tweezers. She dropped the buckshot onto a bloody cloth laid out beside the wounded man. On another gurney against the wall lay Tubbs, the wagon driver. Two large bloody bandages lay covering his wide, fleshy chest.

"Morning, Dad," Darren said in a weak voice, turning sad eyes up at his father. Bloody patches of cotton gauze dotted the side of his face.

"I'll 'morning' your lousy hide," Dad Crayley growled, his fists clenched at his side. "You're lucky I don't beat you with a chair right in front of everybody!"

The Mexican girl cowered away in fear, the tweezers in her bloody fingertips.

"What — what did I do?" Darren said, also cowering, pulling away on his gurney. He raised a hand as if to protect his face.

"You didn't do a *gawl-damn* thing, evidently!" Dad shouted. "I sent you and three men out with a wagon, and Tubbs to help you load it! You didn't bring back a damn thing — no furnishings, no bay fillies, nothing."

"Jesus, Dad, we were attacked," said Darren. "Look at me. I was shotgunned! Look at Tubbs. He nearly died on the way here."

"Give me that chair!" Dad reached around for the straight-backed chair as the young Mexican girl jumped away from it. He grasped the top edges of the chair to swing it back, but one of his gunmen, a Tex-Mexican named Hico Morales, raised a hand, attempting to stop him.

"*Facil, facil,* Dad, do not beat him now," he said, almost touching Dad's reaching hands. "You will kill him."

"So?" said Dad. "Are you taking his side?" He looked sharply at Hico's hands. Hico withdrew them and held them chest high.

"I take your side, Dad, as always," said Hico in a rough but soothing voice, trying to defuse the volatile gunman leader. "If you kill him now you will never know what happened."

Dad calmed a little, took a deep breath and rubbed his red face with both hands, removing them from the chair back. On the gurney, Darren looked relieved. The girl stood back against the wall.

"You're right," Dad said to Hico. He turned to Darren and said, "I warned all of you that was no parlor game I sent you out on. I told you I needed results!"

"He shot me, Dad!" said Darren. "It's hard to load a wagon with a face full of buckshot."

Dad calmed a little more; he motioned the girl back into her chair.

"Who shot you?" Dad asked.

"It was the horse trader Dallas Tate warned us about," said Darren, "the one bringing the bay fillies to Ansil Swann. We rode up, I told him what we were there to do — he shot me right out of my saddle. The Swanns' ranch hands shot Tubbs. I'm telling you, Dad, I was lucky to get out alive. So was Tubbs."

Dad looked around at Tubbs on his gurney, watching. "Tubbs, are you ready to go back and get those horses and furnishings?"

Tubbs thought about it, but only for a second; then he swallowed a tight knot in his throat.

"Soon as I can walk, I'll go, Dad, sure enough," he said.

"You ain't going nowhere until I say you can," said a gravelly voice.

At the door to the room, a bent and aged doctor with a head of wild white hair stood leaning on a hickory cane. Blood smeared a white apron he wore over his suit trousers. He looked from Tubbs to Dad Crayley and said, "These men have lost too much blood to do anything today."

"When can they ride?" Dad asked. He stood glaring back and forth between Tubbs and his son. "I need men, not convalescents."

A gunman named Leon Yates pushed his way past the doctor into the room.

"Dad, Sheriff Miller and his posse are back, riding in right this minute. Looks like they've all had a rough trip. The sheriff is riding bowed over like he's got shot."

"Good," said Dad, "I wish the Belltraes had killed them, probably saved me the trouble." He looked at his son. "Get yourself up and well. We're going back to the

158

Swanns' spread as soon as you can sit on a horse."

"All right, Dad," said Darren Crayley.

Dad looked at Yates, Hico and the third gunman, former Abilene town marshal Jasper Trent.

"You three men come with me. It's damn time we sent Swann's worthless sheriff packing — put one of my own security men in to replace him."

The three men followed Dad outside and walked with him, all four of them abreast, up the stone-tiled street where Sheriff Miller, his deputy, Endo Clifford, and the other posse men crawled down from their horses. Two of the Mexicans had lowered Miller from his saddle. They stood him between them and looped his arms over their shoulders. They helped him toward his office as Dad and his men arrived.

"Hold it right there, Miller," said Dad, pointing a finger at the bowed half-conscious sheriff. "You left here chasing the Belltraes and that racing stallion. Where the hell are they?"

Sheriff Miller gasped and coughed. Dad saw the dried vomit on the front of his slicker, his lower trouser legs and boot tops.

"I don't know . . . and I don't give a damn," Miller rasped, the two Mexicans

159

keeping him from falling.

Dad looked at the sheriff's pale white face, flecks of dried sickness in his beard stubble.

"What the hell happened to you, Miller?" Dad asked. Then, as he looked at the others, his expression soured. "What happened to *all* of you for that matter?"

"We damn near drowned, Dad," Red Warren said, sounding sick and exhausted himself. "Hadn't been for these vaqueros, I expect we all would have. The sheriff took the worst of it, swallowed half the Río Azul and caught water fever."

"Take the sheriff inside," Endo said to the Mexicans, stepping forward as if taking charge. To Dad he said, "He spent the night shaking, puking and carrying on. But to answer your question, we lost the Belltraes at the river crossing." Behind him the Mexicans led the sheriff into the adobe office building.

"Did you at least *see* the stallion?" Dad said as the office door closed. They heard a gagging sound come from inside.

"Oh yes, we saw him," said Endo. "Saw what was left of him anyway. Those horse-eating sons a' bitches gutted him and boned him asshole to appetite. We tried to bring his head back with us, but wolves got ahold of it. I hate telling Ansil Swann about it. He

160

loved that stallion like it was close kin."

"To hell with Swann," said Dad. "That stallion was the property of Finnity and Baines. I was taking possession of the racing stallion soon as you brought it back."

Endo just stared upon hearing Dad's words.

"That's right," Dad said. "Ansil Swann is broke. Everything he owned is now the property of Finnity and Baines, north of the border and south." He gave a nasty grin. "That also means you and Miller are out of jobs. I'm appointing a new sheriff here."

"Who — who do you figure you'll appoint?" Endo asked.

"Whoever damn well suits me, Endo. Why," he said, "you interested in holding the office?"

"I am," Clifford said flatly. "Just because Miller is gone doesn't mean I want to be. To tell the truth, him and I ain't in agreement on how to uphold the law. He let the Belltraes get away when he should have hanged them first thing. He did the same thing with one of their pals, Will Summers. The Swann woman showed up, and Miller let Summers ride right off with her and her cowhands, free as a bird. Bay fillies and all."

"You don't say. . . ." Dad gave a glance toward the doctor's office, then back at Clifford, putting two and two together in his mind. Finally he looked back at Clifford with a sharp expression. "Endo, this might be your lucky day. If I pin a badge on you, are you going to do everything I say, when I say it, so help you God?"

"You got it, Dad," said Endo.

Crayley gave a chuckle.

"Consider yourself sworn in," he said. "First thing you need to do is go inside and yank Miller's badge off his chest and pin it on yours." He looked around Dark Horses. "Then get right back out here. We've got lots of changes to make here. I'm running this town for Finnity and Baines, but by thunder, I intend to make them proud."

"Just one question, Dad," said Clifford. "If Miller gives me any guff over taking his badge, how far can I go to straighten him out?"

"Hell, Endo," said Dad, "you're the sheriff now. You go as far as you think is necessary."

Endo Clifford grinned and hiked up his damp, dirty trousers.

"I was hoping that's what you'd say," he said, loosening his Colt up and down in its holster as he turned toward the sheriff's office door.

"Stand here, watch this, you want to know

162

how to get ahead in this world," Dad said to Jasper Trent, Hico Morales and Yates, who had now joined them. "You too, Red, Buster," he said to Red Warren and Buster Saggert, who he knew had been listening, "unless you're both all set to throw in against us."

"Against you, hell no," said Warren. "I shoot for whoever pays the most."

"And lets us run the biggest bar tabs," Buster Saggert put in with a stonelike expression.

"That's me on both counts." Dad grinned and added, "Listen up now."

The two Mexicans stepped out of the office at Clifford's command and stood at the closed door with grim looks on their faces.

From inside they heard Sheriff Miller yell, "No! Please, Endo!"

A single shot rang out inside the office; Dad gave a dark chuckle and shook his head slowly.

"And there it is, men," he said. "A man who takes orders usually ends up giving them. Let that be a lesson to all of you."

Endo Clifford stepped out of the office with a crooked grin and his Colt smoking in his hand.

"He gave me *guff,*" he said. "I *straightened* him out."

CHAPTER 12

Will Summers called Lonnie Kerns and Little Ted aside when the two had ridden back to the bunkhouse at daylight. He explained to them that they would need to empty loose hay and other items from the spread's large freight wagon and prepare it for the trail. The wagon sat inside the work barn near the bunkhouse. While the three got the wagon ready, Bailey, Summers and Rena Reyes went through the hacienda picking and sorting through furniture, silverware, ornate platters and gold candle-holders, anything of value that would serve to cover the real treasure they would have loaded beneath the household goods on their return trip.

"Why today?" Kerns asked. "It's looking like we've got more rain coming in."

"Because today we've still got wagon horses," Summers said, nodding at the team of large powerful-looking wagon horses standing to the side. "The collectors could take them any day."

"Not without a fight," Kerns said.

"True," said Summers, "but it's better this way. Why fight if we don't have to?"

"Can I ask why we're taking this big, heavy freight wagon?" said Little Ted, he and Kerns standing beside the wagon, watching mice run and dive from the wagon bed as Summers swept it out. "We've got a buckboard that will carry a load of furniture just as well. It'd only take one horse, and it doesn't need cleaning out first."

"No, you can't," said Summers.

"Can't what?" asked Little Ted, looking confused.

"No, you can't *ask why*," said Summers, starting to sweep out the wagon bed with a broom. "I'll tell you when we get the load of belongings to where we're taking them."

Ted gave a sly grin and looked at Kerns.

"I get it now," he said. "We're going to hide the load from the collectors. And Mrs. Swann doesn't want us to know where until we're nearly there."

"She doesn't trust us?" Kerns asked Summers.

"Look at it this way," said Summers, "wouldn't you rather not know, just so if the collectors found out, nobody could

165

suspect you telling them?"

"Makes sense," said Kerns.

"Ha! So I was right," said Little Ted. "We are going to hide the load?"

Summers just looked at him, poker-faced.

"How'd the practice go?" he asked, instead of acknowledging his question.

"Don't ask," Little Ted said, looking disappointed. "Lonnie wouldn't let me practice on him last night while we were watching the trail."

"I'm not getting my arm wrenched out of my socket," said Kerns. "I saw the shape Dallas Tate was in after getting flipped."

"I wasn't going to flip you, fool," said Ted, "just grab your gun hand when you drew on me." He looked back at Summers. "Anyway, I practiced by myself, acted like a gun was drawn on me, grabbed the make-believe hand and held it up and twisted as I stepped under it." He went through the motion as he spoke. "It wasn't like having a real person to practice on, but it'll do."

Summers stepped down from the swept wagon, broom in hand, and stood with the two ranch hands, looking the freight wagon over good.

"Would you like to know how to take a knife away from a man trying to stab you?" he asked Little Ted.

Little Ted's eyes turned excited. So did his voice.

"Oh man! How I would!" he said to Summers. "I have always wanted to know how to do that! I saw an army scout do it to a fellow in a saloon one night in El Paso — knocked him cold as a wedge with his own knife handle. You can show me how it's done?"

"Yep, I'll show you," Summers said, "if you'll stop asking questions until we get to where we're going."

"Deal," said Ted.

"Yep, deal," said Summers. "Now go get the four bays ready for the trail while Lonnie and I take the wagon up to the hacienda."

"The four bays are going with us?" said Little Ted, curious. "Why are we taking them —" He caught himself and stopped when he saw the look Summers gave him. "I didn't ask," he said quickly. "I started to, but I didn't." He turned and walked to the stalls where he'd placed the bays last night. The fillies stood in a row, watching, chewing hay.

"I might like to learn that trick myself, how to take a man's knife away from him," Kerns said as he and Summers walked to where two large team horses stood chewing hay, ready to be hitched to the freight wagon tongue. "Will you teach me too?"

"Why not?" said Summers. "I'll teach you both. You can practice on each other when you've got time."

"Same deal you offered Little Ted?" said Kerns. "Keep my questions to myself till we get where we're going?"

"Same deal," Summers said.

The two hitched the team of wagon horses to the empty freight wagon and climbed up into the wooden seat. Kerns jiggled the wagon reins to the horses' backs and drove them to the side door of the Swann hacienda.

At the side door, Bedos and his daughter, Rena, met them, having already carried out and stacked a few pieces of smaller furniture and wooden crates. Kerns set the wagon brake. Summers stepped down and began handing the items up to him. As the men worked, Summers looked at the side porch and saw Ansil Swann sitting slumped in his wheelchair. Swann stared out at the wagon, but his flint-colored eyes were hollow and glazed. The eyes of a dead man, Summers thought grimly to himself.

He watched Bailey come down the stone walkway and gesture him to the side. Summers stepped away from the loading and joined her.

"I hope I've chosen the right items, Will," she said just between the two of them, while the others continued loading. From the barn, Little Ted walked up, leading the four bays on a lead rope.

"It all looks good, ma'am," Summers said. "If you took your best valuables you might lose them if we get in a bad spot and have to give them up. If you don't bring some things of value, it could cause suspicion." The two of them gave the furnishings and housewares an appraising look.

"What do you think, Will?" she asked him in a hushed tone. "How'd I do?"

Summers nodded, watching the others load the wagon.

"You did just fine, ma'am," he said, noting a large painted portrait of a younger, powerful Ansil Swann leaning in an ornate gilded frame. "These are not items a person would easily toss aside." He paused, then said, "Are you sure you wouldn't want to keep the portrait here?"

"No," she said without a second thought. "Like you said, if we get caught in a spot, something of value has to go in order to make this whole thing look good."

In Dark Horses, Endo Clifford, Red Warren

and Buster Saggert had been going from business to business after dragging Bert Miller out in front of the adobe office and leaning him against a hitch-ring post. Endo had stuck Miller's earless head through the wide iron hitch ring and left him sitting, his dead eyes staring out at the street. Hico stood beside Evert Crayley in front of the sheriff's office, the two watching Endo break the news to the citizenry that he'd become their newly appointed sheriff.

"Dad, this man is an imbecile," Hico said quietly. "I hope he doesn't turn on you someday."

"No problem," Crawley said with a careless shrug. "There's nothing wrong with Endo that a bullet in his head won't cure."

Hico nodded with a slight grin and glanced at the town mercantile with a curious expression.

Moving along the street with Bert Miller's ears in his shirt pocket and his hands smeared with blood from cutting them off, Endo and the two gunmen made their rounds. They met no objections from the town's business community when they explained to the store merchants that Miller was out of office for good and that Endo had now taken over.

"And, by the way," he told Melvin Smith,

170

the Dark Horses Mercantile owner, "Ansil Swann is no longer running the mines or anything else here. If you take any notes signed under Swann's name, you'll likely never get paid." He grinned, then added, "And don't say you never *heard* me say it. You see what happens to men who don't *listen.*" Patting Miller's severed ears in his shirt pocket with a bloody hand, he turned to leave.

"But — but I came here and settled specifically because of Ansil Swann," Smith stammered, before Endo walked away.

"Uh-oh," Red Warren said under his breath, he and Buster Saggert stopping on either side of the new wild-eyed sheriff. Endo turned to face Smith with a strange, enraged look in his beady eyes.

"What did you just say to me?" Endo said slowly, each word evenly delivered. One hand went to his Colt, his other, bloody hand to the handle of his knife sheathed at his waist.

The store owner's face turned pale and drawn.

"I'm not trying to start trouble, Sheriff Endo," Smith said. "It's just that Ansil Swann lent me money to help open an American-style mercantile store here in his settlement venture. Without him, who do I pay each month?"

It took Endo a second to understand. When he did, his rage cooled quickly. He chuckled as he looked at Red Warren and Buster Saggert. They returned a sly grin.

"Grab his ears, Deputy Red," Endo said, his bloody hand wrapped around the knife handle.

"No, please no!" Smith screamed, unable to duck away and run before the deputies grabbed his forearms and yanked him over the counter. While Buster jumped behind him and wrapped his arms around him in a bear hug, Red reached out, grabbed both of his ears and held them stretched out. Smith screamed again, loud and long.

"Are you listening now?" said Endo, only inches from the store owner's face.

"Yes, *God* yes!" Smith screamed.

"All right, pay attention," said Endo. He went back to a slow, evenly delivered voice. "You come *pay me* the same amount, *every month,* as you *were* paying Swann." He took a step back, his bloody hand still poised on the knife handle. "Did you hear every word real clear?"

"Yes, Sheriff, yes!" Smith said in a trembling tone. "I will. I will. I swear I will!"

"I know you will," said Endo. "I've got faith in you — in this whole town for that matter."

He motioned for Buster and Warren to turn the terrified man loose. When they did the store owner collapsed and caught himself with both hands on the long counter. His breath rushed in and out.

"Need some water?" Red asked Smith, putting his hand on the store owner's bowed back and patting it kindly.

"I'm . . . all right," Smith said, panting heavily. "I just need a minute . . . to calm down some."

"Take your time," Endo said in a feigned tone of concern. "Getting out of breath can kill you, as hot as it is here." He paused, then said, "I want you to keep paying attention 'cause I've got something for you to pass along to the other business owners. Will you do that for me?" he asked politely.

Smith swallowed hard and straightened himself up.

"Yes, anything you say," he said, rubbing his reddened ears with both hands.

"What was *that*?" Endo asked, a smoldering look coming back into his eyes.

"I meant, anything you say, *Sheriff Endo,*" Smith said, correcting himself quickly.

Endo looked at Red and Buster. The two deputies looked at each other and gave a smirk.

"That's lots better, Melvin," Endo said. "That shows you've got respect for the law. I admire that in a man. It shows that a Mexican town can be run just like it's American. With Americans running it, of course," He smiled proudly. "I believe that's what Ansil Swann was out to prove coming here. Don't you?"

"Yes, I do," Smith said humbly, his head bowed slightly.

Red and Buster watched Endo at work, liking the idea of people having to do what they told them to.

"I want you to tell them what I just told you, Melvin," Endo said to Smith. "Anybody owing Swann money, just come on up with it. Pay it to me, same as you paid it to him."

"I'll tell them," Smith said.

"That's good. I'm counting on you, Melvin," said Endo. "The sooner everybody gets into the spirit of this, the better. You all came here following Swann, wanting to see things run like this is Texas or Arizona Territory. I aim to run it just that way." He turned and walked out, the two deputies flanking him.

On the street, Dad Crayley and Hico Morales watched the three newly appointed lawmen walk purposefully from the mercantile store to the large Dark Horses Cantina and step through the open double doorway.

"So far, so good," said Dad to Hico. "Anytime there's no gunfire where Endo Clifford just left, it's worth celebrating." He chuckled, reached into his coat pocket, took out two cigars and gave one to Hico. "Come on, let's get a drink."

"What about the screaming?" Hico asked as the two started walking to the cantina.

"A little screaming never hurt anything," said Dad. "Far as I'm concerned, that's just a part of making folks understand." He grinned and shoved the cigar into his mouth. Nodding toward the open double doors of the cantina, he added, "I've got a feeling we're going to see some big changes in this town's attitude on drinking, gambling and whores."

"I believe you," Hico said, the two of them walking on. "Endo Clifford has always had huge cravings for all three."

"And what red-blooded man doesn't?" Dad asked.

From the open doors of the cantina they heard a loud cheer and a heavy round of applause resound out along the street as they walked on.

"What about Ansil Swann's place, the horse trader who buckshot your boy, Darren?" Hico asked. "When are we going to ride through and strip that place to the bone?"

"Soon enough," Dad said. "Finnity and Baines has put the word out we're taking over everything Swann owns. Thomas Finnity is rehiring some of the old railroad gun monkeys who used to work for them, sending them all this way. This is a big deal for Finnity. He might show up himself."

"I have never met him," Hico said.

"Well, be prepared to anytime," said Dad. "Taking over something as big as Swann Enterprises is no light piece of work." He grinned. "We'll have gunmen straggling into Dark Horses two and three at a time before long. And that suits me. The more men I've got at my command, the better. As far as the horse trader goes, if I wake up with a big mad-on, we might ride out and shoot holes in him. For now, let's enjoy the hospitality of Dark Horses." He gestured a sweeping hand all around at the Mexican hill town that had been made over to look like a smaller version of El Paso, or Denver City.

CHAPTER 13

In the afternoon, crossing a flat stretch of sandy plain, Little Ted rode up alongside the wagon on the driver's side, where Will Summers sat with the wagon reins in his hands. His Winchester rifle stuck out from within the furniture stacked tightly in the wagon bed. Bailey Swann sat on the seat beside him. Behind the wagon Lonnie Kerns rode along, leading the four bays and Summers' dapple gray. The gray clopped along saddled, ready to ride.

"Don't look around right now, Will," Little Ted said sidelong to Summers, "but I think somebody's watching from the ridgelines to your right."

Summers nodded without looking.

"Good call, Ted. I've been thinking that myself," Summers replied. Listening, Bailey Swann had to catch herself to keep from turning in the wagon seat and searching along the ridges.

"Apache?" she said, almost with a gasp.

"No," said Summers, "I doubt it. I first thought I saw somebody skylighted a little ways back."

"No Apache would do that," Little Ted cut in.

Summers nodded in agreement.

"Besides, if it was Apache," Summers said, "they'd be after these horses. Us crossing this plain would have been too good a chance for them to pass up."

"Who, then?" she said, still fighting the urge to look. "Maybe some traveler headed for Dark Horses? Maybe they watched us for a minute, then moved on?"

"No," said Summers, "I wish that was the case. But whoever it is up there, they've been moving right along with us the past couple of miles."

"Dang, Will," said Little Ted in surprise, "then you spotted them long before I did." He looked Will up and down. "Why didn't you say something sooner?"

"I was waiting for you to ride up here," Summers said quietly. "I was also thinking it over, deciding the best thing for us to do this time of day." Without turning toward Bailey, he asked sidelong, "How much farther to the mines?"

"We can be there by dark, easy enough,"

she said.

Summers looked at the sandy plain, at the hills a short distance in front of them, at the slant of the sun.

"Three hours . . . ," he said, thinking out loud.

"Yes, three hours, I'd say," Bailey replied.

"Too close to stop for the night, if our destination is that near," Summers said.

"Yes, it wouldn't make sense, us being this close and making camp for the night," Bailey said, "not when we'll be there by nightfall."

"Right, it would make no sense at all," Summers said. "But that's exactly what we'll do if we're still being followed when we reach the end of this flatland."

They rode in silence for a moment as Bailey and Little Ted thought it over. Finally Bailey nodded and smiled, staring straight ahead.

"I get it," she said. "Whoever's up there will figure we must be headed farther away than we are if we're stopping here for the night?"

"Yep, that's it," Summers said. "And if they stick with us until morning, they'll be surprised to learn that we cleared out overnight." He gave the team of horses a tap of the reins just to keep their attention.

"Pretty clever," Bailey said. She looked past Summers at Little Ted.

"I knew that was the plan, all along," Little Ted said with a slight shrug.

Kerns galloped up beside him, leading the five-horse string. The horses bunched around him as he slowed his horse back to a walk.

"I just saw the sun flash on something up along the ridges," he said, not looking up at the hillsides. "Thought I ought to say something."

Little Ted gave a chuckle.

"We've known that for an hour, Lonnie," he said. "Were you sleeping back there?"

"Hell no, I wasn't sleeping — pardon my language, ma'am," Lonnie said. He looked past Little Ted at Summers. "What do you think we ought to do, Will?"

"Spread out," Will said, tapping the reins to the wagon horses' backs, pulling the wagon ahead of the two ranch hands a couple of yards. "We'll make camp as soon as we reach the hills."

Lonnie gave Little Ted a curious look as the wagon rolled on ahead of them.

"Make camp?" he said. "Did I hear him right?"

"Of course you heard him right," Little Ted said. "It's the only thing that makes

180

sense. Now spread out like he told you. We'll make camp just up ahead." He grinned to himself as he rode on.

Watching from high atop a cliff shelf overlooking the stretch of sandy flatlands, Dallas Tate was glad to see the wagon stop at the bottom of an up-reaching hill trail. Through a battered telescope, in the shadowy evening light, he saw the two ranch hands carry downfall wood behind a tall stand of rock. In a moment he saw firelight glowing along the upper edge of the rock.

"Good," he murmured to himself, lying stretched out on the rock shelf, a nearly empty whiskey bottle in his left hand. He didn't know how much farther he could have made it, had they continued on up into the hill line. The pain in his right arm was sharp and constant. The arm felt broken at shoulder level. He had to hold the telescope up with one hand, his right arm dangling loose, sore and throbbing. The whiskey had helped the pain some. But now, with the whiskey supply diminishing quickly, he knew he would be in trouble the rest of the night.

Luckily, while he was in Dark Horses, he'd picked up two bottles of rye at the cantina and a small bottle of opium extract at the

181

apothecary. He took out the bottle of opium and looked at it and shook it a little. He had just about enough to get him through the night. Then he gauged the whiskey. Between the two he might be able to quell the pain, for a while anyway, he told himself, uncorking the whiskey with his left hand and taking a long swig from it.

Come morning, he would continue following them. He placed the whiskey bottle on the rock shelf and opened the opium, taking a generous drink of the bitter-tasting drug. *That'll help. . . .* He corked the blue opium bottle, stood it beside the whiskey and lay back facing the graying evening sky, the telescope on his chest.

Oh yeah, he thought as his head began to swim, it's helping already.

He had no idea where Summers, Bailey Swann and her ranch hands were going, but seeing the bays, the furnishings, and the silverware, he would bet they were taking the fillies and the household goods somewhere to keep the collectors from getting them. That would suit me fine, he thought. He'd follow them in the morning, find out where they were going, first thing. Then he'd ride back and tell Dad Crayley.

Smart thinking.

He smiled dreamily at the darkening sky.

He was pretty sure Crayley would pay well for that kind of information. He rolled onto his stomach and stared for a moment at the whiskey and opium bottles. His hands relaxed at his sides, the pain in his left arm melting away as his eyes crept slowly shut.

In a moment he had fallen into a sound opium-alcohol stupor. His eyes did not open again until sunlight stood above the hill line on the eastern sky. When he did open his eyes and blink them to get them working, he found himself lying facedown on the rock shelf and struggled to push himself up using only his left hand. Once up, he staggered back and forth in place and looked out with his naked blurry eyes toward the place where he'd seen the party make its campfire last night.

Damn it!

He rubbed his eyes with his left hand and tried to focus again. Then he cursed and bowed at the waist and looked all around for the telescope. It was gone, and so were the bottle of rye and the opium. He looked at the edge of the rock shelf, visualizing all three items rolling off in the night and plunging down the hillside.

Damn it to hell!

He stared back out across the flatland below. He had no idea if the wagon had

pulled away or was still sitting there. Without the telescope he couldn't even look for
the wagon tracks. Still, he held his hand
above his eyes as a visor and tried to look
through the bright sunlight.

Nothing. . . .

He started to lower his hand, but he froze
when he heard a voice behind him.

"Keep your hand right there," the voice
commanded. "Raise your other hand too."
The voice paused, then said, "I'm Texas
Ranger Boyd Matthews. I've searched all
over Mexico for you."

"I — I can't raise my right hand," Tate
said, staring straight ahead. "My arm's
broken." He started to turn around. "Anyway, you've got the wrong man."

"Don't turn around," the voice demanded.
"Oh, I've got the right man all right, *Dallas
Tate.* I'm just wondering if I should shoot
you now and let you fall, or waste my time
taking you back."

"Don't shoot, Ranger, please. You're making a big mistake," Tate said.

"Oh?" the voice said, as if the Ranger was
considering his words.

"You see, I'm not Dallas Tate," Tate
replied quickly. "My name's Harvey . . .
Jonas Harvey." He instinctively started to
turn around again.

"I told you to stand where you are," the voice barked.

"You are Dallas Tate, and you are wanted for robbery, murder and having intimate congress with a milk goat," another voice called out sharply.

"What? Jesus, God, no!" said Tate. "A milk goat? I've never done nothing like that. I swear to God — !" His words cut short as he heard muffled laughter behind him. "Wait a minute," he said. Again he started to turn.

"I said don't turn around," the first voice warned, "you goat-loving lowlife —"

But this time Tate turned anyway, cutting the man short.

"You sons a' bitches," he said, seeing the familiar grinning faces of two Texas gunmen, Rodney Gaines and Gil Rizale. Even as the two laughed at their little joke, they both held their sidearms drawn and aimed at him. Tate took note and held on to his temper. These two were not men to fly off the handle with, especially with a bad gun arm.

"You notice he didn't deny robbery or murder. It's just his goat consorting he took offense at," said the tall, hefty Rizale, his hairless head hidden beneath a wide-brimmed slouch hat. They both let their guns sag in their hands. A long brown duster hung to his bootheels. Tate caught a glimpse of a sawed-off shotgun hanging behind the duster's open front.

Rodney Gaines chuckled and lowered his big Remington a little more. He stood as tall as Rizale, but lean and gangly. He wore a short embroidered Mexican waistcoat and a tall battered derby. Tate's telescope stuck up from his waist.

"Did you even know that goat's name?" he asked Tate. He took the telescope from behind his belt.

"All right, that's enough," Tate said. He took the telescope Gaines held out to him. His head throbbed with a whiskey-drug hangover. His temper had stretched as far as he could take it. He saw his nearly empty whiskey bottle hanging in Rizale's gloved hand.

"I need that last drink something fierce," he said, stepping forward.

"We figured you would, soon as you woke up," Rizale said, holding the bottle out to him. "We've shown restraint with it."

Dallas Tate took the bottle, drained it and pitched it away.

"I suppose the opium's gone?" he said.

"You supposed right on that, son," said Rizale. "Some things don't keep." He holstered a short-barreled Colt. He took off his hat, rubbed his slick head and put the slouch hat back on, looking all around. "The hell you doing out here anyway?"

Tate stretched out the telescope with his left hand, turned away, raised it to his eye and looked out across the flats below.

"Everybody's got to be somewhere," he said over his shoulder.

The two gunmen looked at each other.

"Who are you watching out there?" said Gaines.

"Nobody now," said Tate. "I was watching some drovers and a wagon moving toward the hills there. But they're gone now."

"Yeah?" said Rizale. "There was a fire burning when we got here before daylight. They must've left it burning and moved out of there early."

"Damn it," said Tate, lowering the telescope, closing it with his left hand, his right arm hanging down at his side. He paused, then asked, "What are you two doing out here?"

"Headed for Dark Horses," said Rizale. "Thomas Finnity hired us by telegram over a week ago. Told us to go there and help Dad Crayley take possession of some mines and whatnot."

"Yeah, I'm going to work for Dad too,

soon as I finish up some business and get my hand working again," said Dallas.

"What's wrong with your gun hand?" Gaines asked.

"It's not so much my hand as my arm," said Tate. "Some bastard jumped me from behind the other day, broke my arm up high — hurts something awful."

"Imagine a fellow does something like that," said Gaines, not believing him. "He might travel the frontier, jump folks from behind, break their arm and move to the next. . . ."

"Let me look at it," said Rizale, stepping forward.

"Huh-uh," said Tate, taking a step back, "I'd sooner you didn't."

"I'd sooner *I did,*" Rizale insisted. He took another step forward; Tate stepped back, closer to the rock shelf's edge.

"I said *no,*" said Tate. His left hand crossed over clumsily to the Colt holstered on his right hip. But he wasn't quick enough. Gaines stepped in and grabbed the gun up from its holster. Both he and Rizale stepped forward.

"He's going to look at it," Gaines told Tate. "You just as well give it up, unless you can fly."

"Damn it to hell, stay back!" Tate shouted

as the two sprang upon him and took him to the ground.

The pain in Tate's arm caused him to peal out a scream as Gaines lay atop him, pinning him down, and Rizale grabbed his right arm by the wrist.

"Please, for God sakes!" shouted Tate.

Rizale's big fingers felt up and down his arm and found no broken bone.

"Just like I thought," he said, "it's not broke. I had a cousin this used to happen to."

"I'll kill you! I'll kill you both," Tate shouted, seeing that begging got him nowhere.

"Hold him good, Rod," said Rizale. He stood, stretching Tate's arm up with him, and clamped a boot on Tate's chest up under his armpit. Tate screamed loud again. "This is going to hurt *bad,*" said Rizale. "But you'll be glad."

"What the hell does that mean — ?" screamed Tate. But his words turned into a louder scream as the big gunman held him in place with his boot and gave a long pull on Tate's wrist.

Through his scream, Tate heard, and felt, a pop inside his shoulder joint. Rizale turned his wrist loose and took his boot off Tate's chest, stepping back with a grin.

"How's that, son?" he said down to Tate, whose scream had turned into a whimper. "I can do it again," he offered.

Tate fell silent, but found himself able to work his arm without the blinding pain he'd had only seconds earlier.

"Oh my," he said in amazement, "it's gone. I can move it! Jesus, Gil, what did you do?" He was nearly tearful in his sudden relief.

Rizale grinned. He reached down and pulled Gaines to his feet. The two of them took Tate's left hand and pulled him to his feet.

"The fellow jerked it out of the socket," Rizale said. "I jerked it back in, like I used to do to my cousin."

Tate let out a breath, rounding his shoulder. He couldn't believe it. The arm was a little stiff, still a little sore, but otherwise the pain was gone.

"Are we good here, amigo?" Gaines asked, holding up Tate's Colt in his hand.

"Yeah," Tate said, still rounding his shoulder. "I'm real sorry about all the threats. I didn't mean none of it."

"I know it," said Gaines, shoving the Colt down into Tate's holster. "If we thought you meant it, guess what we would have done instead of pulling your arm into its socket."

"I know," said Tate, cooled out now, glad to have his shoulder fixed. "Can I boil you some coffee?" he asked.

The two looked at each other.

"Can't see why not," Rizale said. He took off his hat and slapped it against his leg; dust billowed. "Need something to cut this Mexican ground powder."

CHAPTER 14

Over coffee, Dallas Tate told the two gunmen what had happened between him and
Will Summers. He told them about how he
and Bailey Swann had been slipping around
behind Ansil's back. He knew that the old
man was ill and had been using a wheelchair. He didn't realize that Swann would
not have known what was going on between
him and his young wife if he'd been staring
straight at them.

"One sniff of that horse trader," he said
bitterly, "and she threw me over for him.
I'd have done anything for her. I'd have
stuck a gun in the old man's mouth and
pulled the trigger, if she'd asked me to do
it." He swirled his coffee around in his cup
and finished it in one gulp. "I thought about
doing it anyway. Then everything she had
would have been mine."

Rizale and Gaines looked at each other.

"That's a hell of a story," Rizale said when

Tate was finished. He stood up and slung grinds from his empty coffee cup. "But then you always were a man who had a knack for drawing close to womenfolk."

"The hell is that supposed to mean?" Tate asked, staring up at him.

"Nothing to take offense at," Rizale said. "It's just an observation." He grinned.

"It's not like he's accusing you of having congress with a milk goat," Gaines put in. "I've never seen the Swann woman, but I hear she's a looker."

"She's all of it," Tate said, staring intently at his empty tin coffee cup. "Sometimes I felt like she was only using me. But if she was, it was the best using I ever had." He paused, felt them staring at him. "Damn that horse trader to hell," he murmured.

"All right, then," said Gaines, "we'll be riding on to Dark Horses, get ready for this job with Dad Crayley." He stood up. "Sure you won't ride with us?" He picked at the seat of his trousers.

"No," said Tate, "I'll ride in later." He sat rounding his shoulder a little, getting it back in shape. "I've got something to take care of first."

"You're going off after that woman and the horse trader, aren't you?" said Rizale. He grinned. "I'd hate to think fixing that shoulder has set you off on a *cruel path of violence.*" He and Gaines both laughed at his little joke.

Tate's face reddened a little, but he gave a thin, half-hearted smile.

"No, I'm done with her and the horse trader," he said, lying, eager to get rid of them. "I've just got some stuff that needs doing."

"Not that milk goat? Please," said Rizale, with his wide-faced grin, still sticking it to Tate.

"No, not the goat," said Tate, without acknowledging the humor of it.

"Well, we never ask a man's personal business," said Gaines, stretching a little. "I expect we'll see you soon in Dark Horses."

"I expect so," said Tate, standing, slinging grinds from his empty cup. He scraped out the small fire with the side of his boot.

In moments the three were mounted and riding away. They guided their horses to a place where the trail forked, one trail leading off toward Dark Horses, the other leading down toward the stretch of sand flats below. Gaines and Rizale gave a toss of their hands to Tate.

"Don't do nothing crude in public," said Rizale.

"You neither," said Tate, turning his horse,

touching his fingertips to his hat brim.

The two rode up the trail a few feet, out of sight around a stand of rock and pine. But then they stopped, eased their horses out a few inches and watched Dallas Tate ride down away from them.

"Think he believes we're just getting here?" Gaines asked in a lowered voice, even though Tate was out of listening range.

"Yeah, he does," said Rizale. "Why wouldn't he? He never saw us in town. If he had, he'd have been too drunk and hurting too bad to remember." He shook his big head. "I hate ever helping anybody. But I couldn't stand seeing the shape he was in. I had to fix his shoulder or shoot him in the head."

"We're going to stick with him, then?" Gaines asked, crossing his wrists on his saddle horn, getting comfortable.

"Yep, for a while, see what he's up to," said Rizale. "I don't want to tell Dad he shook us off his trail."

"Me neither," said Gaines, the two of them staring at Tate as he faded in a rise of dust. "He's a squirrel, ain't he?"

"Yep, a straight-up squirrel," said Rizale in reflection. "He's woman-struck to the bone." He sighed heavily, saying under his breath, "Likes the womenfolk *awfully.*"

Gaines looked at him narrowly.

"So?" he said. "Don't we all?"

"Not the way he does," said Rizale. "He's ate up by them. Don't know what to do if one ain't leading him around by his crotch. That's why he didn't join Dad Crayley right away."

"Yeah, he should have jumped at the chance to ride for Dad when Dad invited him," Gaines said. "What kind of gunman turns down Dad Crayley?"

"A *squirrel,*" Rizale restated. "I figure Dad knows it, and that's why he wants us following him — thinks he's up to something. And I expect he is too. Don't forget he was ramrod for Swann, before the woman dropped him, that is."

"Figure that's why the Swann woman dropped him for the horse trader?" Gaines said. "Saw he's a squirrel, couldn't stand it no longer?"

"We don't know that she really *did* drop him for some horse trader," said Rizale, "just that she *dropped him.* Might be the horse trader part was all in his mind. Might be she got tired of his nose poking her in the behind every time she stopped too fast."

Gaines chuckled and nodded.

"He's wanting onto those wagon tracks real bad, ain't he?" he said, nodding in

196

Tate's direction.

"Oh, *son,*" said Rizale, "so bad it's torturing his guts."

"How you want to follow?" Gaines asked.

"Stay up here and skirt around behind him on this hill line," said Rizale. "We'll drop down and get on the other hill trail when he's off the flats."

The two turned their horses as one and rode out around a high, steep ledge, out of Tate's sight.

"Damn squirrel," Gaines said under his breath.

Just before noon, Summers drove the wagon-load of furniture off the high trail onto a flat spot of ground in front of a row of closed and rock-sealed mine shafts. The night before, he'd told Lonnie and Little Ted where they were headed, but so far he hadn't told them why. As soon as he stopped the wagon out in front of the mine shaft Bailey Swann had pointed out to him, he set the wagon brake and stepped from the seat. As he gave Bailey a hand down from her seat, Ted and Lonnie drew their horses up beside him.

"All right, men," Summers said, "let's get the wagon unloaded here and clear the rocks away from the mine opening." He nodded at the correct mine.

The two ranch hands nodded at each other, then looked back at Summers.

"We've got a sneaking suspicion why we're here," Little Ted said, stepping down from his saddle. Beside him Lonnie stepped down holding the lead rope to Summers' dapple gray and the four bay fillies.

"I knew the two of you would likely figure it out by the time we got here," Summers said. "Tell me what you come up with." He looked at Little Ted.

Little Ted gave a sly grin back and forth between Summers and Lonnie.

"You figure on opening one of the mines and hiding the hacienda furnishings and valuables there until the collectors give up and leave Dark Horses," he said.

"You couldn't be more wrong, fellow," Summers said. He nodded at the rocks piled thick against the front of the mine shaft. "We're unloading the furniture so we can hide something beneath it." He turned to Bailey Swann. "They work for you, ma'am," he said. "You want to tell them?"

"Lonnie, Ted," said Bailey, turning to them. "My husband, Ansil, had a lot of ore smelted into gold over the last two years. He had it placed in the mine shaft here for safekeeping —"

"Over *two years*?" said Lonnie, interrupting her. "How much gold are we talking about here?"

"A lot," Bailey said. "I don't know exactly how much, but Ansil assured me it would be enough to take care of him and me for the rest of our lives, in spite of what we've lost in the business world." She looked at each of the ranch hands in turn. "Help us get it to Don Manuel's. I promise you will both be well paid for you efforts."

The two looked at Summers, who nodded toward the mine shaft. "Let's get the mine open and see what we've got," he said.

Little Ted grinned and leveled his hat on his head and walked toward the rock-sealed mine.

"That's what I say," he replied, excited, rolling up his shirtsleeves.

Summers took the lead rope from Lonnie and Lonnie caught up with Little Ted. As the two ranch hands walked toward the sealed shaft, Summers led the five horses to the side and hitched them to a long wooden hitch rail. When he walked to the shaft, Lonnie and Little Ted were already carrying large stones away from the front of the mine shaft entrance and piling them along the face of the hillside.

The shafts of the commercial mines had

been cut almost eight feet high and heavily shored up with local cut pine timbers over a foot thick. By the end of an hour's worth of heavy lifting and toting, the three had only cleared away four feet of the mine shaft, finding the sealing rocks to be well stacked, almost interlocked into place. Bailey Swann, determined to do her part, picked up any smaller rocks as they fell from within the loosening pile and carried them outside the shaft. When she wasn't helping with moving the rocks, she kept busy unloading less heavier items from the wagon.

The four of them had each raised a bandanna up over the bridge of their nose against the stirred-up dust. At the end of the second hour, having gained another seven feet of cleared entrance shaft, Little Ted stopped and leaned back against the shaft wall and looked up at the thick support timbers overhead.

"How deep do you suppose they seal a mine shaft?" he asked Summers, his voice muffled by the dust-caked bandanna.

With the point of a pick he'd taken from the wagon bed, Summers stepped up onto the pile, reached up against the timber-lined ceiling and pried down a thick rock from its spot and let it tumble down past him to the ground at his feet.

"As deep as it dang well suited Ansil Swann," Lonnie answered before Summers could. "If it was my gold, I'd have buried it pretty deep."

Summers reached out with the pick and pulled down another rock. He stepped aside out of its way as it tumbled from the timbered ceiling to the ground. From the blackness behind the rock he felt the first breath of cool air from deep inside the cavern.

"I think I just found out the answer for us, Lonnie," he said. He looked around the open space they had created. Almost twelve feet of piled rock had been removed. "About *this deep,*" he added, nodding at the open hole in the rock pile.

As the two stepped up onto the pile and gathered closer to him, Summers took out a match from his shirt pocket, struck it and held it carefully to the black cavity the rock had left. Without risking putting his head or forearm into the opening, he looked in and caught the flicker of match light on the open cavern in front of them.

"All right," he said, leaning away and handing the match to Little Ted. "How does that look to you?" He pulled down his dusty bandanna and sank back on the rock pile.

"Whoo-ee!" said Little Ted. "We've done it! I feel like a prospector who's just struck

gold on my own!" he added.

He whooped and shouted aloud. So did Lonnie Kerns. Holding the match while Lonnie looked into the blackness, the two noted the cool out-drifting air bending the flame back toward them.

"It's about dang time," Lonnie said, dust puffing from his bandanna as he spoke through it.

"All right," Summers said quietly, not wavering from the task at hand. "Now we'll start pushing the rocks in and letting them fall away from us, instead of pulling them loose and letting them fall at us."

"Sounds good to me," Little Ted said with renewed energy.

At the front of the cleared shaft, Bailey Swann stepped in and looked at the three.

"What's the cheering about?" she asked.

"We've gotten through the rocks," Summers said. "Soon as we push this layer down, we'll be inside."

"Thank goodness," Bailey said. "I have the wagon nearly empty. We should be loaded and able to leave before dark. With luck we'll get on toward Don Manuel's spread."

"Yes, ma'am," Summers said. He stepped onto the rock pile, reached up to the highest point and pushed, feeling the rock give way toward the other side.

CHAPTER 15

For another half hour, the four continued working, Ted and Lonnie going at a fevered pace now they knew the gold was so close at hand. Bailey Swann brought in an oil lantern, lit it and held it up. In the circle of lantern light Summers rolled away one last stone and the four of them stepped forward into the open shaft. They walked forward deeper into the shaft, the hillside entrance growing smaller behind them. On the floor at their feet they saw overlapping donkey prints and two small iron track rails running through the center of the shaft.

"This row of shafts on this hillside is the oldest the company owns," Bailey said as they rounded a slight turn in the shaft and started following the cart rails downward. "Usually they seal the worked-out shafts with blasting powder. But Ansil had this one sealed by hand. From the outside you can't tell the difference. Only when you go to reopen one, you'll find the ones blasted shut are completely filled."

"This makes a good hiding place," Summers said, looking all around, the two ranch hands right beside him, the woman a step ahead with the raised lantern.

Around the slight turn, the four looked in the shadowy circle of light at an overturned ore cart lying on the tracks. Beyond it stood a fifteen-foot-long, four-foot-high stack of crates alongside the iron cart rails. A dusty canvas tarpaulin half covered the crates. They stopped and stared. Past the stack of covered crates stood a large iron three-man strongbox.

"My goodness," Bailey said, almost gasping at the sight of the crates, "can that be the ingots?" She took a slow step forward, like a doe stepping into a wood's clearing. "Is that the strongbox?" she murmured.

"Ain't but one way to find out, ma'am." Ted chuckled in his excitement. He hurried to the crates, Lonnie alongside him. The two threw back the dusty tarpaulin. Before the dust had settled, Lonnie had picked up an iron pry bar lying on the stack of crates and opened a lid.

Summers joined the two as Lonnie held up a gold ingot the size of his hand.

"My oh my!" he whispered to himself.

"It's plumb beautiful." He held the ingot over for Little Ted to see. But Ted had already reached in and grabbed an ingot for himself. He turned it back and forth in his hand. The gold bar glittered softly even in the dim lantern light.

Summers looked along the row of crates through the wafting dust. At the end of the rows he saw Bailey Swann standing at the large strongbox. She took a large iron key from inside her coat and stuck it into the box's lock and twisted it.

The ranch hands looked up from the gold at the sound of the door creaking open on the large iron box.

Bailey held the lantern close to the inside of the box, the light falling on stack upon stack of American greenback dollars.

"Ansil was right," she said without looking around. "There's a fortune here." She put a hand forward and ran it down the stack as if the bills were alive and in need of affection.

Summers started walking toward her in the dim light. But he stopped abruptly and walked past the last of the stacked crates. His eyes traveled to the lower edge of the mine's stone wall.

"What's this?" he said aloud. He stood looking at three ragged, dust-covered bodies lying in a row. The seriousness of his voice caused Bailey to turn away from the open strongbox door and hurry to him, the lantern held up in front of her. Little Ted and Lonnie scurried over to Summers from the other direction.

"Holy Joseph!" said Ted, staring down at the bodies.

"Give me the lantern," Summers said over his shoulder to Bailey as she moved closer.

Bailey handed him the lantern; he held it above the three dried bodies for a better look. The bodies lay sprawled, dressed in ragged mining clothes and boots, half-mummified, half skeletons. Summers moved the lantern back and forth slowly.

"What in the world!" Little Ted exclaimed as if in awe.

Summers stopped the lantern and held it over each body in turn, revealing a large bullet hole in each fleshless forehead.

"Exit wounds," he murmured quietly, almost to himself.

"Shot from behind, you're saying?" said Lonnie.

"Yes, I believe so," Summers said. He half turned and looked up at Bailey. "Would your husband have gone this far to keep this shaft a secret?"

"You mean — you mean murder, Will?"

the woman asked in disbelief.

"Yes, Bailey, I do mean murder," Summers said. He nodded toward the stacked crates. "If these three loaded this shaft and were killed just before it was sealed off, that made three less people your husband had to worry about."

"No, Will, Ansil would never do such a thing," said Bailey, sounding shocked at the prospect. But her voice didn't sound convincing, Summers thought. There was too much hidden here to be trusted to three miners. "If he had he would've known I'd see the bodies when we came here for the gold."

"Maybe he wasn't going to bring you here," said Summers. "Maybe he would've brought help for the rocks and left you at the hacienda."

Ted and Lonnie stared at him in the lantern's glow.

"Whoa," said Ted. "Is that what we would have gotten had we come here with Mr. Swann?" He and Kerns almost stepped back, as if suddenly concerned for their safety.

"Is that the way Ansil Swann does things, ma'am?" Kerns questioned Bailey.

Bailey looked too stunned to answer.

"I don't know what Ansil might have had

in mind," Summers replied quickly, "but that's not the way I do things. You can believe that."

The two settled a little.

Bailey shook her head, looking at the bodies in disbelief.

"I don't think my husband would have had anything to do with this," she said. "He wouldn't kill anyone."

"Somebody sure did," Little Ted said cynically. "These three didn't get together and commit suicide."

"Enough about what Ansil might or might not have done," said Summers, standing up and looking all around. "If these crates are all full, we've got a lot of gold to move. Not to mention cash." He nodded at the strongbox against the wall. Then he looked at Bailey. "There's no way we can get it all in one wagonload."

"I know," she said, looking all around, overwhelmed by the huge number of gold crates. "What on earth was Ansil thinking?"

Summers looked all around too.

"I don't know," he said, shaking his head. "But let's get what we can this trip. Keep the rest of it hidden here. If this Don Manuel will buy the rest, we'll have to come back and make another run with it."

"You mean we'll have to carry all the rocks

back, reseal the shaft before we leave?" Lonnie asked.

"Yep, I'm afraid so," said Summers. "Let's get to it. Don't forget there was somebody trailing us yesterday. For all we know they might have picked up our wagon tracks this morning. They could still be following us."

"I don't see how," said Kerns. "We crossed every stretch of stone and rock-hard dirt in this desert hill country."

"A good part of that gold is going to be yours, Lonnie," Summers replied. "Are you willing to take that chance?"

"I get your point, Will. Let's get to it," Kerns said, turning toward the shaft's entrance. As Summers followed the two over a low pile of the remaining rocks and toward the entrance, Bailey walked behind him with the lantern raised.

"Will, please don't think that poor Ansil and I had anything to do with those dead miners lying there. Please don't think anything bad would have happened to Ted and Lonnie, had Ansil and I brought them instead of you and I."

"I have no reason to think you and your husband are murderers, Bailey," he said. "I only know what I saw." He nodded sidelong back toward the three bodies.

"I know how bad this looks," Bailey said.

"But would I have brought you here if I knew the bodies were here?"

"I don't know," said Summers, walking on.

"Think of how foolish that would be, how much my husband's enemies would like to see him and me facing murder charges."

"When people get desperate . . . they take foolish chances," Summers said.

"But I need you to believe me, Will," she said.

"Whatever I believe makes no difference," Summers said over his shoulder, "especially not to the miners. We came here to get the gold. We've got it. Now we need to get out of here, go to Don Manuel's, settle up and go our separate ways. This solves your financial problems, doesn't it?"

He looked at her hand on the back of his arm and turned toward her.

"I hoped there would be more between us than just settling up and going our own way, Will," she said.

"The sooner we get away from here, the better for all of us," Summers said. "Like you said, your husband's enemies would like to see you charged as murderers. I've got a feeling they wouldn't mind seeing me and your ranch hands charged too, after we shot two of their collectors." He walked on, letting her drop her hand from his arm. "I remember how I felt, thinking I was going to face a hanging the other day. I don't want to do that again."

"You're right," Bailey said, walking a little faster with the lantern in order to keep up with him. "We need to get the gold and go. We can talk about this another time." Ahead of them at the entrance to the mine shaft, Lonnie and Little Ted stood waiting.

When Summers and the woman arrived, Lonnie and Little Ted looked to Summers for instructions.

"I'll bring the wagon around," Summers said, looking over to where the wagon sat empty twenty yards away, Bailey having unloaded and stacked the furnishings and other items alongside it. "The two of you turn that mine cart upright and on the tracks. We'll use it to bring out the crates." He spoke looking up at the afternoon sky. "We've got a lot to do if we want to get out of here tonight."

With one of the wagon horses harnessed to the ore cart, the four worked nonstop loading the crates inside the mine shaft and unloading them again outside, onto the wagon. Bailey worked right along with the three men; she pried open each crate and made sure it was filled with smelted ingots instead of raw ore still laced into broken chunks of rocks.

As Little Ted laid the last crate of ingots down into the wagon bed, he and Lonnie stood back and watched Summers and Bailey walk out of the mine shaft with large canvas packs full of cash strapped over their shoulders. Each pack had a large black dollar sign painted on it. They had left an open space among the crates large enough to house the packs of cash near the rear of the wagon.

Summers stepped onto the rear of the wagon and unshouldered his pack into the opening. He turned to Bailey standing on the ground, took the pack from her shoulder and dropped it down inside the open space. Then he covered the packs of cash, filling in over them with two crates of ingots.

"This will do," he said, dusting his hands together. He stepped down from the wagon bed and looked at the load. The ingot crates were stacked three feet high in the wagon bed. The wooden sideboards of the wagon stood five feet higher, made to accommodate a tall load of loose hay without losing any of it. With household furnishings loaded atop the crates, the wagon would not appear to be hiding anything.

"It's a heavy load," Little Ted said, standing beside him. "We'd better hope we don't have to leave in a hurry."

"I know," Summers said. "It'll be some tight traveling the rest of the way."

"We'll have to leave about half this furniture behind," Lonnie said, standing on his other side.

"I know," Summers repeated. He nodded toward a weathered lean-to shed across the flat gravelly yard. "Take what we don't load and stack it under there. Cover it with the tarpaulin so it won't look like we dumped it here for something more valuable. We'll sweep all our tracks away from the entrance."

Behind the two ranch hands, Bailey stood with the unlit lantern in hand. She smiled.

"You do think of everything, don't you, Will?" she said. She had unhooked a canteen from a peg on the side of the wagon and uncapped it as she spoke. She swished it around, took a short sip and passed the canteen to Lonnie.

"I try to," Summers said, watching Lonnie raise the canteen to his lips.

Turning, Summers looked out across the graying evening sky, the long black shadows starting to spread east across the rocky land.

"Let's get the mine resealed and get the

furniture loaded," he said. "We've been here too long as it is."

Lonnie passed the canteen on to Little Ted, who poured a few drops into his cupped palm and wiped it over his face and forehead.

"No rest for the weary," Little Ted said. He handed the uncapped canteen to Summers, who took a short drink, capped it and hooked it back on the side of the wagon. He walked around to the front of the wagon and stepped up into the driver's seat. Bailey and the ranch hands walked along behind as Summers drove the wagon forward and stopped beside the furniture sitting on the ground.

"I always heard there's nothing easy about gold except spending it," Little Ted commented. "I believe it." He gave a tired smile and added in a tired voice, "But I'd like to find that spending part out for myself."

CHAPTER 16

Tracking had never come easy for Dallas Tate. Yet what he might lack in trail-craft, he more than made up for in determination, he reminded himself proudly. Atop his horse, he looked out along the mining path leading upward along the hillside through a silvery morning mist. The night before he'd come close to giving up when the wagon tracks and horses' hooves seemed to have vanished across a two-mile stretch of long stone flats reaching out onto the desert floor.

The flats had ended where a sandy trail led off in three directions. Three sets of hill lines to choose from, and damned if he hadn't chosen the right one!

He grinned shrewdly to himself. It never occurred to him that he had discovered the right trail by sheer luck. So what if he had? The main thing was, he had gotten back on their trail now, and he wasn't giving up until he had Will Summers in his gun's sights. He hadn't thought that much about killing Summers before, but now that his arm was back in working order, why not kill him? Rage still smoldered hot in his belly every time he thought about how the woman had treated him — how the horse trader had humiliated him.

Kill them both? Sure, why not? Maybe he'd kill Little Ted Ford and Lonnie Kerns while he was at it, and anybody else who had anything to do with them. *That whole stinking bunch . . .*

He nodded to himself and nudged his horse forward. The horse traveled up the steep mining trail at a walk for the next half hour. Tate kept an eye on the wagon tracks until he could see the row of Ansil Swann's deserted mine shafts standing along a widened, terraced stretch of rock hillside. He stopped the horse and stepped down and drew his rifle from its saddle boot.

Rifle in hand, he led the horse the rest of the way and didn't stop again until he stood at a weathered hitch rail inside the mine yard. Looking all around, he saw only the wagon's tracks and the horses' hooves in the dirt. Across the yard he spotted the tarpaulin-covered furniture sitting under the tin roof of the lean-to.

What the — ? He stared curiously at the furniture, wondering why Bailey Swann would try to hide her furnishings and valuables from the collectors in a place like this.

"Hello the mines," he called out. He looked all along the row of sealed mine shaft entrances, each of them with large stones spilling out of them. There were no wagon tracks, hoofprints or boot tracks in the gravelly dirt around them.

"Hello the mines," he called again. He saw where the wagon had stopped and where it had swung to the lean-to. Nothing here made any sense to him.

Stupid sons a' bitches.

He stood waiting for a moment, listening intently. The only reply he heard was his own voice echoing back to him as it fell away into the distance.

All right, they're gone, he concluded. Walking over under the lean-to, he untied a corner of the tarpaulin and flipped it back. He stood looking at the stacked and piled-up furniture with a puzzled expression.

So much for the furniture. Where're the bays?

He looked all around again, as if having found the furniture and household goods

218

meant the bay fillies would be somewhere near. Trying to make sense of it all, he became so absorbed that when he heard a voice boom out from behind him he was caught completely off guard.

"Throw your hands up high, you son of a bitch!" the voice demanded.

Tate, startled beyond control, threw his hands up instinctively before he could stop himself. No sooner were his hands up than he realized what a mistake he'd made.

Damn it to hell. . . .

"This is Texas Ranger Boyd Matthews, *again,*" the voice called out, muffling a hard belly laugh. "I've found more charges of you and the milk goat —"

"This ain't funny, damn you, Rizale!" Tate shrieked. He spun toward the two gunmen who stood at the edge of the trail, barely containing their laughter. Tate's hand started to grab the butt of his holstered Colt. But seeing Gaines and Rizale, their guns already drawn, cocked and pointed at him, he stopped himself and tried to cool down quickly. Grin or no grin, he knew they would kill him where he stood.

"Damn, son," Rizale said, chuckling, "that's twice in a row!" The two of them walked forward, leading their horses. "I'm starting to wonder if the milk goat rumor ain't true."

"There is no *rumor* about it — never was," Tate said, cooled down but still seething at Rizale for tricking him. "I don't want it getting started," he added with a bit of a warning tone.

"Easy, now," said Rizale, still digging at him. "We know how some men don't talk about their love life." He raised a gloved finger and touched it to his lips. "I will not bring it up again." He gave Tate a sincere look. The two stopped a few feet away and looked all around the mine yard, at the furniture under the lean-to.

"The hell are you doing here anyway?" Gaines asked, lowering the hammer on his big Remington Army and cross-holstering it. Tate noted that Gil Rizale kept his Colt in hand, still cocked.

"The question is," Tate said in a testy tone, "why the hell are you following me?" He stared at Gaines.

Gaines shook his head, still grinning.

"Huh-uh, me first," he said, his Remington holstered, but his hand resting on the bone handle.

Tate breathed deep and calmed himself down a little more. These were not men to get testy with, he reminded himself.

"All right, here it is," he said. "The wagon

tracks we saw? They belonged to the horse trader, Bailey Swann and her hired hands. I was following them." He gestured toward the furniture. "This is their doing. I figure the Swanns are hiding their possessions from Finnity and Baines' collectors."

"From *us,* in other words," Rizale said, "soon as we take the job with Dad Crayley."

"Well, yeah, I suppose so, putting it that way," said Tate. He looked down at his boot toes.

"Why?" Gaines asked. "Are you trying to get the jump on a job with Crayley? Make the rest of us look bad?"

"Naw, it's not like that," said Tate. He cleared his throat and shrugged and looked back down at his boots.

"Ha!" Rizale laughed, rearing back. "I told you, I told you," he said to Gaines, beaming. "Didn't I tell you?"

"You told me," Gaines confirmed.

Tate looked back and forth between the two. Gunmen or not, they weren't going to ridicule him and treat him like a fool.

"What do you mean, *you told him*? You told him *what*?" he demanded, glaring narrow-eyed at Rizale.

Rizale eased his chuckling laugh down a little and tried to get serious.

"I just told him when we found you passed out that you're known to have a great fondness for womenfolk, that's all," he said.

"A great fondness for women . . . ?" Tate cocked his head and gave him a strange curious look. "What the hell does that mean?" His voice rose. "Yes, I do have a fondness for women. What are you trying to turn that into?"

"Whoa, son, whoa!" said Rizale. "It's not a bad thing I was saying. It's just that you're known to get a little . . . steered off course, womanwise." He held his free hand in front of him and zigzagged it back and forth. His other hand still held his short-barreled Colt. "Nothing to be ashamed of."

"Yeah," said Gaines, "it ain't like he called you a *squirrel* or something."

Tate saw the look the two passed back and forth to each other. But he let it go and simmered down some more.

"Anyway," he said, "she's done with me and I'm done with her." He sighed. "She's taken up with the horse trader."

"Let me ask you something," Rizale said. "She's done with you. You're done with her. Why are you following her?"

Tate thought about it and shook his head.

"I don't know," he said. "What else can I do . . . ?" He let his words trail.

Gaines and Rizale shook their heads in disgust and stepped closer to the furnishings under the lean-to. Rizale lifted the edge of the tarpaulin more and took a closer look.

"They brought all this out here, to keep us from taking it for Finnity and Baines?" he said. "I can't believe that. There's a trick in the works here. I just can't get it figured."

"If this was my stuff, why would I leave it out like this?" said Gaines, looking around again.

"I was asking myself that," said Tate, "when you came in with your funny stuff."

"All right, no more funny stuff," said Rizale, a serious look coming to his face. "We're already working for Dad. He sent us to see what you're up to, make sure you're not in cahoots with the Swanns anymore."

Tate just stared at him.

"Don't evil-eye me, Dallas," Rizale warned. "I can still unload this gun right into your belly. *Comprende?*"

Tate nodded and raised his hands slightly, knowing his limits with these two.

"Okay, I expect I would have done the same if I was Dad Crayley," he said. "But I'm through with the Swanns — both of them."

"So you say," said Gaines. "But how do we know it's true?"

"Ride there with me," said Tate. "They'll be getting back there by now. I'll show you I'm through with them."

The two gunmen looked at each other.

"How do you know they're headed back?" said Gaines.

"It's the only thing that makes sense," said Tate. "Anyway, the ground's all stone, hill line and hardpan dirt the next fifty miles. You can't track nothing from here. They went back."

"He sounds awfully cocksure," Gaines said to Rizale. "Think we ought to ride to Swann's ranchero with him?"

"Hell, son," Rizale said to Gaines. "You know me. I'll ride any-damn-where, with any-damn-body, to do any-damn-thing." He laughed and spun the short-barreled Colt on his thick finger. The Colt looked small, almost like a toy in his huge hand. "Only thing is, you best show us something when we get there," he warned. "I hate riding somewhere for nothing."

"Follow me," Tate said flatly. With no more to say on the matter, he gave Rizale an even gaze, turned and mounted his horse and put it forward with a touch of his boots.

"Well, all right, then," Rizale said to Gaines. He grinned and turned to his horse. Between himself and Gaines he said in a lowered voice, "Let's see what the squirrel's got in mind."

Late in the afternoon, Bedos Reyes walked from the empty bunkhouse to the hacienda, where Rena stood cooking dinner for the two of them. On the fiery grill of an open adobe-and-stone *chimenea,* beef sizzled. Beans and peppers bubbled in a pot. Off to the less-heated side of the grill top, a smaller pot of beef gravy with small bits of beef and mild, chopped desert herbs sat simmering.

On his way to where Rena stood cooking, he caught sight of two riders rising into sight and stopping their horses. The two sat watching as he hurried his steps to Rena.

"Set the food aside quickly," he said. "There are two men coming. I think one of them is Dallas Tate."

Hearing the sound of concern in his voice, Rena turned, wiping her hands on her apron.

"Dallas Tate?" she said. She gazed long and hard at the two men. They sat as still as stone, looking small against the evening sky. She frowned as they sat staring back at her. "Yes, Papa," she agreed finally. "I believe it is him." She turned quickly back to the food on the grill. She stabbed the beef with a long fork and pitched it up onto the next highest rack above the flames. She set the pot off the grill, from above a bed of glowing mesquite.

"Señora warned us that this one might come back," said Bedos. "I will get the shotgun from inside the front door and meet them. You get upstairs at the gun ports, like always."

"Yes, Papa," Rena said, hurrying, taking off her apron as she crossed the yard to the porch, her father right behind her. As she bounded up the porch steps, she stopped at the front door and gazed out at where the two sat staring. "Why is Dallas waiting there?" she said. "Why does he not come in? He knows we see him. He knows his way around here."

"I don't know why he waits," Bedos said, bounding up the porch steps behind her. "He knows that the longer he waits, the more prepared for him we will be." Bedos stepped past his daughter, opened the front door and ushered her inside. "Go up, close all the shutters," he said, nodding at the stairs leading to the long row of upstairs windows. "Stay with Señor Swann in his office."

Bedos watched as his daughter hurried off up the stairs. Turning, he picked up a shotgun from beside the door, checked it and walked from window to window, closing shutters. At the window nearest the front door, he looked out through the gun port and saw the two men still sitting, their wrists crossed on their saddle horns.

"What are they waiting for?" he asked himself out loud. He stood watching in silence for a long moment. "I have never liked you, Dallas Tate," he murmured to the distant figure, "and I have never trusted you." His voice rose in the empty room. "Of all the men this Swann *puta* has taken to her breasts and her thighs, I have disliked you the most."

He stood watching, waiting, the shotgun ready, his strong aged hands opening and closing around its wooden stock. He glanced around, up the stairs, knowing his daughter was up there waiting at the window port in Ansil Swann's office. There was nothing to fear here, he reminded himself. Two men could not ride in and take over this hacienda. It was built to withstand an attack by the desert Apache, or the Mexican rebels. They would be all right. He waited.

"Why don't you come on?" he asked again through the gun port. This time, as if hearing his words and acting on them, the two nudged their horses into a walk and rode forward slowly. "All right," Bedos said, "you want to show me you are in no hurry, that you are bold and fearless? Then so am I." He opened the front door halfway and stood staring out at the two as they drew nearer to the house.

"*Hola* the house," Dallas Tate called out, seeing the old Mexican step out onto the porch with the shotgun up across his chest. "Bedos. It's me, Dallas," he said.

"I see who you are, Señor Tate," Bedos said. "I am told that you are no longer welcome here. So *vamonos.*" He stood firm.

Tate grinned at Gaines seated on his horse beside him; then he looked all around, seeing no sign of the ranch hands, or of Summers or the woman.

"I saw Señora Swann on the trail this morning, moving furniture. We cleared the air between us," he lied, straight-faced. "She told me to come get my things from the bunkhouse." He grinned. "I thought she'd be back by now. Where'd they go? She told me. I forgot," he said, fishing.

But the old Mexican would have none of it. He stepped forward to the top of the porch steps.

"You and your amigo turn your horses and go, or I will shoot you both," Bedos said with resolve.

Tate's grin melted; his expression turned harsh.

"I came here offering to be real friendly, old man," he said. "I know you and your pretty daughter are alone here. Don't push your luck with me." He turned to Gaines as if in afterthought. "Did I mention his daughter, Rena? She's hotter than a pepper sprout."

"Really? A pepper sprout?" said Gaines. "I'd be obliged to make her acquaintance."

Anger flared in Bedos' eyes. His grip on the shotgun tightened.

"You will *die* if you go near my daughter!" he warned, stomping down the porch steps. He stood with his feet spread, ready for a fight. "By the saints, I will —" His words stopped short as the front slammed shut from inside and the iron latch fell into place. He spun and ran up the steps to the door and pounded his whole body against it. "Open this door! Rena? Is that you? Open the door this instant!"

"Uh-oh," Dallas Tate said from his saddle. "Bedos, ol' pard, it looks like you've let a wolf into the meat house." As the old Mexican pounded on the door, the two drew their guns and sat waiting.

From inside the hacienda they heard heavy boots running up the stairway. Then they heard a rifle shot resound inside the rifle port, followed by Rena's scream.

"I got her, sons," Rizale called out through the gun port. "She damn near shot me. What do you want me to do to her?"

"I will *kill* you!" Bedos raged, swinging the shotgun around at the two. But Tate and Gaines only sat smiling at him, as if they knew he wouldn't shoot.

Tate wagged his gun at Bedos.

"Get that shotgun out of your hands, Bedos, before I tell my pal up there to lift his knife and go to work whittling on your family tree."

"Do not hurt her, Tate!" the old man shouted. "She has done nothing to you!" As he spoke he threw the shotgun aside.

"That's not true, Bedos," Tate said. "Before I took up with Señora Swann, I tried sticking my hand up her dress and she strongly rebuffed me."

"That was plumb mean, her doing that," said Gaines.

"I know it was," said Tate. "But I'm here to set things right today.

Upstairs, the window shutter in Ansil Swann's office opened.

"What do you want me to do to her up here?" Rizale called down, sticking his head out.

"Bring her down," said Tate. "This food smells so good, I know they'll be inviting us to stay for supper."

Rizale chuckled and drew his head back inside, holding Rena to his broad chest.

"You heard him, little darling," he said, pressing his pale hairless face to the side of Rena's throat. "Let's go see what you've got cooking."

In his wheelchair, Ansil Swann sat slumped, his eyes as blank as a dead man's.

"How does this lump of wood get up and down the stairs for supper?" Rizale asked the woman on the way out of the office.

"My — my father carries him," she said in a frightened tone. "I roll the empty chair."

"Ha!" said Rizale. "I can show you a quicker way than that."

CHAPTER 17

As Rena finished preparing dinner, adding more beef to the grill and slicing more peppers into the pot of beans, Dallas Tate and Rodney Gaines stood out in front of the house, staring at the open front door. Between the two Bedos stood with his hands tied in front of him, a large knot on top of his bare head. They'd watched Rizale drag a six-foot-long wood sled from the barn into the hacienda. The wood sled was what the ranch hands used to lower firewood down from the steep rocky hillsides.

"How long do we have to stand here waiting on him?" Tate asked Gaines, glancing toward the *chemenea,* the sizzle and smell of grilling meat.

"Hard to say," said Gaines. "He comes up with an idea, he can't put it off. He has to show somebody right away."

From inside the hacienda they heard Rizale's voice cry out to them, "Watch this!"

The two stopped talking and turned their full attention to the front door. Between them Bedos crossed himself with his tied hands and murmured something under his breath.

They heard Rizale suddenly let out a loud *"Yii-hiiii!"* above the sound of wood on wood skidding, bumping and screeching as the big sled raced down the inside stairs. They stared awe-stricken, seeing the big sled streak out through the open door, across the front porch and shoot straight out above the porch steps into the front yard.

"No! No, Señor Swann!" Bedos cried out, bolting from between the two and running to Ansil Swann, who lay limp, tied down to the wood sled. From the *chemenea,* Rena came running, a long wooden bean spoon clutched in her hand.

On the front porch, Rizale stepped out, pushing the high-backed wheelchair. He gave a dark chuckle, looking at Bedos and his daughter stooped beside Swann and the sled lying in the dirt.

"That's a lot faster than this," he called out, gesturing at the empty wheelchair. The sled's two skid marks lay fifteen feet long across the hard earth to where the sled stopped.

Tate stood staring as if dumbstruck.

"Jesus," he whispered.

Gaines gave a short laugh.

"Believe me, I've seen him do worse," he said.

Tate turned, facing Gaines, wearing a strange stunned expression.

"It's true," Gaines said, seeing Rizale step down from the porch, pushing the wheelchair in front of him. "That's why it's important to never get on his bad side."

Stooping over Swann lying on the sled, Bedos cried out, "By the saints' mercy, he is alive!"

"How can you tell?" said Rizale, stopping and looking over at the limp body on the sled.

"His heart still beats!" Bedos said, tearful with gratitude, his eyes darting upward.

"So," said Rizale, "why wouldn't it beat? People take rougher rides than that every day."

"But poor Señor Swann is so ill," said the old Mexican, "so *very* ill."

"Oh? I hadn't noticed," said Rizale.

Even with his hands tied, the old Mexican worked feverishly to untie Swann from the wood sled. Rena helped. She looked over at Rizale.

"Please, give us the wheelchair," she said to the big hairless gunman.

"Come get it, little darling," Rizale said. "I'm through with that sick ol' bastard, 'less you want me to shoot the ropes off him." He laid his big hand on his short-barreled Colt.

"No, señor, please! Don't shoot him, I beg of you," Bedos shouted, bending down over Swann with his tied hands covering Swann's face, as if to shield him.

"Damn, son," Rizale said to Bedos, "I hope the old fool is paying you *well.*" He gave the chair a stiff shove toward Rena as she hurried over to get it, and walked on to Tate and Gaines.

"The trick will be getting him upstairs the same way." Gaines grinned.

Rizale glanced at the hacienda as if considering it for a moment.

"Yeah, I suspect it will be," he said. "I figured anything I do now will soften them up — make them answer quicker when we ask them something."

"You think so?" said Gaines. "Let's just see." He took a step forward and watched Bedos and Rena lift Swann into his wheelchair and dust him off.

"Señorita," he said, "did the Swann woman take the household goods to the old mines to hide them from us?"

"No comprendo, señor," Rena said, looking

235

baffled. She shook her head.

"See?" said Gaines to Rizale and Tate with a shrug. "A while ago, she spoke better American than I do. Now she don't know nothing I'm saying."

"I speak English, mister," Rena said clearly. "But I did not understand your question. I don't know where they took the wagonload of goods. The señora didn't tell us."

"Oh, I see," said Gaines, sounding dubious. "The four bays neither, I don't expect?"

"That's right. She told us nothing," Rena said. "We are paid house servants here. We ask no questions. We are told what to do, and we go and do it. That is all."

"All right, then." Gaines gave a sly grin. "You go finish fixing supper. After that, I've got something for you to do." He ended in a dark suggestive laugh.

"Wait a damn minute," Tate said just between himself and the two gunmen, not liking the way these had taken over. "This is supposed to be my show. I brought you here to show you how I go about handling the Swanns."

"That is true," said Gaines. "But I suppose we should have warned you, me and Rizale here just have natural ways of taking things over when it suits us." He stared at

Tate with a thin smile. "And right now it *suits* us, eh, Gilbert?" He gave a nod toward the woman.

"Ah, son, son," said Rizale, looking the woman up and down as he spoke. "It *suits* me, front, back and sideways."

The two stood flanking Tate as the woman pushed the wheelchair to the porch steps and helped her hand-tied father lift the chair, Swann and all, onto the porch.

"No palavering up there," Gaines cautioned, seeing both Bedos and Rena bent over Ansil Swann, adjusting him into the chair.

"We are not talking," Rena said, straightening and turning toward the men. "We are only doing what must be done." She placed a hand on her hip.

Rizale chuckled.

"I like her. She's got real sand," he said sidelong to Gaines, Tate standing in between them. To Tate he said, "A pepper sprout, you said?"

"Yeah, a pepper sprout," Tate said grudgingly.

They watched Rena step down from the porch; behind her Bedos finished adjusting Ansil Swann's shirt and trousers.

"What is this?" Bedos whispered to himself, feeling the shape of a small jackknife in

Swann's pants pocket. He gazed into Swann's blank lifeless eyes as he fished the knife out with his tied hands and hid it quickly inside his shirt. Swann's dead eyes did not change as the old Mexican looked down at him and stepped back from the chair.

"Get done with that chair, old man," Gaines growled, " 'less you want to be strapped in it beside him."

"Come, Papa," Rena whispered to her father. "Don't do anything to anger them. Can't you see they are madmen? We must protect Señor Swann and get these monsters away from here."

When the meal was served and Gaines gestured for Bedos to sit across the table from him, the old Mexican did as he was told. He ate with his hands still tied, and upon every opportunity he reached his hands under the table and tried to hold the knife in a way to cut the ropes from his wrists without being seen. Next to Bedos sat Tate; across from Tate sat Rizale. On the porch, Ansil Swann sat in his wheelchair, staring lifelessly at the gathering. On the table in front of each gunman sat a bottle of Swann's fine select bourbon, imported all the way from Kentucky.

Gaines lifted his bottle of bourbon, swished it and took a long swig. He set the bottle down and let out a whiskey hiss.

"I admire a man who likes good bourbon," he said. He raised a spoonful of beans and peppers, blew on them to cool them, then grinned and spoke to Rizale.

"So, Gil," he said, "do you suppose that old rooster bumped his stone against this young pepper sprout every chance he got?"

"Son, if he didn't," said Rizale, "he's not like any rich man I ever heard of. He'd be a disgrace to American business barons."

The two laughed; Tate only gave a token half grin.

Pepper sprout?

Bedos heard what they were saying but had only a slight idea they were talking about his daughter. He stared curiously, wanting to cut at his ropes under the tables but knowing better than to try right then.

"Señorita, you are working too damn hard," Gaines said, grabbing Rena's wrist as she laid down a platter of hot flatbread. "I want you to sit right here on my knee —"

"No, turn me loose!" Rena said angrily, trying to jerk her arm away from him. "I am not some *puta* —"

"Sure you are, honey," said Gaines. "You just need some friendly coaxing, is all." He groped at her breasts; her blouse tore down the front. Bedos jumped up from the table.

"Get off her, you pig!" he bellowed.

"Stay out of this, old man!" Gaines shouted, turning his face away from Rena long enough to warn Bedos.

Rizale said, "What does a man have to do to eat in peace around here!"

When Gaines turned his face back to Rena, she slapped him hard across his face; beans flew from his mouth. The sound of the slap resounded all around the yard. Gaines staggered in place but held on to her wrist.

"Oh, son!" Rizale laughed. "She just brought you your hat and sent you packing!" He gave a deep belly laugh, seeing the red handprint on Gaines' jaw.

"She didn't hurt me!" Gaines flared. Holding Rena's wrist, he stood up quickly and backhanded her hard across her face.

Rena shrieked, not because of Gaines' hand across her face, but because she saw Bedos lunge up from his seat and land atop the table like some aging mountain cat.

"No, Papa!" she shouted. But it was too late. Bedos launched himself onto Gaines' back. His tied hands looped down over the unsuspecting gunman's head. His left hand gripped Gaines by his shirt. With Swann's jackknife open in his right hand, Bedos stabbed Gaines repeatedly in his upper chest, his shoulder, his throat and face — short vicious strokes. Dallas Tate sprang up from his seat. But he only stood staring in stunned disbelief.

"Whoa, son!" shouted Rizale, also up from his seat, his Colt out and cocked. But the big, hairless gunman couldn't take a clear shot at Bedos that didn't run the risk of shooting Gaines instead.

"Shoot! For God's sake, *shoot*!" Gaines screamed, running in short broken circles, his arms flailing wildly. Bedos clung to his back like some lethal insect, delivering blow upon blow with the wicked three-inch knife blade. Blood flew; a piece of Gaines' left eye came out of its socket on the tip of the knife blade.

Seeing Rizale's short-barreled Colt search back and forth for a shot, Rena hurled herself at the gunman. But Rizale knocked her away with a swipe of the gun barrel. Swinging the Colt back at the tangle of limbs, blood and gore, Rizale took a chance and pulled the trigger, sending a bullet through Bedos' head in a spray of blood and brain matter.

The impact of the shot flung Bedos sidelong. The weight of the dead Mexican hanging around his throat sent Gaines to the ground, the bloody jackknife blade buried in his upper lip.

"Son, son!" said Rizale. "Looks like he's took an eye out." He stooped beside his fallen partner, lifted Bedos' bloody arms from around his neck and laid him flat on his back. Gaines lay convulsing in pain, his left eye a pool of dark blood. His face was covered with blood, stabbed, shredded and carved to pieces.

Tate stooped down beside Rizale and winced at the sight of Gaines.

"Uake id out . . . ," Gaines begged, his words deformed by the knife blade inside his mouth.

"The hell's he saying?" said Rizale.

"I think he's saying 'take it out,' " said Tate.

"The knife?" said Rizale, appearing bewildered at what to do for the wounded man.

"That would be my guess," said Tate. He stared in horror, amazed that in a few passing seconds Gaines' normal face had turned into a bloody mass of sliced meat and exposed bone matter.

"Jesus, son!" said Rizale, rubbing his hand up and down his thighs nervously. He looked around at where Rena was knocked out on the ground. She was gone. "I don't think you're going to live either way, ol' pal," he said. "Maybe we ought to just . . ." He stopped short and looked all around for Rena again. "Where the hell did she go?" he said.

"I don't know," Tate said, "but this knife's got to come out."

"Uake id out . . . ," Gaines repeated, his body shuddering like a man stricken with a terrible fever.

"I hate doing this," Rizale said. He gripped the bloody knife blade and pulled, feeling it grit across the roots of Gaines' upper teeth. As soon as he had the blade out, he slumped, but only for a second. Then he and Tate both leaped away from Gaines as a rifle shot rang out and a bullet hit the ground beside the wounded man's head.

"Damn it, woman! Stop it!" Rizale shouted, rolling in the dirt, his Colt coming back up from his holster as the second rifle shot resounded and dirt flew up beside his knee. "Are you loco?" He fired quickly; so did Tate as a third round thumped into Tate's shoulder. Tate flew backward; his next shot went wild into the air.

Rena stalked forward, firing, sobbing, her breasts half-exposed through her torn blouse. Her next shot grazed Rizale's thigh. He yelped like a dog.

"The hell with you, then!" he shouted.

His next shot sent Rena's head flying sideways. She fell to the side beneath a red mist of blood. The rifle flew from her hands.

"My God, son!" Rizale said to Tate and the wounded Gaines lying shaking on the ground between them. "See how it is with these people? You never know what's going to set them off."

Tate staggered up and stood unsteadily on his feet, his right hand gripped his bleeding shoulder wound.

"Jesus, Rizale," he said, "looks like we've killed the only help we've got."

Rizale wagged his gun toward Rena lying on the ground. Her bloody hand scratched toward the rifle lying in the dirt near her.

"Look at this," he said. "She ain't even dead." He raised his voice for Rena to hear. "But she's going to be, if she don't forgo grabbing for that rifle!" He aimed the short-barreled Colt as he spoke. "Get over there and get her, damn it, Dallas."

"I — I can't hardly walk," Tate said, staggering in place, his chest and shoulder covered in blood.

"You'd *better* get yourself to walking, son, if you know what's good for you," Rizale said menacingly. "Somebody's got to attend to all this." He gestured the Colt all around at the bloody table, the dead and wounded.

Tate staggered forward, one slow step at a time, until he stopped beside the slow-crawling woman and clamped a boot down on the rifle just as she clasped a hand on it.

■ ■ ■ ■

PART 3

■ ■ ■ ■

CHAPTER 18

Will Summers stood at the corral and watched the three bay fillies playing in a large corral under a blue and perfect Mexican sky. Across the corral, he saw the big black stallion he thought he'd eaten the day he found ol' Hendrik wounded and dying in one of the many abandoned mines above Dark Horses. At this point he wanted to say "all's well that ends well," but something cautioned him against it. True, he'd not only escaped the hangman; he'd delivered his horses to the Swanns as promised. Not only that, but he'd helped Ansil Swann by accompanying his wife and delivering the gold to Don Manuel.

All right, he'd made a lot of money for delivering it, he reminded himself. But that was nothing to be ashamed of. He'd saved the Swanns from becoming completely insolvent after a lifetime of hard work and accumulating an empire. He'd also helped the two ranch hands make a lot of money in the process.

Good enough. . . .

Down the corral rail a good thirty feet, Bailey Swann stood beside Lonnie Kerns, her hand on his forearm. Summers looked at the two, then lowered his eyes and shook his head slightly. When Don Manuel had told her that he had investors who would buy the rest of the gold ingots, Bailey had come to Summers and asked him to go back to the mines and make one more delivery with her. He'd turned her down. They had been fortunate enough to get the first load here without running into either Mexican bandits, American outlaws, Apache, *rurales* or *federales.*

Besides, he'd reasoned, they had brought the first load here to Don Manuel. He should be willing to send his own men for the second load at a reduced price, and she should be willing to take that reduced price for not taking the risk herself.

But Summers knew Bailey Swann didn't see it that way. Now that she had collected a fortune, she wanted more. Maybe that's the way it is with folks like the Swanns, Summers thought. He wasn't judging her; he was just seeing her differently now. He'd seen before how she played men one against the other, the way she had with him and Dallas Tate.

Time for you to go, he heard a voice say inside his head. And he knew that voice was right. He had a feeling she thought she'd make him jealous seeing her play up to Lonnie Kerns. Let her think it, he told himself, looking back at the bays playing in the morning sun. He had done his part. Once the wagon was back at the ranch, he would take his money and go. Fair enough, he told himself.

"Señor Summers," said Don Manuel, smiling widely, walking across the yard to him, "the man who has brought me such a wonderful business opportunity — not to mention such fine breeding animals." He swept a long dapper hand toward the corral.

"It was my pleasure, Don Manuel," said Summers. He gave a respectful nod. The don wore a pale blue suit embroidered on the shoulders, cuffs and trouser legs with gold filament. He stood poker rigid behind a wide pearly smile, and raised a long finger for emphasis. Sunlight flashed off a large gold ring.

"On the way over here I ask myself," he said, "why does this man look so unhappy, after all the money he has made here today?" He shrugged and spread his hands. "Yet I have no answer for myself. So I must ask you, if I am not being too forward, why do you look so unhappy?"

"Didn't realize I did, Don Manuel," Summers said. "But just for the sake of being factual, I didn't make all that money today, just a portion of it." He paused, then said, "For helping the Swanns out, by bringing it here."

"Ah, then you did not make enough?" the tall, graying Mexican aristocrat asked.

"I made plenty, Don Manuel," said Summers, "more than I'll likely make all year dealing horses. So I can't complain."

"Good, good," said the Don, "then I was mistaken. You were *not* unhappy."

"No," Summers said, "far from it. I accompanied Señora Swann here on her husband's behalf, and I'm glad I could step in and help."

The don cast a guarded glance along the corral fence where Bailey and Lonnie stood side by side.

"It is kindness that tells one when to step into a situation," the don said. "It is wisdom that tells one when to step out." He gave Summers a knowing smile. "You have a good eye for horses. How long have you

252

been a horse trader, Will Summers?" he asked.

"A little over a year," Summers replied. "I tried a couple of other things first — carried a deputy's badge, wrangled for a big spread. But I'm best at doing this."

"And how is horse trading working out for you?" the don asked bluntly.

"Not bad," Summers said. He wasn't going to tell the man much about his business or himself.

Sensing Summers' reluctance, the don placed a hand on the young horse trader's shoulder.

"You have done yourself much good coming here," he said. "I am a man who is always looking for good horseflesh, like Swann's stallion and the young mares you brought here. I would like you to bring me any horses you find of this quality." He nodded at the fillies and the stallion. "You will be made welcome at my casa. Let us see more of you, and your finely chosen horses."

"You can count on it, Don Manuel," Summers said, shaking the man's strong thin hand.

"And now I must bid the señora adios," he said elegantly. He nodded toward the barn where the wagon stood reloaded with furniture, the team of horses standing hitched to it, ready to go. "Your wagon and horses have been prepared for the trail." He turned away and walked along the corral fence toward Bailey Swann, who saw him and walked forward to meet him, Lonnie Kerns walking a few feet behind her.

Summers walked away and stood at the barn checking the wagon and horses when Little Ted and a Mexican houseman came from the outdoor *cocina,* Ted carrying a large white canvas bag filled with food and provisions for the trail. The houseman beside him carried a leather and canvas bag filled with cash, partial payment for the gold ingots. The cash was enough to pay the ranch hands and himself and give the Swanns some much-needed expense money. In a long folded business wallet, Bailey Swann carried a promissory note from the don, to be deposited in the Banco Nacional in Mexico City.

"I hope you don't get a mad-on at Lonnie over her the way Dallas Tate did at you," Little Ted said to Summers, the two of them watching the don accompany Bailey Swann toward the barn, Lonnie following closely.

"I'm not going to," said Summers, not wanting to offer any more on the matter. He didn't even want to tell Little Ted that nothing had happened between him and the woman. It was nobody's business, he'd already decided. He wasn't Bailey Swann's judge. She had used him, but only as far as he'd allowed himself to be used. She'd offered herself to him, yet the Belltraes had shown up and prevented anything from happening between them. Looking back, he was glad they did. He hadn't come here looking for a woman, especially not another man's wife.

"She is a fine-looking woman," Little Ted said quietly. "I can't say I'd blame you if you did get ugly mad —"

"Bring the wagon out front, Ted," Summers said, almost cutting him short. "I'll bring the horses."

In moments Summers rode his dapple gray at a walk and led the other horses to the front of Don Manuel's sprawling hacienda, Little Ted right beside him, riding along in the wagon.

Before Summers could step down from his saddle and hitch his horse to the rear of the wagon, Bailey smiled up at him.

"Don't bother, Will," she said pleasantly enough. "You've done so much already. Lonnie will be driving the wagon back for me." She looked at Lonnie and said, "That is, if it's all the same to you, Lonnie."

"Yes, ma'am," Lonnie said dutifully. He

glanced at Will as if to make sure it was all right with him.

Will only looked at the two of them, nodded and touched his hat brim.

"Yes, ma'am," he said. He glanced at Don Manuel, who stood watching. The don only gazed at him with a thin smile, his dark eyes caged, yet knowing.

"Adios, Señor Summers," said the don.

Summers gave a nod and waved him adios.

The don turned and waved at Bailey Swann seated in the wagon beside Kerns. She returned his wave and settled back onto the wagon seat.

Summers nudged his dapple gray forward and led the wagon and Little Ted toward the trail, Bailey's and Lonnie's horses walking along behind the wagon, their reins hitched to the wagon's tailgate.

The wagon moved along smooth and easy and without delay throughout the morning. It was noon before Lonnie Kerns brought the loaded rig to a halt and the party gathered alongside a water hole on the bottom slope of a hill. Summers stood looking off along the trail ahead of them, watching two large buzzards circling high in the distance. At the water hole Lonnie and

Little Ted unhitched the wagon horses and led them forward to the water's edge. Summers' dapple gray and the other three horses stood beside the team horses drinking their fill. Seeing Summers standing alone, Bailey stepped down from the wagon seat and walked over to him.

"Will," she said hesitantly, "I hope I haven't done a foolish thing, having Lonnie drive the wagon. I certainly didn't intend for it to upset you."

"It didn't, ma'am," Summers said, turning his eyes away from the buzzards to the woman.

" 'Ma'am,' is it now?" Bailey said. "I thought we were closer than *that,* after all we've been through together."

Summers just looked at her for a moment, deciding whether or not to tell her that he saw through her games. Deciding not to mention it, he finally responded.

"You're right. We've been through something," Summers said in a gentler tone. "Pardon me, *Bailey.*"

"Of course, and thank you, Will," she said. "I was afraid that choosing Lonnie to drive the wagon, with me beside him, might have you upset."

"No," Will said, "it's your wagon. You're the boss. You can choose who you want to drive it," he said.

Seeing that Summers was sincerely not upset by Lonnie taking over the job of driving her, she took another try at recruiting his help for the next load of ingots to Don Manuel's.

"Oh, Will, I *do* wish you were coming with us this next trip," she said. She wrapped her arm in his. Lonnie stood staring from the water's edge. "I feel safe with you at my side —"

"I'm not going to," Will said sharply. "Another trip is pushing your luck. The gold's not going anywhere. You can wait a couple of weeks, a month. Let the dust settle. These two will stick around and go with you when you're ready." He gestured toward Little Ted and Lonnie.

"Yes, I know they will," she said. "Lonnie has already given me his word. But it's not the same. I want you, and I don't mean just to deliver more gold. I want you with me, near me." She squeezed his forearm. "How much plainer can I make it?"

"For how long?" Summers said, unmoved. "For a month, a year? You're a married woman, Bailey. What about your husband?"

"You've seen my husband's condition," she said. "How long do you say he'll be around? He's old, Will. I don't love him. I never did. But he doesn't matter. He's already dead to me. This money, the gold, it's not enough. I want it, but I want it with you."

Summers shook his head.

"How much is enough?" he said. "You said this trip would be enough now to clear your husband's debts — or enough to go somewhere and start over if you choose to."

"It's true. The one load is enough to make things right," she said. "But why would I settle for that now that I know there's more, just lying there for the taking?" She smiled and hugged his arm to her. "There is no such thing as enough," she whispered. "Only losers and fools settle for a portion when the whole treasure trough is laid before them. You're a young man, Will. That's what makes me want you so badly. But you still have things to learn. No man of wealth and substance ever looked at anything and said, 'That's enough.'"

Summers slipped his arm from within hers.

"I'll remember that," he said. "I don't know if I'll remember it as a lesson to live by or a lesson to avoid. But I'll remember it."

"All right," she said, turning angry, "be a young fool, then. See where it gets you.

Lonnie and Ted have agreed to go with me back to the mine. You can take your money tonight when we make camp and leave in the morning when we reach the fork in the trail."

"I think it'd be wise to go back to the hacienda first," Will said. "At least long enough to get the cash off the wagon and put up safe somewhere."

"I have had more dealings with large sums of money than you," she said haughtily. "I think *I know* what I'm doing." She turned and walked toward the wagon.

"Yes, ma'am," Will said quietly. "Everybody knows what they're doing till they find out they've done it wrong."

Bailey planted a hand on her hip. "I don't think I need to hear any homespun advice. I'm managing pretty well."

"Yes, you are," Summers agreed dismissingly, looking off toward the buzzards in the distant sky. There were now four of the big birds circling, two more flying in from farther away. He looked over at Lonnie and Little Ted, who had also been watching the buzzards circle all morning. "I'm going to ride forward, see what's waiting up ahead." He nodded at the circling scavengers.

"I'm going with you," Little Ted said.

Summers gave Lonnie a look.

"Go ahead," Lonnie said. "It's not that far. We'll be all right this close."

Summers and Little Ted walked to their horses. Bailey joined Lonnie at the water's edge.

"This is good," she said with a smile. "It gives us more time to be alone and talk."

Lonnie only smiled. They both watched as Summers and Little Ted rode away.

CHAPTER 19

Ezra and Collard Belltrae rode their horses down from a stone cliff, hidden by a hillside of tall, sparse pine and a thicker colony of scrub cedar brush. In moments they moved their horses onto a valley floor where the dark shadows of buzzards above circled slowly on the wild grass at their feet. A hundred yards out they saw a big roan standing alone, saddled, its reins hanging when it raised its head from grazing and stared at them.

"Holy Jorn and Alice," said Collard, looking at the figure lying half-hidden in the grass ten feet from the roan. "Bust my hide if that's not a woman lying there."

Ezra grinned and nudged his horse on a walk in order not to spook the grazing roan.

"I'll say for a fact it's a woman," Ezra replied, "without even lifting its leg." He gave a little laugh of delight at their good fortune. "Pa always told us, 'You'll never go wrong following buzzards. . . .' "

" 'They might not eat the best, but they never go hungry,' " Collard said, finishing their father's quote for them. They both chuckled.

Ezra's grin turned into a puzzled look.

"Wait a minute," he said. "We're not talking about eating a dead woman, are we?"

"Jesus, no!" said Collard, giving his brother a strange curious look. "What goes on in your mind, Ez? I'm talking about following these buzzards and coming upon a roan worth fifty dollars standing or twice that butchered out to the hill people — not counting braided out."

"So was I," said Ezra, stopping his horse a few feet back from the woman in the wild grass.

"Anyway, how do we know she's dead?" Collard said, crossing his hands on his saddle horn, getting comfortable.

"We don't, yet," said Ezra, swinging his horse over slowly and sidling close enough to the roan to reach out and gather its loose reins. "But we're going to know, soon as you step down and check her over."

Collard stepped down from his saddle and walked over to the woman and stooped down beside her. He laid his hand on her breast to feel for a heartbeat, then jerked his hand up, startled, when the woman groaned and turned her head to the side.

"Damn it! Scare the bejeez out'n me!" he said down to the dazed woman. He saw the dirty, bloody bandanna tied around a head wound and recognized Rena. "Hell, Ezra, it's that Mexican house girl of the Swanns'!" He looked closer at Rena. "She's been shot," he called out. "Stabbed too," he added, looking her over closer.

"Now what?" Ezra muttered under his breath. He stepped down from his saddle and led his horse and the roan over to where Collard squatted beside the woman. He looked at the woman, then up at the circling buzzards, then back down. Seeing her move her head a little and groan again, he stepped back and unhooked the canteen from his horse and uncapped it.

Collard stared at the wounded woman intently.

"Keeping her alive is worth something to us. Think of what we can do to her if we've a mind to," Ezra said, stooping down beside Rena with the canteen.

Collard gave him a dark serious look.

"You don't mean we're going to . . . ?" He let his words trail and held out a stiffened forearm.

Ezra shook his head as he poured a trickle

of water onto his palm to apply to her dried and cracked lips.

"No, Collard! You raving lunatic," he said. "And you wonder what goes on in *my* mind." He gave Collard a frown as he touched the tepid water to Rena's lips. "We're not animals — leastwise, I'm not."

"Neither am I," Collard said. "I just figured while she's knocked out —"

"Shut up, Collard. I don't want to hear such talk. The woman's badly hurt," said Ezra. "What I meant was, if we can keep her alive, nurse her along a little, we can sell her to one of the brothels south of here." He poured a thin trickle of water into Rena's slightly parted lips. "I've thought of it different times, but the old man was always too close."

"Yes, we could do that, come to think of it," said Collard, "sell her, sell her horse." He reached out a rough hand as if to feel her partly exposed breast. Ezra shoved his hand away.

"What the hell is wrong with you?" he said angrily. "Have you never seen a woman before?"

"Woman, horse, it doesn't matter. I'm just checking what we're selling," Collard said.

"Well, just *don't,* damn it!" said Ezra. "She is in bad shape. We'll have to get her well if we expect to make anything."

"If she dies we keep her hair to braid," said Collard.

"Yes, but we want the whole woman," said Ezra. He reached in to pour more water on Rena's lips. *"Braid her hair . . . ,"* he growled under his breath. "You pitiless wretch."

"Papa . . . ?" Rena groaned in a weak whisper. Water trickled pink from her swollen lips.

"We're not your pa, little lamb," Ezra said, wiping a wisp of hair aside on her bruised forehead. "But we're the next best thing. We're going to take you somewhere where they'll look after you —" His words stopped short at the sound of a Colt cocking close behind him.

"Get your hands off the woman," Will Summers said in a tone that offered nothing but sure death if they refused.

Both of the Belltrae brothers' hands sprang up chest high.

"Whoa!" said Ezra as they rose in a half crouch and turned facing him. "You might not believe this, Will Summers," he said, "but I recognized your voice — sure did."

"Step away from her," said Summers. As he spoke, Little Ted Ford came riding up at a gallop, having seen what was going on from farther up the hill than Summers had been. He bounced down from his saddle with his pistol in hand.

"I know this looks bad, Summers," said Ezra, "but we just come upon her. Followed those buzzards just hoping for potluck and here she was." He raised his eyes to the buzzards overhead.

"That's the gospel truth," said Collard. "We would not harm a hair on this young woman's head."

"Over there," said Summers, wagging them away from Rena with the barrel of his cocked Colt. He said to Little Ted, "Check her heartbeat, Little Ted."

Little Ted started toward Rena. She groaned; he saw her try to raise a hand.

"She's alive, Will!" he said, hurrying forward. "Come see. I've got these two covered."

"Of course she's alive," said Collard. "Brother and I saved her life, the truth be known."

"You're all heart, fellows," Summers said, stepping forward as Little Ted walked closer to the Belltraes.

"Señor . . . Summers," Rena whispered in a failing voice as Summers kneeled beside her. He picked up the canteen that Ezra Belltrae had left lying on the ground beside her.

"Just help yourself to our water there, Summers," Ezra said, a little grudgingly, as Summers poured water into his cupped palm and let it trickle into Rena's mouth.

"You . . . you found me," Rena said.

"Hey, over there," said Ezra, leaning a little. "He didn't find you. We did."

"*I* did," said Collard, "to be exact on the matter. So, if anybody here deserves some appreciation . . ."

Rena didn't seem to hear or see the Belltraes. Her eyes opened and closed slowly. Her blood-crusted hand found Summers' hand and held on. "Don't . . . leave me," she whispered.

"Don't worry, Rena," Summers said. "I've got you. I'm not going to leave you. You're safe now."

"So, this is what we get for all our good intentions," Collard said to Ezra. "Remind me never to do nothing good for nobody ever again —"

"Shut up, both of you," Summers said. He looked over his shoulder and saw Ted standing too close to them. "Ted, get back some before one of them —"

But Summers' warning came too late.

Already preparing to make a move on Little Ted, Ezra shouted as he slapped Ted's Colt away and snatched his own from its holster. Collard jumped back, ready to make the same play. But dropping his Colt, Little Ted clamped his hand down over Ezra's gun, hand and all, and did exactly what he'd practiced ever since Summers had shown him the flip.

The small ranch hand moved like a streak of lightning. Ezra let out a squall as he sailed high in a full circle and landed hard, flat on his back, his gun now in Little Ted's hand. Collard, stunned, backed up a step, his hands springing back to chest high.

"I'm done!" Collard said quickly, seeing his brother writhing in pain on the ground.

"My arm's broke!" Ezra groaned, clutching his shoulder in pain.

Little Ted gave Summers a sidelong grin.

"You're lucky I didn't break them both," he said to Ezra. He asked Summers, "How was that, Will?" As he spoke he took a step back away from the gunmen and motioned for Collard to help his brother to his feet.

"Risky, that's how it was," said Summers. He considered it and added, "Otherwise, nicely done." They both looked toward the hill trail as the wagon rolled into sight. "Keep an eye on those two while I attend to Rena." He reached out and gently raised the corner of the bandage covering a nasty bullet graze on the side on her head.

"The collectors . . . Dallas Tate . . . they killed my papa," Rena murmured. "Papa stabbed . . . one of them to death."

"Take it easy, Rena," Summers whispered. He could see she was fighting to remain conscious. He laid the bandage back into place on the side of her head. He pulled back another bloodstained bandage on her side where she'd been stabbed. "We're going to get you to town, get you taken care of."

When the wagon had rolled up and stopped, Bailey Swann stepped down and looked at Little Ted, who stood holding a gun on the Belltraes. Lonnie stepped down from the wagon and stood beside it. Little Ted motioned Bailey toward Summers and the wounded woman.

"It's Rena, ma'am," he said. "She's taken a bullet graze to her head. It looks bad."

"Oh no," said Bailey. Her eyes went to the Belltraes as she turned to hurry to Rena's side.

"It weren't us who harmed her, ma'am," Collard called out behind her.

"No, indeed," Ezra called out, kneading his injured shoulder. "It was us who found her. Good thing we happened along. A head wound ain't nothing to fool with. She'll be

270

an idiot from now on, she ain't careful."

At Rena's side, Bailey kneeled beside Summers. Finding Rena had slipped into unconsciousness, she reached out to hold the woman to her. Summers stopped her.

"The less moving around, the better," he said. "She's been shot, stabbed, beaten pretty bad. She said they killed Bedos."

"This poor darling," Bailey said, almost sobbing. Then she caught herself. "Who did she mean, *they*?" She glared around at the Belltraes.

"She said Dallas Tate and some collectors," said Summers. "She said Bedos stabbed one of them."

"Oh, this poor, wonderful angel," Bailey sobbed softly. "Of course we're going to do everything we can to save her." She saw the canteen lying beside Summers and snatched it up. She quickly untied her trail bandanna from around her throat and held it down to the uncapped canteen. She wet the bandanna and began wiping Rena's bruised and battered face with it.

"Don't you worry about anything, Rena, darling," she said to the unconscious woman. "We're going to take good care of you, see to it you have everything you need—"

"Ma'am," Summers said, taking Bailey's

wrist, stopping her, "you can do that in the wagon as soon as we get it unloaded and get under way."

Bailey stopped suddenly and gave him a stunned, bemused look.

"Unloaded? Under way?" she said, the wet bandanna in hand. "Will, what are you talking about?"

"We've got to get her to a doctor," Summers said. "Head wounds are serious business." He looked around at Lonnie and said, "Start unloading, Lonnie. We're headed for Dark Horses."

"Whoa, now!" said Ezra Belltrae, holding his injured shoulder. "You can't be taking brother and me to Dark Horses. They'll hang us sure as the world."

"We're not taking you anywhere, Ezra," Summers said. "You two didn't do this. She told me so." He gestured at Rena.

Ezra gave Little Ted a hard stare.

"It'd been nice if she'd said something before this fool broke my arm," he said.

"It's not broken if you can round it," Summers said. "Keep working it. The soreness will go away." He said to Ted, "Unload their guns and let them go." Ezra stood rounding his arm and flexing his sore shoulder.

"Will," said Bailey in a lowered voice, "we can't take her to Dark Horses. I'm taking

272

this wagon back to the mines. I'm taking the rest of the gold to Don Manuel's as quick as I can."

Summers stared at her.

"She can die if she doesn't get to a doctor," he said.

"I'm sorry, Will," Bailey said stiffly. "If you feel you must, you can take her to Dark Horses on horseback. This wagon is going back to the mines."

"It could kill her traveling by horseback," Summers said.

"Oh?" Bailey pointed out the roan standing nearby. "And how did she get here?"

"You want to take a chance on killing this woman, after all she and her father have done for you and your husband?"

"You don't understand people like these, Will," Bailey said. "She and her father are strong people — Guatemalans. Ansil made arrangements for them to be sent through the church, to be our servants. We've given them everything, work, a place to live." She paused, then said, "My God, I am sorry for what's happened to her and Bedos. But what about me? Don't I deserve something? With all that gold I can bring many more servants like her here. That's how we help these people — they become domestic

servants. Clean her up, get her on a horse
—"

"We'll take her," Collard Belltrae cut in.
"We'll see she gets looked after somewhere.
That's what we was discussing when you
rode in on us."

Summers looked back and forth from
Bailey to the Belltraes as if seeing something
of the same fabric in common between
them.

"There, you see," Bailey said, "the problem's solved. They'll take her and see she
gets cared for. I'll give her some money to
get south back to her people —"

"I have . . . no people," Rena murmured,
drifting in and out of consciousness. "Only
mi padre. . . ."

"All the more reason for me to give her
some money," Bailey cut in. "She won't be
able to work. She'll need a way to live —"

"We're going to Dark Horses," Summers
said with finality, cutting her off. He looked
at the Belltraes. "Unless you're going there
with us, you'd best skin out of here."

"We're gone," said Collard, taking his and
Ezra's unloaded guns as Little Ted held
them out to him. "Last you saw of us, we
were hanging on to a log floating down the
Río Azul."

"I've got it," Summers said. "Now get out

of here. You come back around me again, I'll shoot you."

The Belltraes looked surprised.

"*Shoot* us? Why?" said Collard, reaching for his horse's reins.

"Because I just don't like you," Summers said flatly. He turned to Lonnie as the Belltraes hurriedly mounted and rode away. "Lonnie, you and Ted get the wagon unloaded, make room for her." He gave a look toward the Belltraes riding out of sight. "We'll hide the money at the hacienda on our way. Make sure those two horse thieves can't get to it." He gestured toward the Belltraes.

Lonnie started to make a move toward the rear of the wagon.

"Stay where you are, Lonnie!" Bailey said, springing to her feet. "In case either of you has forgotten, you're hired hands. You both work for me. Your jobs are to see to my husband's and my interests and well-being."

Lonnie and Ted looked at Summers, then back to Bailey.

"Ma'am," Lonnie said, "this is the first I've heard your husband's interest and well-being mentioned since we got here. You didn't even ask if he's still alive. If he's alive when we get there, maybe we can keep him that way. We know he can't lift a finger for himself."

Bailey stared back and forth between the two ranch hands. "Well, I'm — I'm certain he is all right. That is, I mean —"

"Will," said Lonnie, cutting Bailey off, "are we stopping by the ranch to see about Ansil? It's right on our way."

"You know we are, Lonnie," Will said. "I figured that goes without saying."

Bailey started to say more on the matter, but Lonnie gave her a firm stare.

"Ma'am, either get on your horse or get back in the wagon. We're unloading here and headed for Dark Horses."

CHAPTER 20

Rodney Gaines lay trembling on the ground, muttering incoherently on a pallet of blankets Rena had made for him beneath a cottonwood tree, after cleaning his wounds and patching his face together as best she could. Empty whiskey bottles lay strewn about the yard. Full bottles stood on the wooden table.

Dallas Tate lay with his face down on the wooden table beneath a gray cloud of flies. His shoulder wound had been dressed; his arm lay cradled in a sling Rena had made for him out of torn strips of bedsheet. Both wounded men had benefited from Ansil Swann's office liquor cabinet. So had Gil Rizale.

Rizale sat on the ground, leaning against the cottonwood beside Gaines' pallet, his bandanna tied around the graze on his right leg. A bottle of expensive bourbon stood between his thighs.

"Where's . . . the woman?" he asked anybody listening. "I need this leg cleaned and bandaged."

"She's gone," Tate said, raising his face a little, looking all around, then dropping his head with a thump. "She left yesterday sometime . . . I think," he said, his voice muffled, speaking down into the tabletop. "You beat her up . . . He stabbed her while she tried to bandage him, remember?" He gestured at Gaines, who muttered and whined in pain.

"If I remembered . . . I wouldn't have asked," said Rizale.

"You shot at her some when she ran away," Tate said. He raised his head and this time managed to hold it up. "It's all been like a bad dream."

"Where's old man Swann?" Rizale asked.

"The woman carried him upstairs," said Tate, "stuck him back in his chair. Cleaned him, fed him, threw a blanket over his shoulders. Then she lit out of here. I expect he's still up there. He can't go nowhere."

"Why didn't you try to stop her?" Rizale asked.

"Stop her?" Tate stared at him through red-rimmed eyes. He gestured at his bloody shoulder bandage.

Rizale shook his head. He stuck the bottle

inside his shirt and pushed himself up the cottonwood tree with his palms. He staggered there for a moment.

"That old turd knows his whiskey," he said with a groan. "I'll give him that." He looked down at Gaines, who lay shuddering, muttering and reaching his trembling hands around aimlessly above his bloody chest. His face was a thick bundle of bloody bandages. Dark blood covered the pallet beneath his head. A large part of his eye lay a few feet away, dark and dried in the overnight air, like some withering grape.

"He had a terrible night," Tate said, "calling out to his ma, his pa, crying, screaming under his breath. That Mexican sliced him up like a Mississippi watermelon."

"He ain't going to live," said Rizale. He paused for a moment looking down at Gaines, then said to him, "Hear me, Rodney? I told Tate here you ain't going to live."

Gaines rocked his head back and forth, muttering, whining, his senses gone, given over to pain. Whiskey vomit showed through the bandaging covering his sliced lips.

"To hell with this," said Rizale. He raised his short-barreled Colt from its holster, cocked it and fired a bullet down between Gaines' eyes. Gaines' body bucked once, then seemed to melt inside.

"Jesus!" said Tate, jumping at the sudden break of silence in the big side yard.

"I don't want to hear nothing about this," Rizale warned. "He'd've done the same for me."

"I know it, the poor sumbitch," said Tate. "He carried on all night."

"I should have shot him sooner," said Rizale, with a look of regret. "But better late than never, I expect." He lowered his Colt into its holster. "Things sure went bad here in a hurry," he added, looking all around, at Bedos' body, at Gaines.

Tate pushed himself up from the table with one hand, his wounded shoulder throbbing in pain.

"What now?" he said. "There's nobody left here to clean this mess up."

Rizale looked around again, kicked an empty blood-splattered bottle away and gave a dark grin.

"What mess?" he said. On the cold *chimenea* grill a large sand rat sat chewing on leftover beef. "Let's get our horses and clear out of here." He picked up a blood-splattered bottle and hurled it at the rat. The bottle crashed on the *chimenea.* The rat screeched and vanished off the stone edge, its tail whipping the air behind it.

Tate stood staring after the rat, blurry-

280

eyed. So did Rizale.

"Dad Crayley's going to want to hear about this place being picked over, missing furniture and all," said Rizale. "Another few days it'll be an empty hull sitting here."

"What about him up there?" Tate asked, nodding toward the upper floor of the hacienda.

"What about him, son?" said Rizale. "I didn't take him to raise, did you?"

"No." Tate shrugged his good shoulder. "It's just, having worked for him and all . . ." His words trailed.

Rizale chuckled.

"Son, wake up," he said. "You were stiff-legging the man's wife. What do you think he'd do to you if he could?" He spread his thick hands.

"I hate leaving anybody in that shape," said Tate. "How long before the rats and coyotes get in, start chewing on him?"

"I left that cocked Colt lying in reach," said Rizale. "That's all he gets from me." He stepped over and grabbed two more whiskey bottles by their necks.

"The gun won't fire — it's froze up," said Tate. "Anyways, I don't think he's able to move a muscle."

"There're two things he'll need to work on, moving a muscle and firing a gun," said

Rizale, swinging the bottles up under his arm and reaching for two more. "Are you riding with me, or what?"

Rizale limped on his bullet-grazed leg to where the horses had stood at a hitch rail all night. Dallas Tate quickly stuffed two full bottles into the sling around his arm. He looked over at the upstairs windows of the hacienda. *What the hell?* Then he grabbed a third bottle and hurried along behind him.

Summers had heard the shot echoing out from the direction of the Swann hacienda. But it was another two hours' ride before he and Little Ted Ford stopped their horses and looked out at the hacienda from the low rise. They saw afternoon sunlight glisten off the empty whiskey bottles lying strewn about. They saw buzzards overhead, circling low — never a good sign. A coyote who'd given up the shelter of his den in the glaring light of day sat staring at something lying under the cottonwood tree.

"Easy-like, Ted," Summers cautioned. "You wait here till I wave you in. I need you to wave in the wagon."

"All right, if you say so," Ted said with reluctance, "but you watch your backside. I'm going to keep you beaded." He drew his Winchester from its boot, checked it and held it ready across his chest with both hands.

"Obliged," Summers said. He nodded and put his dapple gray forward at an easy gallop, his rifle in hand. When he got close enough to see the two bodies lying on the ground, he slowed the gray a little and kept an eye on the gun ports on the hacienda's second floor. Ten yards from the cottonwood, he stopped his horse, stepped down from his saddle and slipped his Winchester into its boot. He drew his Colt and walked forward, leading the gray by its reins.

A buzzard standing on the wooden table lifted on its thrashing wings and batted away into the sky. Summers stopped again when he stood over Rodney Gaines' body on the dark bloody pallet of blankets. He looked at the thick bandages covering Gaines' mangled face, the bullet hole between his eyes, the dried, shriveled half of an eye lying in the dirt. He winced and looked at Bedos Reyes' body, lying where Rizale's bullet had left him, hands still tied together at the wrists. Flies circled the blackened blood on the old houseman's face. Summers fanned away the flies and stooped and closed Bedos' eyes.

He walked through strewn whiskey bottles, dried blood, bits of bone and brain matter to the hacienda. Inside the front door, his eyes searched upward along the stairs, the upper landing. Then, climbing the stairs, he walked down the hallway and through the open doorway into Ansil Swann's office. In his wheelchair behind his wide desk, Ansil Swann sat slumped, staring lifeless at him through blank unblinking eyes. Chafe from dried streams of tears stained the old man cheeks. A fly stood on his nose.

My God. . . .

Summers walked past the desk and fanned the fly away on his way to the windows. He opened the shutters, let fresh air into the baking-hot room and leaned half out the window and waved at Little Ted.

Seeing Summers' signal, Little Ted turned in his saddle and waved the wagon forward. Summers went downstairs and met the wagon as it rolled into the side yard. Lonnie stopped ten yards back from the cotton-wood tree.

"My goodness," Lonnie said as if in awe, stepping down from the wagon seat and looking around the yard. Little Ted, down from his saddle, helped Bailey climb down from the wagon seat. The three stood beside Summers for a moment looking at the dead, the strewn bottles, the buzzards flying low overhead.

"You know what struck me a while ago?" Bailey said quietly in a somber tone. "Instead of taking this poor woman to Dark Horses, one of us should ride in and bring the doctor back here." She looked at Summers. "It makes more sense, doesn't it, Will?"

Summers looked at her.

"No. Who's going to attend to her until the doctor arrives, if he comes back here at all?" he said.

"Well, I will, of course," said Bailey. "I do know how to attend to someone who needs attending."

"That's good to hear," Summers said. "Your husband is upstairs. He needs attending real bad." As he spoke he walked to the wagon and hitched the dapple gray to the tailgate.

"Oh . . . ? Real bad?" She worked at keeping a pleasant expression.

"Yes, *real* bad," Summers repeated. He stepped up into the wagon bed to check on the unconscious woman. "Looks like he's been there a long time. He needs water and food . . . among other attending. I expect you'll want to get on up there."

"Well, you know . . . I suppose —" Bailey Swann was at a loss. Struck speechless, she

285

touched nervous fingers to her hair. "You know something . . . This is not what I'm best at doing. . . ." She looked toward the wagon as if she hoped Rena might rise and attend to her husband for her. "These are such unusual circumstances. I find myself unprepared." She looked at Bedos' body lying on the ground. She looked up at the window to Ansil Swann's office in horror.

Summers and the two ranch hands stood silent, staring at her, Summers standing over Rena in the wagon bed.

"Why are all of you looking at me?" she said, almost shrieking her words. "What have I done wrong? Nothing, that's what!" She looked back and forth, her eyes welling up and glistening. "I am not a house servant!"

"I'll go see to Ansil," Lonnie said finally. He unhooked a canteen from the hook on the side of the wagon and walked toward the hacienda.

"Ted," said Summers, "are you up to riding with me, scouting the trail ahead till I get this woman to Dark Horses?"

"Right you are, Will," Ted said, proud to have been chosen. "I'm ready when you are."

"Let me remind you again, Little Ted," said Bailey, "you still work for the Swann

286

Ranch. You will take orders from me, and only me. Are we clear on that?"

"Begging your pardon, ma'am, but I don't work for you no more," Ted said. "I've seen how little you care for people when they need your help, or when they're not serving your interests." He walked toward the wagon and looked up at Summers. "If it's all the same with you, Will, I'd feel better taking my part of the money now."

"How dare you, Little Ted!" said Bailey. "I resent you implying your money is not safe here with Lonnie and me."

Little Ted ignored her and stared up at Summers.

Summers looked at Bailey, then down at the small ranch hand.

"It's your money, Ted," he replied. "Take your part. We'll take the rest into the house for Lonnie and Bailey here to hide."

"Obliged, Will," said Little Ted.

"I have a personal draft from Don Manuel that is a larger amount than either of you has ever seen!" Bailey said. "So, go, Little Ted, take your paltry share. Take it and get out of here. You're fired!" She turned to Summers. "You can take your share too, as far as I care."

Summers looked at her for a moment.

"Yes, ma'am, I think I will at that," he

287

said. He looked up and saw Lonnie at the window to Ansil Swann's office. "Have you got everything covered here, Lonnie?" he called out. "If you do, Ted and I are taking our cut and headed for town. Have you got any problem with us doing that?"

"None at all," Lonnie replied. "Sorry I'm not going with you, but somebody's got to attend to Ansil and look after the place." He looked at the dead on the ground. "I need to bury Bedos and drag this one off somewhere before these buzzards eat him where he lies."

"We're out of here," Summers said. He slapped the reins to the horses' backs and put the wagon forward, Ted Ford riding along beside him.

CHAPTER 21

At dusk Gil Rizale and Dallas Tate rode into Dark Horses, seated low in their saddles. Having ridden all day in the scorching Mexican sun, both men and their animals were drawn instinctively to the stone-sided well in the heart of the town. The two spilled down from their horses' backs and knocked any number of gourd dippers out of their way. They fell upon the short stone wall and plunged their faces, hats and all, into the cool water. A bottle of bourbon slipped from the sling on Tate's shoulder and bobbed like an ocean buoy.

"What the hell is this?" said Evert Dad Crayley. He stood slowly from his cushioned rocker on the porch out in front of the Dark Horses Hotel. He and the gunmen standing around him stared diagonally across the stone-tiled street as Rizale's and Tate's horses stuck their sweaty muzzles into the well itself instead of into a runoff trough designed for just that purpose.

"Were these filthy sons a' bitches raised out of doors?" Dad said, jerking his cigar from his mouth. On his left stood Hico Morales and Jasper Trent. On his right stood Leon Yates and Lajo Alvarez.

"Hico, go bring those fools over here before our jackrabbit loco sheriff sees what they're doing and shoots them both. I'd like to hear what Rizale has to say about the Swanns." He paused and watched, curious as to where Rodney Gaines might be, and why Dallas Tate was now riding in his place.

As Hico stepped down from the porch and started toward the well, beside Dad, Jasper Trent spat a stream of tobacco and nodded toward the far end of the street.

"Speaking of jackrabbit crazy," he said, "here comes our *Sheriff Endo* right now."

"Damn it all," said Dad. "Does he see them?" He swung his head toward Endo Clifford, who walked poker-stiff up the middle of the street. "Hell, of course he sees them," Dad answered himself. "He ain't missed seeing a thing ever since he stuck that badge on his chest."

"He still ain't got it through his head that he works for the same folks we do?" said Yates, his fingers tapping on the butt of his holstered Colt. "He still thinks Ansil

Swann's footing the bills here, or some-thing?"

"Nobody knows what he thinks," said Dad with disgust. "There are some men in this world you can't figure, because there's just not enough to figure with." He shook his head. "Nothing you say ever sticks. It's gone before you said it."

"We can kill him most anytime you give us a nod," Yates said, his fingers still tap-ping.

"Yes, you *can,*" said Dad, "and most likely *will.*" He let out a patient breath. "But not today." He took a draw on his cigar, let out a stream of smoke and blew on its red fiery tip. "I'd like to finish a smoke without get-ting blood slung all over it." He smiled thinly. "Besides, we've got Thomas Finnity coming to town any day now. We need to make a good showing of this spit-in-your-eye Mexican dung hill."

He eyed Rizale and Tate following Hico across the street, leading their tired horses behind them, Rizale limping, both of them wounded and bandaged. Water still dribbled from their horses' muzzles. From the other direction Endo Clifford continued walking, poker-stiff, veering away from the well and stalking toward the hotel, the same place Tate and Rizale were headed.

"Everybody stand down, for now," Dad said. He looked at Rizale and Tate. They stopped and tied their horses to the hotel's hitch rail.

"Pay attention, both of you," Dad said. "The sheriff's getting ready to give you a hard time about how you watered your horses. Keep your mouths shut and don't go for your guns."

Rizale shrugged, looked at Tate, then back at Dad.

"All right, whatever you say, Dad," he replied.

The two stood watching as Endo Clifford walked closer, staring at Rizale and Tate. But instead of coming up to them as Dad expected, Clifford turned a sharp right, walked stiffly into a nearby alley and disappeared.

"See? He just walked on," said Dad to Trent and Yates. "How can you figure an idiot like that?" He looked at Rizale and Tate with a scowl. "Were the two of you raised by polecats?"

"What'd we do?" Rizale said.

The rest of the men chuckled.

"Hell, never mind," said Dad in disgust. "Where's Gaines?" He looked around the street as if Gaines might appear.

Rizale shook his head with regret. "Poor

Rodney is dead, Dad." He gestured toward Tate. "The three of us rode to the Swann spread after seeing their ranch hands running a load of furnishings along the high trails. Thought we'd take a look-see. Turns out they hadn't got back yet. Only ones there was Ansil and his houseman, the old Guatemalan."

Dad gave a grin. "Ansil's fit to be tied over us taking his stuff, I imagine?"

"Hard to say," said Rizale. "The old man ain't got the mind of an iron skillet."

"Oh?" said Dad, cigar in between his fingers. He looked to Tate as if for confirmation.

"It's true," Tate said. "We knew he'd been ill. But I think Mrs. Swann was hiding it from us." He shook his head, one arm in the sling but his hand holding the wet bottle of bourbon he'd just pulled from the well. Water dripped to the ground. "Ansil's a gone duck — stroke is what I'm thinking."

"Anyway," said Rizale, cutting in, "the old Guatemalan commenced stabbing Gaines in the face. We couldn't get him stopped. Finally I killed the old man." He gesture at his grazed leg. "His daughter did this . . . and that." He pointed at Tate's bandaged shoulder and chest.

"Let me make sure I understand," Dad

said. "The old man carved Gaines up. The young woman handled you two . . . by herself?" He gave them a look of disbelief. *"Jesus!"* he added. "Do I want men like you working for me?"

"It was something you had to see to understand, Dad," said Rizale.

"I bet it was," said Dad. He looked at Tate. "So, the old man is down and you want to come work for me?" He wore a thin, unreadable smile. He nodded at the bottle of bourbon in Tate's hand. "I see you managed to liberate some of Ansil's excellent corn renderings?"

"Well, yes, I did at that," said Tate. He swished the bourbon in his hand. "I couldn't see it left lying out there, something other than a white man getting his hands on it."

"Come closer," Dad said coolly and evenly, flagging the two in with his hand. As the two stepped forward and stopped again at the porch's edge, he said, "Drunk a lot of it, did you?" He still smiled.

Rizale sensed something in the works and stayed silent. But Tate wasn't as perceptive.

"All I could, and then some," he said proudly.

"Oh. . . ." Dad nodded, still coolly and evenly. Then his words started to turn sour as he continued, saying, "Let me ask you something, you son of a bitch. Didn't you know that bourbon now belongs to Finnity and Baines?" As he spoke, Yates stepped forward and snatched the bourbon bottle from his hand.

"You're going to pay for that bourbon," Dad said. He took the bottle from Yates, uncorked it, took a drink and stared, red-faced, at the label.

"I had no idea we —" said Tate. He shut up when Rizale shook his head warning him to.

"All right," said Dad, "both of you get over to the doctor's. Tell my boy Darren to get his hind end up out of there so's you two can get patched up." He shook the bottle of bourbon. "You got any more of this put away?"

"A few more bottles in our saddlebags, Dad," said Rizale. "You want them?"

"Hell yes, I want them," said Dad. "Bring them over here before you go to the doctor's. You'll be lucky I don't tell Finnity what you've done. This is just a bottle of *knock-down* to you. To Finnity and Baines it's Swann's *marketable assets,* just like everything else of the Swanns'."

Dad watched as the two hurried to their saddlebags to retrieve the bourbon.

"Here," he said, handing the bottle of

bourbon to Yates. "Take yourselves a shot and give it back. Some things Finnity and Baines don't have to know about."

It was after dark when Will Summers drove the wagon onto the stone-tiled street and stopped out in front of the large adobe-and-clapboard house where a brass-trimmed medical shingle read L. L. LABOE, M.D. Beside the wagon, Little Ted stepped down from his saddle and looked back and forth along the empty street. Somewhere a dog barked twice, then seemed to lose interest. Farther up the street, torchlight broke the darkness and the town's cantina and two Texas-style saloons spewed music and laughter into the soft Mexican night.

Summers set the wagon brake handle and stepped down from the seat, Ted from his saddle.

"We might should have come in through the back alleys," Ted said in a guarded tone, knowing the men who had done this to Rena were very likely in the Dark Horses saloons or cantina at that very moment.

"Huh-uh," said Summers, hurrying around the wagon and scooping the young woman up in his arms. "We've wronged no one here. We've got nothing to hide, especially not Rena here." He walked up a stone walkway and up three steps onto the front porch. Ted hurried around him, got to the door and knocked on it twice. Then he opened the unlocked door and walked inside as a lamp came on inside.

"Bring her back here, hombres," said the elderly white-haired doctor, seeing the unconscious woman. He stood in a hallway in a long bed shirt, holding up the oil lamp to see what the night had brought him. "Horse kick or snake bite?" he asked as Summers walked past him and followed his guiding hand into a side room.

"Neither," Summers said. "She's shot and stabbed, and wrung out by the heat and elements." He laid her onto a high-standing surgical gurney and stepped back. Little Ted stood inside the door, his hat in hand.

"Is she your woman?" the doctor asked, stepping into a pair of trousers and pulling them up beneath his nightshirt. He pulled suspenders up over his stooped shoulders. He took wire-rimmed spectacles from his pocket, hooked them behind his ears and wrinkled his nose to adjust them. They watched him step over and pour water from a pitcher into a pan.

"No," Summers said, "she's one of Ansil Swann's house servants. We found her along the trail like this."

The doctor dipped a corner of clean white cloth into the water and leaned in over Rena. As he did so, he glanced around at Little Ted beside the door.

"You work for the Swanns, don't you, young man?" he asked, then turned back to Rena's bullet-grazed head, lifted the bandage from it and examined it closely. "Ted Ford, I believe?"

"Yes, that's me," Little Ted replied, first looking to Summers as if making sure it was all right to say so.

The doctor glanced around at Summers.

"I'm Dr. Lyman Laboe," he said. Looking Summers up and down appraisingly, he said, "You must be the horse trader, Summers something or other — the one with the shotgun who peppered Darren Crayley?"

Summers only stared at him for a moment.

"Oh, don't cull up on me, young fellow," the doctor said with a slight chuckle. "I see all the bruised, maimed and punctured flesh that passes through Dark Horses. Far as you getting to shoot Darren Crayley goes, you must have won a lottery to get at the head of the line."

Summers relaxed a little.

"I'm Summers . . . Will Summers," he

said. "I did shoot him. But he pushed me to it."

"Not quite how he told it, but probably close enough," said the doctor. He stepped over, picked up his black medical bag and opened it on the gurney. He said to Little Ted, "I heard you or Lonnie shot Tubbs?"

"Are you going to charge me his bill?" Ted asked.

"No, he paid it," said the doctor.

"Yep, one of us shot him," Ted admitted. "I sort of hope he's not dead."

"He's not," the doctor said. He checked Rena's heartbeat with a stethoscope he fished from his medical bag. When he'd finished, he sighed and went back to cleaning the bullet graze. He said, "It might interest you to know that Dallas Tate was in here, him and Gilbert Rizale — both wounded, both drunk." He shook his head. "Drunk enough to admit that it was Swann's *house servant* who shot them." He gestured at Rena. "I'd be very surprised if this is not her."

Neither Little Ted nor Summers replied. The doctor shook his head slowly.

"I ought to warn you," he said. "I heard them saying they were going back there, soon as they could get horses under them."

"We can't let that happen," Summers said to Ted.

"If I know Rizale, he'll go back," the doctor said. "I know there's enough bad things afoot at the Swann spread as it is. Rizale is just going to make it worse, the way I figure. Finnity and Baines is out to get what's owed to them. They don't give a hoot what Rizale or any of their gunmen do, so long as they get what's coming to them." He frowned. "It's a terrible way to do business. Me being a doctor, it's my job to shore up and anticipate how bad things are going to get."

Summers considered things for a moment.

"You're looking at the worst of it, for my part," he said. "We're getting this woman taken care of, that's all. Soon as she's all right, we're out of here with her."

"Not looking for revenge, are you?" the doctor asked.

"No," said Summers, "all I'm looking for is the border. I came here on business, took care of it. Now I'm headed home."

The doctor appeared not to hear him. He continued cleaning the young woman's wounds.

"You know, this town was Ansil Swann's experiment," he said. "He wanted to see this become like an American town, like Springfield or even Denver City — not as big, of course, leastwise not right away. I know he's got himself in financial trouble, but I'm hoping he'll pull out of it." He smiled down at Rena as he attended to her. "He's a determined man. I don't see this knocking him off his feet for long."

Summers and Ted Ford looked at each other.

"Soon as you can, Dr. Laboe, you need to ride out and check on Ansil," Summers said. "I'm afraid he's awfully ill."

"Oh?" said the doctor, looking around at Summers, seeing the concern in his eyes. "Then I will ride out there first thing come morning, now that I know you hombres aren't going to be shooting each other all over town."

"Obliged, Doctor," said Summers. He stepped in closer when he heard Rena moan and saw her open her eyes. "Is she going to be all right?"

"She is," the doctor said. "Sometimes the impact of a bullet graze to the head can keep a person addled for a few days — not to mention bleeding from a knife wound. I've seen folks go a day or two like normal, then suddenly come off their feet and go unconscious off and on for a week." He nodded at Rena. "She's lost blood, but she's showing good signs. Right now she needs to rest, let her head clear. Come morning I believe she'll be much better — a little bit more each day until she's over it."

Summers gave a sigh of relief; so did Little Ted.

"Meanwhile," the doctor said, "why don't the two of you go to the kitchen and find yourselves something to eat while you wait? You can rest on the sofa and chairs in the waiting parlor."

"If it's all the same with you, Doctor," Summers said, "I'd like to be right here when she wakes up, keep her from being frightened by her new surroundings."

The doctor nodded.

"Sounds good to me," he said. "Get yourselves fed. We'll discuss her condition when I'm through here." He nodded at an empty gurney against the far wall. "Then you can make yourself at home." He turned back to his patient and continued cleaning her wounds.

CHAPTER 22

In the gray hour of dawn, Summers, dozing, opened his eyes and sat up on the gurney when he heard Rena Reyes murmuring under her breath. Standing, he stepped over beside her, took her hand and stood quietly looking on her face when her eyes opened. He felt her tense up slightly at the sight of him in the dim-lit room, at the touch of his hand on hers.

"Rena, it's me, Will Summers," he said quietly. "Don't be afraid. I'm right here with you."

She took a second to look around the shadowy darkness, already calming herself as she recognized his voice.

"Where — where are we?" she asked sleepily.

Summers could tell she was having difficulty gathering her thoughts.

"We're at Dr. Laboe's in Dark Horses," he said. He watched and waited while she looked around the room some more. She touched her fingertips to the bandage the doctor had placed high up on the side of her head, above her ear. "He told me you're doing fine. You might not remember much right now, but he says you'll come back with a little rest."

"But I do remember," she said. "I remember my father's death, the men who killed him. They made me dress their wounds. . . ." She paused, then said, "I remember the Belltraes. They said they would sell me in Mexico City."

Summers clenched his teeth, but he managed to keep his anger to himself. Bailey Swann had been willing to leave Rena with the Belltraes without batting an eye.

"They're all gone now, Rena, so put them out of your mind," he said.

"You said you would stay with me . . . and you did," Rena said, clasping both of her hands in his.

In a corner in a cushioned chair, the doctor stirred from dozing at the sound of their voices. He leaned to a small table beside him and lit a lamp.

"Well, now, what have we here?" he said in a tired voice. He stuck his socked feet into a pair of battered leather house slippers, stood up and hooked his suspenders over his shoulders. "How are you feeling, young lady?"

Before Rena could answer, a quiet knock caused them to turn their attention to the closed door.

"Will . . . ?" Little Ted said from the other side of the oak door. Summers stepped over and opened the door a few inches. He saw a worried look in Little Ted's eyes.

"I think you'd better come look out here," Little Ted said almost in a whisper.

Summers eased through the door, keeping it closed as much as possible, and walked with Little Ted to the front window and peeped out between the long curtains.

Sheriff Endo Clifford stood in front of the empty hay wagon, rubbing his hand on one of the team horses' muzzles. Red Warren stood a few feet away, a rifle in his hand. Summers and Little Ted watched Clifford walk slowly around the wagon, inspecting it closely in the grainy morning light. When he got to Summers' dapple gray, he looked it over and laid a hand up behind the saddle as if taking note that there were no saddle-bags there.

"Good thing we hid our bags on the way here," Little Ted said to Summers. "I wouldn't trust Endo Clifford with a steel bolt." He stared for a second longer, then said, "What do you think, Will? Are these two going to give us trouble?"

"I don't know," Summers said, "but we're going to find out." He started to turn and walk to the door.

"Wait, Will," said Little Ted. "Endo Clifford wanted to kill you when we showed up that day. Don't forget you kicked the man in his rack."

"I know," said Summers. "But he was in the wrong. He saw my paperwork. Now I've even got a statement from Ansil Swann that I was bringing him horses." He patted his duster where he'd stuck the bill of sales and the letter Bailey Swann had given him with Ansil's signature on it. He realized Bailey Swann had forged her husband's signature. But it would have to do.

"That might not cut it with Endo," said Ted. "He's a bully, always was. Only now, he's a bully with a badge, maybe even a sore rack still."

"I'm in the right, Ted," Summers replied. "When I'm in the right I tend to stand my ground, bully or no."

"Then I'm going with you," Little Ted said, "to keep the sides even. It never hurts to have a rifle cocked, no matter how *right* you are."

"I can't argue with that," said Summers.

He considered things, then looked back out the window, at an alley across the street behind Endo and Warren. "Think you can go out the back door, circle around behind them into the alley?"

"I know I can, if that's what you want," said Ted.

"It is," said Summers. "When you get a signal from me, I want you to cock your rifle in one hand, then count to three and cock your Colt."

"You got it," Ted said, already headed for the back door. "I'll be right there." He tugged his hat down on his head and walked on. Summers waited, judging the minutes he knew it would take for Ted to get in place.

On the street, Red Warren looked around as he heard the front door begin to swing open. He raised his rifle into both hands and laid a thumb over the hammer.

"Uh-oh. We've got company coming, Sheriff Endo," he said under his breath.

"Suits me," said Endo, stepping around to face Will Summers as Summers walked down off the porch toward him. Summers stopped ten feet away. He saw the shadowy outline of Little Ted in the darkened alleyway across the street behind the two men.

"Morning, *Sheriff*," Summers said in a

flat, no-nonsense tone. His hand rested poised near his holstered Colt, Summers letting Clifford know from the start that he wasn't going to take any guff.

Endo gave Summers a sly, menacing grin. Then he let the grin drop as if the memory of their last harsh encounter came to his mind.

"Well, now," he said, staring coldly at Summers. "We meet again, just like I hoped we would." Without looking at Red Warren he said over his shoulder, "Deputy Red, you remember Will Summers, the horse trader, don't you?"

"I do," said Red. He stood ready for whatever happened next. "I remember him from riding with those two horse thieves, Collard and Ezra Belltrae."

Summers let it go. He knew this was nothing to do with the Belltraes anymore, nothing to do with horse-thieving either. There was a gunfight coming, right here and now, whether he liked it or not. There was no ducking it, no putting it off. *Here goes. . . .*

"Are you still sore, Sheriff," he said flatly, "from me kicking your balls into your belly?"

Endo Clifford's face flared with rage. He tensed all over.

"You're making killing you too easy, Summers," he said. Over his shoulder he said to Red Warren, "Get ready, Red. Let's start shooting." He started to slap leather. But he froze as he heard Summers call out to the alley across the street behind him.

"All right, boys," Summers said, "are you ready to take them down?"

Red Warren's eyes widened at the sound of Ted's rifle cocking; so did Clifford's. Then they both froze when the sound of the Colt cocking followed right behind the rifle.

"Hold off!" shouted Clifford over his shoulder. "You're letting this horse trader get you into bad trouble! I'm the sheriff here, damn it!" He glared at Summers. "So this is a damn setup? An ambush? You dry-gulching —"

"It's all that," said Summers. His Colt came up and barked loud in his hand. Endo Clifford flipped backward and landed face-down on the hard tile street. Blood slung high from the exit hole in his back. Then it melted to a halt. Red Warren had started to throw his rifle to his shoulder, but he saw it was too late as Summers swung his smoking Colt toward him, cocking it, pointing, ready.

"Stop! Stop right here!" Red Warren shouted. He pitched his rifle forward onto the street and threw his hands high. "That was Endo's play, not mine!" As he spoke he walked backward step after step, each one getting quicker until he turned and bolted away in a dead run.

Summers fired a shot into the air, causing the fleeing gunman to speed up even more. He disappeared from sight as he veered sharply from the grainy morning light into the shadows still draping the front of the hotel.

"Come on out, Ted," Summers said, walking over to Endo Clifford's body and standing over it, his Colt still out, still smoking in his hand. "That looks like the end of it, for now anyway."

"That's the slickest ambush I ever heard of," Ted said, stepping out from the alley, looking off along the street. "I don't think Red Warren's going to stop running till his boots wear out." He looked at Summers as he walked over. "I never saw a man get so small so fast in my life. He wasn't an inch tall when he turned into the hotel."

Summers turned Endo Clifford onto his back with the tip of his boot. Clifford's stunned eyes stared blankly into the gray sky.

"You didn't put much time into it, did you?" Little Ted said, looking greatly impressed.

"As much as it took," said Summers. He dropped the two spent rounds from the gate of the Colt and replaced them with fresh bullets from his gun belt. He closed the Colt's gate, spun the cylinder free of smoke and slipped the gun into its holster.

On the front porch, the doctor stepped out with his medical bag in hand. He hurried down, then stopped when he looked down at Endo Clifford's gaping chest and wide-open eyes. He sighed and stooped down anyway and felt for a pulse. Then he stood up and stared at Summers.

"I thought you said the worst of it's over," he said.

"I thought it was," Summers said. "I missed it by a little."

The doctor shook his head.

"We're going to have visitors any minute," he said.

Summers nodded in agreement.

"Why don't you take the wagon around back for us?" he said to Little Ted.

"What are you going to do, Will?" said Little Ted, already climbing into the wagon seat. Dr. Laboe looked back and forth between them.

"I'm going to wait right here, see who shows up," Summers said. "I shot the sheriff. Now we'll find out who's running this town and what he thinks of it."

"I can tell you who's running Dark Horses," the doctor said. "It's Evert Crawley. If I were you I would not stick around to explain anything. You already buckshot his son, Darren. You need to get the hell out of here."

"What about Rena traveling?" Summers asked.

"Wherever you're going, she's better off with you than she is in Dark Horses," the doctor replied, "especially with her father dead."

Summers looked off along the street for a second.

"Have you got a buggy we can use, Doctor?" he said.

"It's back there in my horse barn," the doctor said. "Take it and get out of here. Send it back to me when you can."

"Obliged, Doctor," Summers said. Before Little Ted rode the wagon around the corner of the house, Summers unhitched his dapple gray and led it hurriedly toward the doctor's small barn behind his house.

"What're you doing, Will?" Little Ted asked, ready to put the wagon forward.

"Take the wagon around back," Summers said. "Get Rena out of the back door onto the porch. Be ready when I get there."

"All right, but where are you going, Will?" Ted called out as Summers hurried away.

The old doctor shook his disheveled gray head and waved everything away dismissingly. "I wouldn't be young again for nothing in the world," he murmured to himself. Up and down the street he saw curious faces venture out from doorways onto the street. He watched people walk along the boardwalks toward the front of his house, eager to see what the shooting was about.

At the Dark Horses Hotel, Red Warren spilled into Evert Crayley's office, out of breath, his face flushed, his hands no longer holding the rifle he'd been carrying when he and Endo Clifford walked past only moments earlier.

"Dad! All of yas! Come quick!" he shouted, skidding to a halt in front of Crayley's desk before any of the six men lounging around were quick enough to stop him. "The horse trader is down at the doctor's! He's driving Swann's hay wagon! He's killed Sheriff Endo!"

"The *horse trader*?" said Darren Crayley, standing up with a cup of steaming coffee in his hand. His face was pockmarked red by buckshot Summers had put there. Beside him Tubbs stood up too, his chest bandage showing between the tight buttons on his shirt.

Dad Crayley looked up from his cigar and a thick mug of bourbon-laced black coffee. He eyed Red Warren skeptically, then looked at his son, Darren, and Tubbs.

"The two of you sit down," he demanded with a growl, "unless you're going to do something besides embarrass yourselves." As he stood up he said to Red Warren, "I couldn't care less about Endo Clifford, but Rizale said they've been moving goods from the Swann hacienda in a hay wagon."

"It's sitting there, plain as day," said Warren.

Dad picked up his hat from the edge of the desk, and a rifle leaning near his chair. He looked at Darren and Tubbs.

"Well, my idiot son," he said to Darren, "if you do want to put a bullet or two in him, you can't do it sitting here."

"You told us to sit down," Darren said.

"Well, now I'm telling you to stand up," said Dad.

Darren and Tubbs sprang to their feet. Darren jerked his Colt from its holster, checked it and held it in his hand.

"Here's fair notice to you, Dad," he said. "If I get Summers in my sights, he's a dead man."

"Let's go," Dad said, waving his son's threat aside. "I expect it's time we kill the horse trader and be done with it. He's starting to get in everybody's way."

The men followed Dad Crayley out the hotel door and up the street to the doctor's, where a small group of onlookers had gathered. Instead of seeing the wagon, Dad and his men saw the wagon tracks turn off the stone tiles and down a wide dirt path that ran alongside the doctor's house, back to his barn and to a long alleyway that reached out onto a sandy stretch of flatlands.

"Tell me straight up, Laboe," Dad said to the doctor, "where's Swann's hay wagon and what was it doing here?"

The doctor stood over the body of Endo Clifford while the town barber, Raul Mijares, measured the dead sheriff for a coffin.

"What was the wagon doing here?" the doctor said, addressing the questions in reverse order. "The horse trader brought the Swanns' house servant here in the wagon. Your gunman Rizale shot her. Dallas Tate stabbed her." He held a fierce stare on Dad Crayley. "Where *is it*? The last I saw it, the horse trader was driving it right along that path to my back door, to pick the young woman up and get her out of town." Still

315

the fierce stare. "Might have thought your hombres would shoot her or stab her again."

"Don't get mouthy with me, Doctor," said Dad. "My men and I are interested in gathering the Swanns' assets. We're not out to shoot anybody unless they get in our way."

"Maybe you could have told Gilbert Rizale," the doctor said. "Him and Dallas Tate headed back to the Swanns' the minute I was through patching them up."

Dad looked surprised.

"Anybody seen Rizale and Tate?" he asked his men.

Buster Saggert stepped forward.

"Not since they went to the doctor's last evening," he said.

"Damn it," said Dad. He looked at Darren, who stood off the tile street, he and Tubbs stooped slightly, studying the wagon tracks leading back to the barn and alleyway. "Darren, you and the rest of your men get your horses. We're going to track this horse trader down, take care of him once and for all. Nothing's gone right since I started hearing his name."

CHAPTER 23

Little Ted rode alongside the doctor's buggy in the early-morning sunlight. Will Summers drove the buggy, his dapple gray's reins hitched to its rear. Rena Reyes lay leaning against his side, still coming in and out of consciousness. Summers had started the buggy ride with his arm up around her shoulders in order to steady her. Yet, at one point when he saw her awake and went to remove his arm, she held on to him.

"Please . . . ," she whispered.

Summers drove on with one hand holding the buggy reins.

"How far you think the wagon horses will go without a driver?" Ted asked, riding with his rifle across his lap.

"They can go for miles," said Summers, "especially with the buggy whip tapping them now and then."

He'd propped the doctor's long buggy whip in a way that left the tail dangling an inch from the left horse's rump. The slightest bump in the trail caused the limber whip to jump and slap the horse, an easy reminder to keep up the steady gallop he'd sent the team into with his gloved hand.

Ted grinned.

"A pretty slick move, the way I see it," he said. "Only I'm thinking Dad Crayley ain't going to see it the same way I do."

"Probably not," said Summers. "But it'll give him and his men a nice early-morning ride while we get on out to the Swann spread."

Ted kept his horse at the same quick but easy pace as the buggy horse.

"I hope Lonnie doesn't get caught off guard by Rizale and Dallas Tate," he said.

"He'll be watching the trail from the hacienda," Summers said. "I figure he knows to expect the worst, anything coming from the direction of Dark Horses."

They rode on until midmorning. Rena sat up awake as Summers pulled the buggy off the trail and over to a small water hole.

"Feeling all right?" he asked, taking his arm from around her shoulders and stepping down from the buggy seat.

"Much better," Rena said.

She remained sitting up as Summers led the buggy horse to the water's edge and slipped his rigging loose and watched the animal drink. While the buggy horse drank, Summers untied the dapple gray's reins and led the horse up to the water between the buggy horse and Little Ted's mount.

Summers walked back and stood beside the buggy.

"Do you have much to pack and take with you when we get to the hacienda?" he asked.

"Only a few clothes, my papa's spurs to remember him by," she said. "I want to put a wooden cross on his grave before I leave there," she added, "because I know once I leave, I will never be there again."

"I understand," said Summers. "While you were in and out of consciousness, you said you have no other family. I can take you all the way to the Guatemala border. But where will you go from there?"

Rena gazed out across the water hole and into the southern sky.

"I do not know," she said. "My papa and I have lived at the hacienda, thinking it would be our home from now on. When the Swanns are gone, my home will be too."

"Señora Swann said she's giving you some money," Summers said. "I hope it's enough for you start over with."

Rena didn't reply. Instead she looked down at her hands folded on lap.

"Where is your home, Will Summers?" she asked quietly.

"I travel a lot, Rena," he said. "But when I'm not traveling I keep a small spread near Wind River — nothing fancy, but the roof keeps the weather out." He smiled. "Nothing like the Swann hacienda, but it's home, when I want to take my boots off a day or two."

"And you live there — *alone*?" Rena asked.

"No, I don't live alone," Summers said.

"Oh," Rena said. "You have someone, a wife perhaps, who waits there for you." She sat silent. Summers heard a touch of disappointment in her voice.

"No, not a wife, Rena," Summers said quickly. "A ranch hand. An old waddie named Tuck Mills. He was once a deputy for my father. Now he takes care of my horses while I'm away — keeps the bears and coyotes off the place."

"Oh, I see," Rena said, sounding hopeful.

"He keeps his own place out behind my corrals. It used to be a six-bed bunkhouse, so he's got plenty of room there, just him."

"I bet your place is beautiful," she said, gazing clearly and steadily into his eyes. "I only wish I could see it someday, and you could show me around."

There it was, he told himself. He didn't have to get hit in the head. She was feeling better, no doubt about it. Her eyes were clear, alert. He was sure she still had some pain, a headache, and still would have off and on, according to the doctor. . . .

All that as it is. . . .

"Rena," Summers said, not about to let a chance like this get past him, "when this is all over, there is nothing I would like better than to show you —"

His words stopped short as rifle fire erupted from the direction of the Swann hacienda.

"Uh-oh!" said Little Ted. "Sounds like Lonnie's got his hands full." He grabbed his horse by its reins and pulled it away from the water. "We'd best get there and help him."

Summers started to walk down to the buggy horse and his dapple gray. But before stepping away he looked up at Rena.

"Promise me you will *please* hold that thought, Rena," he said.

She offered him a tired smile and relaxed in the buggy seat.

"I promise, Will," she said. "*Please* promise me you'll hold it too."

Lonnie Kerns stood with his rifle out the

gun port in the window of Ansil Swann's office. He had been in the office attending to Ansil when the shooting erupted and Rizale and Dallas Tate charged the hacienda on horseback. Downstairs, Bailey Swann had first seen the two men galloping down from atop the low rise. She'd hurried, drawn the bolt on the closed front door and run upstairs, shouting at Lonnie.

Lonnie standing at the gun port saw it was Dallas Tate. He recognized Rizale as one of the gunmen who drifted in and out of Dark Horses at Dad Crayley's beck and call.

"What do you want here, Tate?" he'd called out. But it was Rizale who answered.

"Whatever we damn well feel like taking," he'd shouted, raising his rifle from across his lap and firing.

That had been nearly an hour ago. Rifle shots continued to roar from the cover of sage and mesquite brush and thump against the hacienda all around the window of Ansil Swann's office.

"I'm running short of bullets," Lonnie called out over his shoulder. Bailey stood with the front doors of the large gun cabinet open, checking each firearm and every drawer for a box of bullets.

"I know there're bullets here!" she said. "I just have to find them!" She looked at Ansil, who sat slumped in his wheelchair behind his desk, his eyes staring blankly at the floor. On the floor lay two empty cartridge boxes that Lonnie had already used up.

"You'd better find some quick," he said. "I've got to hold them off until Little Ted and Summers get back." He kicked an empty box away as another bullet thumped against the thick, closed wooden shutter.

Bailey came upon a locked door inside the lower part of the cabinet.

"I might have something here," she called out. Having no key, not taking the time to search Ansil's desk for one, she picked up one of the rifles she'd taken out of the cabinet, raised it and struck the iron butt plate down solidly onto the lock and sent it flying away in two pieces.

"Hurry," Lonnie said. "I've got four rifle shots left. My Colt's not going to hold them back far enough to keep them from burning us out."

"Got some!" Bailey called out joyfully, throwing open the cabinet door and seeing box upon box of ammunition stacked neatly.

"Good," Lonnie said. "Load yours and give it to me. I'll stall my last four shots until you get it ready."

Bailey hurried, shoving bullet after bullet into her Winchester. While she worked, Lonnie watched the yard. As Gil Rizale rose into a crouch from behind a stand of brush, Lonnie took close aim and fired on him. But his shot fell short, hit Rizale's bootheel and blew it apart as Rizale ran, limping for cover closer to the front porch.

"Damn, son!" Rizale called out, falling into his new covered position. "I hope you're wearing a pair of big Texas lathemades. When this is over they're mine!" He rose enough to fire two quick shots and fall back into cover. He paused for a moment, then called out to the upstairs window, "You're not doing much shooting up there, son. Could it be there's something amiss?"

Lonnie didn't answer. Instead he looked over his shoulder at Bailey.

"Hurry up. They're gaining ground on us," he said.

"Could it be you're short of ammunition up there?" Rizale said. As he spoke he took close aim through a clump of brush on the small open cross in the thick shutters.

"We've got plenty. Come see," Lonnie shouted. He held his fire.

"It's loaded!" said Bailey, hurrying to the window with the rifle held out to Lonnie.

From the brush, Rizale's rifle roared just as Lonnie reached out for the loaded Winchester. The bullet bored perfectly though the gun port opening and nailed Lonnie high up in his right shoulder. The impact of the bullet sent him staggering sidelong and falling atop Swann's big polished desk.

"Oh my God!" Bailey shouted, running to him.

"Forget about me," Lonnie said. "Get to the window and start shooting. Keep them backed away from the house."

Bailey did as she was told. She ran to the window while Lonnie untied his bandanna from around his neck and tied it around his upper arm. On the ground, Dallas Tate had taken advantage of the lack of gunfire and stood in a crouch and ran to join Rizale closer to the front yard.

"Dallas Tate, you bastard!" she shouted, pulling the trigger. Her shot sliced through the air only an inch from Tate's nose. Tate dived behind a dried downed pine and hugged close to the ground. "I saw what you did while my servants were here alone."

"So what? Can you blame me, after the way you treated me?" Tate shouted out to her. "I suppose now you're telling Lonnie the same things, how much you love him. How you only wished somebody would kill Ansil with an ax handle, make it look like a mule kicked his brains out."

Rizale cackled out loud, hearing the two.

"Son," he called out to Dallas Tate, making sure Bailey heard his voice, "every married woman tells a fellow she wishes he'd kill her husband. That's just part of the courting process with a trifling woman."

A bullet from Bailey's rifle sliced through the brush where Rizale lay.

"Whoa, now," Rizale said with a laugh, "sounds like I struck a vein on that one."

Bailey looked over her shoulder, at her powerless husband, then at Lonnie.

"Dallas is lying, Lonnie," she said, "and this gunman doesn't know what he's talking about."

"I don't care what he says, ma'am," said Lonnie. "All I want to do is keep the three of us alive and hope Summers and Little Ted show up before these two manage to get to the barn."

"Yes, you're right," Bailey said. "Dallas knows there's lamp oil there."

"Enough oil to burn us to a cinder," Lonnie said as he walked to the gun cabinet, holding his wounded arm. He took up a box of ammunition and began loading another Winchester.

Bailey turned back to the gun port and began firing. As she finished firing a round and levered another bullet in the rifle's chamber, she saw Will Summers and Little

Ted ride over the low rise and charge straight for the house. Behind them, she saw Rena bring the one-horse buggy to a halt on the low rise and drop down out of sight.

"Here come Will and Little Ted," she called out over her shoulder to Lonnie.

"Not a minute too soon," Lonnie said, hurrying to the gun port at the next window from her. Looking out, he saw Summers and Little Ted riding hard, firing into the brush where the two gunmen were lying in cover, hidden from the hacienda. But Lonnie knew they were easily seen by Summers and Ted Ford riding down on them from the other direction.

"We've got them in a cross fire now," Lonnie said. He raised the Winchester in his hands, his wounded shoulder not about to keep him from the fight. "Don't let up until these two are dead, or begging to surrender."

CHAPTER 24

Summers and Little Ted split up as they rode down onto the stretch of brush and short rock. Seeing them, Dallas Tate rose into a crouch and tried to run forward, but bullets from the two upstairs windows sent him diving back into the brush. As he tried backing up from the rifle fire from the hacienda, the firing from Summers and Little Ted nipped at the brush all around him.

Ten yards away, Gil Rizale was having the same trouble.

"We're in a bad fix, son!" he yelled at Tate, throwing his empty rifle aside, managing to raise his short-barreled Colt and get off a shot as the bullets whistled in on him. "Looks like that fine bourbon will have to wait." A bullet sliced through his upper arm; another bullet cut across the top of his shoulder, trailing blood.

"Bourbo . . . ?" Tate shouted at Rizale,

above the pounding gunfire. "I didn't come here for no damn *bourbon,* you stupid son of a bitch!"

"By God you should have, son!" Rizale screamed, laughing hysterically, bullets hitting him high and low like angry hornets. Blood flew. He sank to his knees, facing the two riders, still holding up his cocked and pointed Colt in his bloodied hand. "Just one more shot, Lord!" he shouted. "Damn it to hell! Just give me one more —" His words stopped short. His head snapped forward, bowed quickly as a rifle shot from the hacienda windows nailed him in the back of his head, lifted his hat, sent it spinning in a yellow-red ribbon of blood, bone and brain matter.

A bullet had thumped low into Dallas Tate's side. He'd remained standing, but staggered in place, seeing Gil Rizale fall forward into the stiff mesquite brush.

Bourbon . . . ? What the hell did he mean, bourbon?

"Jesus," Tate murmured under his breath. He hadn't come here for more bourbon. Was that what Rizale had thought?

"Don't shoot," he called out to the two riders in a halting, wounded voice. He held his Colt pressed to his side wound in his bloody right hand. The pain was hot, sharp and deep.

Only a fool would have come for the bourbon, he told himself. That was nonsense! He watched Little Ted step down from his saddle as Will Summers rode over to where Rizale lay dead on the ground.

"Throw the gun away, Dallas," Little Ted said in a stiff, serious tone. "Don't make me shoot you." He held his Colt up leveled and cocked; his rifle hung smoking in his left hand.

"Shoot me? Ha," Tate said scornfully. "You little, sawed-off son of a bit—"

Ted's Colt bucked in his hand. The bullet went straight through Tate's upper chest, above his heart. Tate sank backward to the ground on one knee, his Colt still pressed to his side. The world swirled and danced before his eyes.

"All right . . . damn it," he said. He stayed on the one wobbly knee and tried to pitch the Colt away, weak now, not even certain if the gun left his hand. He didn't care. To hell with it. He knew he was dying. Yet he couldn't get Rizale's words out of his mind. *Come here for the bourbon? What kind of fool would have done that?*

He tried to look back over his shoulder toward the hacienda, but his waning strength wouldn't allow it. He hadn't come here for the bourbon, for God's sake. No. He'd come here for . . . His thought trailed. Wait a minute. What the hell had he come here for? He tried to come up with the reason and he almost got it. But before it became clear another bullet from Ted's Colt sent him backward with a solid thump to his forehead.

Little Ted stepped forward the last few feet and looked down at Tate. Then he looked over at Summers, who was walking toward him, down from his saddle and leading the dapple gray's reins through the rounds of mesquite, sage and juniper.

"I told him to throw his gun away, Will," he said. "He wouldn't do it." He gave a troubled shrug that matched the look of regret on his face. "He must've thought I wouldn't do it."

"Well, he's not thinking it now," Summers said, walking in closer. He stooped over Dallas Tate's body, took the Colt from his bloody hand and pitched it over near Ted's feet.

"What's this for, Will?" Little Ted asked, looking down at the bloody gun.

Summers didn't answer. Instead he looked toward the hacienda and saw Bailey Swann running down from the front porch and across the yard. Behind her Lonnie Kerns stepped onto the porch and stood looking after her.

Little Ted stood watching; he shook his head and opened his smoking Colt.

"And here she comes, wondering who to turn to next," he said quietly, reloading the Colt as he spoke.

"I'm riding back to get Rena," Summers said. "She doesn't need to be driving a buggy yet, the shape she's in."

Little Ted nodded. He'd closed the gate on his reloaded Colt and spun the cylinder. Powder smoke puffed and drifted away from his gun hand.

"Go ahead," he said confidently. "I've got everything covered here."

Summers turned, climbed into his saddle and rode away toward the low rise. Seeing him leave, Bailey slowed to a halt and stared after him for a moment. Then she turned to Ted, who stood reloading his Winchester.

"Oh, Little Ted, thank God you're here. I saw what you did. You were outstanding."

"Thank you, ma'am," Ted replied, touching his hat brim. "But don't be wasting your attention on me. I know I'll always be *Little* Ted to you." He turned away from her and walked toward his horse. He gave Lonnie a wave of his gloved hand on his way.

■ ■ ■ ■

When Dad Crayley and his men had tracked the empty wagon seven miles out of their way along an old, seldom-used trail, they found it sitting in a stretch of rock surrounding a small water hole. The team of horses stood grazing on clumps of wild grass, having drunk their fill.

"I hate a smart son of a bitch like this Summers fellow," Dad said, reaching a finger out and flipping the hanging tip of the buggy whip. "This is one of the oldest tricks in the book, and damned if we didn't fall for it."

"Not *we,* Dad, you," said Darren. "I tried to tell you we never should have taken this trail. The Mex won't use it, haven't for a long time. They say it's haunted by the spirits of dead Apache."

"Listen, fool," Dad said. "I'm not a Mex. I don't believe in Apache ghosts, nor does any white man with enough sense to lift a bucket handle. If you do, you'd do well to at least keep your mouth shut about it."

"I never said *I* believe it," said Darren. "I said the *Mex* do." He looked around at the other men, ten of them, dust-covered and tired from chasing an empty hay wagon.

Dad shook his head and growled a curse under his breath. Then he looked around until he saw Hico Morales.

"Hico, get me a driver up here," he said. "We chased this damn rig down. I'm going to get some use out of it."

Hico looked at Lajo sitting on his horse beside him.

"You heard him, Lajo," Hico said. "Tie your horse to the tailgate and drive the hay wagon."

"Where are we headed now?" Darren asked his father as Lajo rode his horse to the rear of the wagon and jumped down from his saddle.

"We're headed for the Swann spread," said Dad. "That's where Summers and Little Ted are headed. They didn't get themselves more than a two- or three-hour start on us, the way I figure it. If we ride hard we'll make that up in no time."

"Our horses are tired and need resting, Dad," Hico said, sounding reluctant.

"There's water, damn it, Hico. Water them," Dad said, pointing at the small water hole. "They can rest while they drink their fill. The longer I put off dealing with the Swanns, the worse things seem to get. We've got a big wagon. We might as well fill it. There're lots of valuables there, if Rizale and Tate haven't gotten it all and cut out with it. Those sons a' bitches."

Hico and the men dropped from their saddles and led their horses to the edge of the water hole and let them drink. Lajo took the buggy whip down and pitched it in the empty wagon bed. He turned the wagon around and waited until the other horses were watered and the men had stepped up into their saddles. He waited for Dad's signal until the men filed past him and Dad waved him out to follow behind them.

At the front of the men, Darren and Tubbs rode along side by side. When Dad rode up to the head of the column, Tubbs pulled away and rode next to Red Warren and Buster Saggert.

"You look like you're 'bout dead, Tubbs," Red Warren said. He nodded at the bandage behind Tubbs' shirt. The wide, dark blood-stain covered half his chest where the blood had seeped through.

"Don't worry about me," Tubbs said haughtily. "I've got something here waiting for that horse trader and the two ranch hands soon as we get there."

They rode on, with Dad signaling them to boot their horses into a gallop to make up for lost time.

Three hours later the riders arrived at the

Swann spread, stopping out of sight below the far side of the low rise. Dad waved them around him. All of them bunched up in front of the wagon.

"I've already told the lot of yas, we've got a right to anything we take from the Swanns. When a man owes the kind of money Ansil Swann owes Finnity and Baines, folks like us have a right and an obligation to take everything he's got to make up for it. If his assets come to more than it costs to seize and sell them, anything left over goes to us for our trouble of having to hunt him down."

"Don't forget," Darren put in, "the law on the other side of the border might not read that way, but this is Mexico and we can do as we damn please —"

"Who the hell asked you to open your idiot mouth?" Dad said, cutting Darren off with a strange, bemused expression.

"Sorry, Dad," Darren said. "I just felt like I ought to say something about it, that's all."

"Jesus," Dad said under his breath. He looked around, then motioned the men toward the crest of the low rise. "All right, follow me," he said. "We're riding in slow. If they turn tail and run, all the better for us. It'll keep the valuables from getting busted up." He grinned. "And don't forget, there's nothing says we can't shoot them in their backs while they're leaving."

In the Swann hacienda, Summers, Rena, Bailey and the two ranch hands stood inside Ansil Swann's office. Ansil sat slumped in his wheelchair, his expression the same as it had been ever since Summers arrived with the bay fillies. The broken engraved Colt still lay in the same spot, its hammer cocked. The gunmen who had been there hadn't even bothered stealing the worthless gun. Ansil's bourbon had been more important to them.

Atop the desk lay the two large packs of cash that had come from the safe inside the sealed mine shaft, each with the large dollar sign on them. Bailey stood with her hand atop the packs, Lonnie Kerns' cut of the proceeds stacked beside them.

"This takes care of everybody," Bailey said coolly. "I thank all of you. And now it's time for me to go to Mexico City and make sure this promissory note from Don Manuel gets properly cashed and deposited."

"Wait a minute," Summers said. "What about Ansil? Who's going to take care of him while you're gone?"

Bailey looked for a second as if she'd

completely forgotten about her husband sitting there. But then she recovered quickly and turned to Rena.

"Actually," she said, "I had hoped Rena would stay here awhile longer, take care of him until I get back. I can see you are feeling much better, eh? Aren't you, darling?"

Rena shook her head.

"I'm leaving," she said bluntly.

"Leaving? Don't be silly, Rena," Bailey said. "You have no family now. There's no one to go home to in Guatemala — your humble little village." She smiled condescendingly. "Where on earth will you go, dear?"

"I'm going with Will," Rena said boldly. "He has invited me to join him and go to . . . Wind River?" She posed it as a question.

Summers looked surprised, but he too played it off quickly.

"Yes, Wind River," he said. He looked from Rena to Bailey. "We're leaving right away."

"Well, well, Mr. Summers," Bailey said in a half-piqued tone. "I can see that nothing slows you down for long, does it?"

"No, ma'am," Summers said. He passed Rena the trace of a smile. "I know good fortune when it comes knocking."

Rena returned his smile; she blushed a little.

"I kept that thought, like I promised," she said.

"Yes, you did," Summers said, "and you must have read my mind while you were at it."

Bailey stood staring rigidly.

"How wonderful," she said, oozing sarcasm.

"So," Rena said, ignoring her attitude, "if you will be so kind as to give me my, and my father's, wages for the past seven months . . ." She let her words trail.

"Well, Rena, really . . . ," Bailey said, caught off guard. "You can't just expect me to come up with the money all at once like this."

Rena looked at the bag of cash on the desk; so did Summers and the two ranch hands.

"You said with Don Manuel's bank draft you have enough to pay off Finnity and Baines and take care of the ranch and some other investments," Summers said quietly.

"Well, I do," said Bailey, "but I won't have, if I fritter it all away."

"It's her and her father's money. Pay her," Summers insisted.

"Hold everything, all of you!" Lonnie said,

having stepped quickly over to the gun port and gazed out. "Look there, coming over the rise."

Summers and Little Ted stepped over to the window and looked out with him.

"Looks like they've come to collect what they think is due to them," Summers said. "They're riding in slow, hoping we'll make a run for it. If we do, we'll be dead before we leave the yard."

The two ranch hands looked at him and stood in silence.

He said over his shoulder to Bailey Swann, "How much money is still in the packs, ma'am? It looks like we'll need it to keep them from pounding us into the ground."

"I'm not giving the money to them," Bailey said with resolve. "It's that simple. I'll need it to travel on to Mexico City."

"There looks to be a dozen or more," Summers said. "You tell me how you plan on all of us getting out of this alive."

"I don't know, but I'm not giving them the money," she said. "Even if I did, what's going to keep them from killing us and not even telling Finnity and Baines about this cash?"

"We are," Summers said, "the three of us." He looked at Lonnie and Ted Ford. "Us three and these gun ports," he added, nodding toward the windows. "That's all that's kept this place from falling a long time ago." He picked up one of the packs from the desk and slung it up over his arm. "Take the other one, Bailey," he said, nodding at the other pack. "You'd better hide it somewhere good and safe. If they catch you holding out on them, they'll take the money and kill you for good measure."

CHAPTER 25

Fifty yards from the hacienda, Dad brought his men to a halt. The hay wagon squeaked up beside him and jolted to a halt as Lajo struggled with the unfamiliar brake handle. Dad gave him a harsh look, then turned his eyes back to the upper windows of the hacienda, its gun ports looking ancient and fortress strong in the afternoon sunlight. Darren rode up beside his father, his horse restless, eager to break into a run at the slightest tap of a heel.

"Why are we stopped, Dad?" he asked, a sawed-off shotgun hanging in his hand, his face still smarting from the buckshot the doctor had removed.

"Something's wrong," Dad said, staring straight ahead. "They should be lighting out by now."

Darren's horse spun another full turn before he got it checked down.

"Wrong, hell! It looks perfect to me," he

said, holding his reins back tight with his free hand. Still the horse jumped up and down in place on its front hooves. "I'm ready as hell to blast that horse trader with both barrels — show him us Crayleys *give back* as good as we *get.*"

Dad looked at Hico and Red Warren on his other side, and gave them a look. Then he turned to his son.

"If you don't get that horse under hand," he said, "I'm going bend that shotgun barrel over your back."

"The hell did I do?" shouted Darren.

Dad didn't answer. He straightened in his saddle as he saw Will Summers step out onto the front porch.

"Speak of the devil . . . ," he murmured to himself.

"Who did?" asked Darren. He looked all around as if someone might admit to it.

"*Please,* shut up!" Dad barked at him. He squinted toward the porch, seeing Summers wave a white pillowcase tied to the end of a double-barreled shotgun. In Summers' other hand, Dad saw the canvas backpack.

"What is this?" Hico asked Dad.

"I don't know," said Dad. "You still got your army glass?"

"Oh yeah," said Hico. He reached back

inside his saddlebags, fished out a battered telescope and handed it to Dad.

Dad spat on the front end of it and wiped it on his shirtsleeve. He stretched it out and held it to his eye.

Hico watched a thin smile come to Dad's face as Dad saw the large dollar sign on the canvas pack.

"Now, I like that a lot," Dad said.

"What is it?" Hico asked.

"It's money, Hico," said Dad. "How much, who knows?" he added with a dark chuckle. "But the horse trader is starting to talk my language. He's got a bag that has a big ol' dollar sign right on the side of it."

"Hold it, Dad," said Darren. "You ain't about to let him buy his way out of this, are you?"

Dad grinned, still looking through the long scope.

"Out of what?" he said. "The longer I look at that dollar sign, the more I forget why we're mad at him."

"Not letting him buy his way out of *shooting me,* damn it — that's what!" Darren shouted.

"Aw, yeah, that's right," Dad said, goading his angry son. He raised a hand for the men behind to see, and moved it forward slowly. "Easy-like, boys," he said to them

344

without looking around. "It looks like we've got us a talker here. Let's go down slow and calm, hear what the man's got to say."

"You mean we're not going to kill him?" Darren asked in disbelief.

"That all depends," said Dad. "Thomas Finnity is headed this way. Might be here tomorrow. It would be sweet as Sunday pie if I could throw a bag of money at his feet, tell him we collected a big payment from Ansil Swann."

"Well, I'll be dipped in shit!" Darren said in disgust, raising his voice.

"Yes, you might very well be," Dad said menacingly, "if you don't shut your damn mouth."

On the porch, Summers lowered the canvas bag and held it in his hand as the riders brought their horses into the front yard at a walk. The wagon followed close behind them. Dad rode at the center of a V formation. When he stopped twenty feet from the front porch, the V turned into a half circle, enclosing the front of the hacienda. One of the men started to move away and go around to the rear of the house, but a nod from Dad stopped him. There was no need to watch the rear door. This place truly was a fortress; these people weren't going to try to make a run for it.

Dad gave a pensive grin and raised a finger and shook it a little as he stared at Summers and the canvas pack.

"You know, I could have flushed all of you out of here if I really wanted to. Sooner or later you'd get hungry, thirsty or your own stink starts getting to you. Am I right?" He spread his hands, affably, the grin still in place.

Summers didn't answer. He wasn't about to reveal how many provisions they had laid up inside for a siege.

"Here's enough money to hold off Finnity and Baines until the Swanns can get to Mexico City," he said, gesturing toward the pack in his hand. "Then they'll pay up the rest." The shotgun was still half-raised in his other hand. The pillowcase fluttered slightly on a hot breeze.

"Oh?" said Dad, realizing Summers was too smart to tell him anything he didn't have to. "What happens when they get to Mexico City?"

"They'll be making a deposit large enough to clear all outstanding accounts with Finnity and Baines," he said.

Dad gave him a curious look.

"Are you some kind of attorney, as well as a horse trader?" he asked.

"No," Summers said, "I'm just a horse trader. I got caught in the middle of this, and I've had to scratch my way out." He held the canvas pack forward a little. "There's the deal. What do you say to it?"

"How much is in there?" Dad asked, nodding at the pack.

"I never speculate on money I haven't counted," Summers said. He hefted the bag up and down. "Weightwise I'm going to say seventy pounds, give or take."

"That is a *chunk* of money, sure enough," Dad said, his eyes lighting up a little as he imagined how good it would look, him handing the pack over to Thomas Finnity. "But you have caused an awful lot of trouble since you sprang onto everybody's path. It'd be almost a shame not to kill you."

"I didn't spring onto anybody's path," Summers said. "I came here to deliver some horses. When I seek to do something I get it done. That's the business I'm in. Who would want to deal with a horse trader who can't deliver what he says he'll —"

"All right, *all right,* I understand all that," Dad said, cutting him off with a raised hand. "You're proposing we take the money and just leave? Leave the wagon sitting empty?"

"That's right," Summers said. "Take the

money to your employers and tell them the rest is coming real soon. If it doesn't, they can take up right here where we left off. Deal?" He let the pack fall from his hand and took a cautious step back away from it.

Dad just stared at him for a moment. Darren sat fuming in his saddle.

"A horse trader, huh?" Dad said, curious as to Summers' youth and savvy in handling himself. "You look young. How long you been at it?"

"A year . . . a little over," Summers said.

"You make the auctions, travel the trade circuit, I suppose?" Dad asked.

"That's part of it," Summers said.

"Damn it to hell, *Dad*?" Darren shouted with a dark, bemused look on his face. "You two *want coffee*? Maybe sit and *visit awhile*?" His face boiled red. "The son of a bitch shot me — have you *heard*?"

"Damn it, fool, that's *all* I've heard!" Dad shouted back, so loud and fierce that all the men seemed to cower a little.

Summers stood poised for anything in the tense following silence. He waited for a second, then ventured, "Deal?" again, to Dad.

Dad let out a much-needed breath of relief and started to reply, but Darren would still have none of it.

"Hell no, it's not a *deal*!" he shouted. Seeing his father giving in, he stepped his horse forward, the shotgun in hand, his thumb over the hammers, ready to pull them back.

"Darren, get the hell back here!" Dad shouted.

"Look at my face!" Darren shouted, his eyes flashing back and forth between his father and Will Summers. "Look what the son of a bitch done to me! Look at Tubbs, shot through the chest! That poor bastard breathes, it sounds like turkeys mating!"

"Easy, mister. You're not the only one heeling a scattergun," Summers cautioned, seeing Darren getting more and more out of hand. "I shot you before. I'll shoot you again." Without taking his eyes off Darren, he said to Dad, "Rein him in, Mr. Crayley! This is all about to go bad on us!"

"Bad on us?" Darren shouted. "I'll show you *bad on us*!"

"Get back here, idiot!" Dad demanded to his raging son.

But it was too late. Darren cocked the hammers back on the sawed-off and swung it toward Summers. But before he got the gun level, Summers' shotgun belched a blast of fire and smoke that lifted Darren from his saddle and sent him flying backward. His shotgun went off sidelong, both barrels, and blasted Tubbs' head to pieces. Hearing Dad Crayley let out a scream, Summers didn't hesitate on where to go next. He swung the gun at Dad and fired. Dad left his saddle like a broken rag doll. A red mist hung in the air.

Hico Morales jerked his rifle up from across his lap, but he had to duck Summers' smoking shotgun as Summers hurled it at him. By the time he'd knocked the empty shotgun away and gotten his rifle to his shoulder, Summers had grabbed the pack of money, his Colt up and firing. As bullets nipped at him, he fell back through the front door, which Ted Ford had thrown open for him. Bullets thumped into the thick door as Ted threw the bolt into place.

"That could have gone better, Will," he said, helping Summers to his feet.

"I know," Summers said. "I'm still learning — working on it." He threw the pack of money aside.

"Are you hit?" Ted asked.

"I don't think so," Summers said. Upstairs, Lonnie, Rena and Bailey Swann had started firing from the gun ports. Outside, bullets still hit the front of the hacienda, shots still exploded, but the sound of hooves dwarfed all else.

"They're pulling back into the brush!"

said Ted. "Likely as not they'll try burning us out, the way Rizale and Tate aimed to do to Lonnie —"

"Huh-uh," Summers said, opening his Colt and letting his spent rounds fall to the floor. "Not this bunch. They came to collect anything of value. They got a sniff of this money. They're not going to burn it up."

"Then what now?" Ted asked.

Summers nodded at the large front window ten feet away. Like with all the other windows, its thick shutters where closed. This window looked out onto the whole front yard. It was large enough to support two gun port openings. Its bottom ledge stood knee-high.

"We're going to wave the money in their faces and start negotiating all over again," Summers said somberly. "We're stuck in this game, Ted. The only way out is to win it."

"Lonnie and me, we're just hired hands. But you tell us how to play it, Will, and we'll win it with you, I promise you," Ted said. He patted the Colt standing in its holster on his side.

"Good men," said Summers, grabbing the money pack and walking to the shuttered window. "First, let's see who answers when I ask who's in charge now."

"What if we give them the money and they don't give it to Finnity and Baines?" he asked, helping Summers unlock the big, thick shutters. He picked up a rifle leaning beside the big window and checked it.

"To tell you the truth, Ted, I don't much care," Summers said. "The Swanns are not innocent victims. This is their world. Everybody else is just visiting." He opened the thick shutter on the right and looked out toward the brush. "Everybody I've come across here, the Belltraes, the Swanns, all these gunmen out here, they're all a string of dark horses. The only righteous folks I've met have been Bedos and Rena and you and Lonnie. Everybody else is ready to stab each other in the back." He shook his head. "Hadn't been for you four, I'd have taken my string of bays back home and called all this a misdeal." He raised the pack of money and held it out for the men in the brush to see.

Beside him, Ted stood ready with the rifle.

"All right, out there," Summers shouted, "who's in charge now?"

A silence ensued. Summers stood ready to jump back with the money at the sound of gunfire. But after a moment, he called out, "Who do I give this money to?"

This time only a second seemed to pass.

"I'm in charge," said Hico Morales. He stood up halfway behind a rock. "I have a bullet graze on my arm."

"Tough break," Summers called out. "Can you carry a backpack full of money, or am I talking to the wrong man?"

"You are talking to the right man," Hico said. "How do I know you won't shoot me when I come to get it?"

"You don't," Summers said flatly. "This much money takes *cojones*. If you don't have them, send somebody else."

Beside Summers Ted gave a nervous chuckle.

"You beat all, Will," he said.

The two watched as Hico walked forward warily from the brush. When he stopped ten feet from the front porch, Summers swung the backpack and hurled it to the ground at Hico's feet.

Without another word, Hico picked it up and backed away the first fifteen feet. Then he turned and walked back to the brush. Ted and Summers closed the big shutters and bolted them. They stood listening. In a moment they heard laughter and hoots of delight, then the sound of hoofbeats as they looked out and saw the men riding away. The empty hay wagon sat at the edge of the front yard.

"Is that it? They're gone?" Bailey Swann asked, walking halfway down the stairs.

"Let's hope so," Summers said. At the head of the stairs, he saw Rena looking wary, a rifle in her hands. "I believe they'll go on back to town now," he said. "There's no reason for them not to." Rena and Bailey both looked relieved. They turned and walked back to Ansil Swann's office, where Lonnie still stood looking out a gun port.

Behind them, Summers and Ted walked in as the sound of hooves faded beyond the low rise. Lonnie turned from the window and leaned against the wall in relief.

"What now, Will?" he asked.

Summers looked at Rena Reyes. She gave him a slight nod.

"Rena and I are leaving," he said. "We're taking the doctor's rig back to him. Then we're gone to Wind River."

"I'm leaving too," Ted Ford said. "Maybe I should ride with you to the doctor's, just in case?"

Summers glanced at Rena for a look of approval and got it.

"You can ride with us," he said.

"Me too?" Lonnie asked. "For a little ways?"

"Yep," Summers said.

"What about me?" Bailey Swann asked.

They all looked at her.

"Take care of your husband," Lonnie said. "We'll tell the doctor to come see about him. He'll know somebody willing to work for you."

"And I'm stuck here until then?" Bailey asked in a tense voice, struggling to keep herself in check. A nerve twitched at her jawline. Ansil Swann sat in his wheelchair, the same blank expression on his face, the same lost and hopeless eyes staring at the floor.

"Afraid so," Lonnie said.

The four of them looked at one another, then turned, walked out the office door and down the stairs. They started for the front door, but Lonnie stopped, let out a breath and turned around. He started back up.

"Where are you going, Lon?" said Ted.

"I can't leave him here with her. She won't take care of him. Send the doctor when you get to town —" His words stopped short at the sound of a gunshot from upstairs. Everybody froze. Lonnie recovered quickly and bound up the stairs, the other three right behind him. At the top of the landing another shot exploded. They rushed into Ansil Swann's office and froze again.

"My, my . . . ," Lonnie whispered, in dread and in awe.

Bailey Swann lay dead in a pool of blood on the office floor, a bullet hole through her heart. Her dead eyes stared straight and mindlessly across the office floor. Ansil Swann lay facedown on his desk, blood and brain matter running down the wall on his left. His right hand lay near the frozen engraved Colt on his desk. Smoke curled from the gun's barrel and rose and weaved its way into the cloud of smoke hanging overhead.

"Oh no!" Rena said. She clasped her hands to her mouth and tried to step forward. But Summers slipped his arm around her and gently but firmly drew her away. He turned her away from the grisly scene and led her out the office door. "Let's go downstairs, Rena," he whispered to her. "There's nothing you can do here. You don't work for them anymore."

The employees of Thorndike Press hope you have enjoyed this Large Print book. All our Thorndike, Wheeler, and Kennebec Large Print titles are designed for easy reading, and all our books are made to last. Other Thorndike Press Large Print books are available at your library, through selected bookstores, or directly from us.

For information about titles, please call:
(800) 223-1244

or visit our Web site at:
http://gale.cengage.com/thorndike

To share your comments, please write:
Publisher
Thorndike Press
10 Water St., Suite 310
Waterville, ME 04901